MY
SUMMONED
BEAST
IS DEAD

PANDORA, LEGENDARY
BEAST OF THE LAST REALM
Feil's summon (corpse)

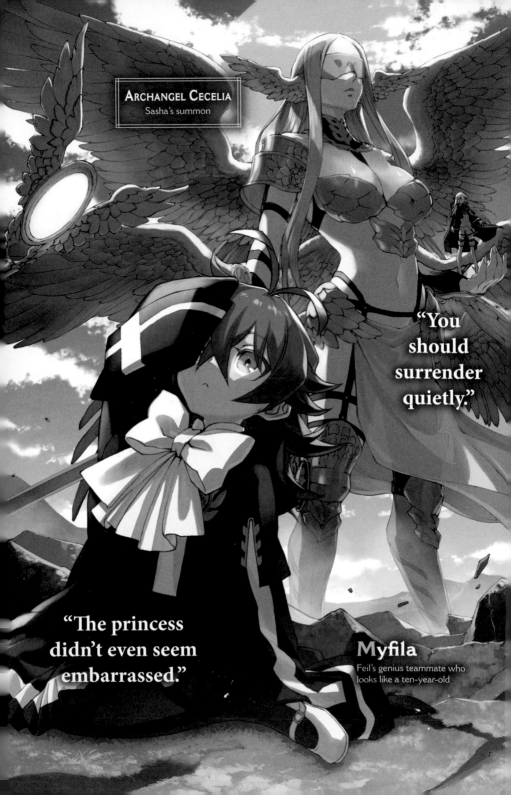

ARCHANGEL CECELIA
Sasha's summon

"You should surrender quietly."

"The princess didn't even seem embarrassed."

Myfila
Feil's genius teammate who looks like a ten-year-old

Cyril
Ojlock

Feil's teammate and
handsome noble

"You're
serious
about
winning
against
Sasha?!"

"'Course
I am! I
wouldn't go
into a battle
expectin' to
lose!"

Feil onaf

Working student at
the Academy

TIGER-SABER
KING ZYLGAR
Cyril's summon

"If I summon
too rapidly,
I'll die, all
right?!"

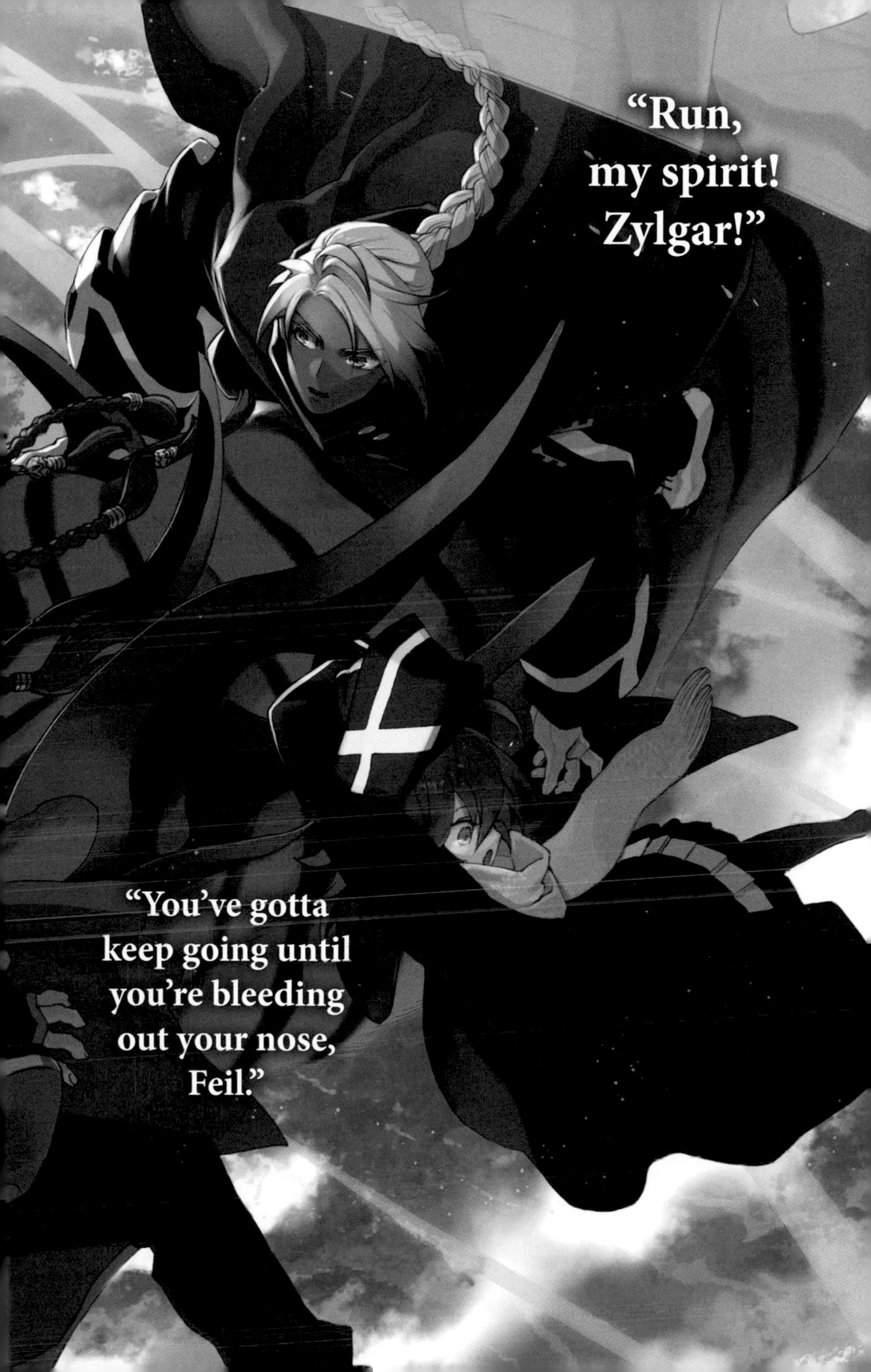
"Run, my spirit! Zylgar!"
"You've gotta keep going until you're bleeding out your nose, Feil."

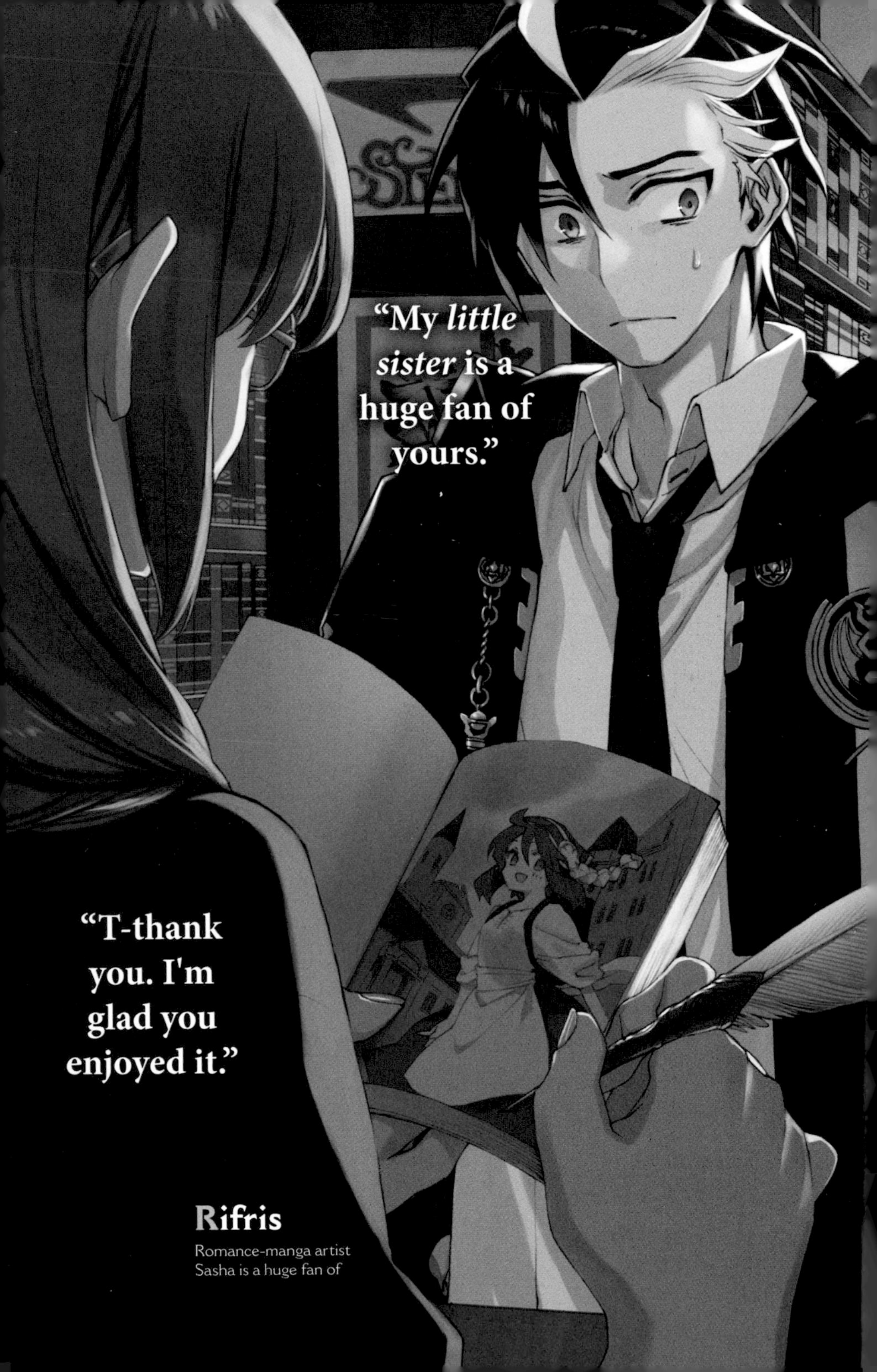
"My *little sister* is a huge fan of yours."
"T-thank you. I'm glad you enjoyed it."
Rifris
Romance-manga artist Sasha is a huge fan of

"Th-thank you so much..."

Sasha Shidoh Zultania

Top summoner at the Academy and third princess of land of Shidoh

SUMMONER

A superior conjurer position. By first summoning the being that will serve as their Counterpart, they learn how to call forth various monsters from history. Because creating a contract with a summon requires complex knowledge and vast reserves of magic, all summoners are also great conjurers.

SUMMONER TRAINING SCHOOL

Educational institutions that not only teach the foundations of advanced spellcraft and summoning techniques but also drill students in practical combat experience using magic. Most present-day summoners attend a school. Though they are fundamentally under government management, not all eight grand kingdoms that divide the world have a school. In the land of Shidoh, they have the Academy; the land of Hadoh has the Tower; and the land of Nodoh has the Gate.

SUMMONER INCANTATIONS

A magical tool to record the contracts between a summoner and their summons. Typically, volumes are a hundred and twenty pages in length, but they are visualizations of the summon contracts and the summoner's capacity, so the page count has little meaning.

PANDORA, LEGENDARY BEAST OF THE LAST REALM

A legendary magical beast who stands three hundred and fifty mejals at his full height. It may be fitting to call him a dragonkin, as his appearance is a cross between a dragon and a human. He abruptly appeared during the age of gods, when humans and deities coexisted. Upon challenging the gods to battle, his head was crushed by the Supreme God, Zen.

In some remote regions, it is passed down that he and Zen were once friends, but the veracity of these stories cannot be confirmed.

MY SUMMONED BEAST IS DEAD

Rakuzan

Illustration by **Miyuu**

YEN ON

New York

Rakuzan

Translation by **Jan Cash**
Cover art by **Miyuu**

ORE NO SHOKANJU, SHINDERU Vol.1
©Rakuzan, Miyuu 2022
First published in Japan in 2022 by KADOKAWA CORPORATION, Tokyo.
English translation rights arranged with KADOKAWA CORPORATION, Tokyo, through Tuttle-Mori Agency, Inc., Tokyo.

English translation © 2023 by Yen Press, LLC

Yen On
150 West 30th Street, 19th Floor
New York, NY 10001

Visit us at yenpress.com ◆ facebook.com/yenpress ◆ twitter.com/yenpress
yenpress.tumblr.com ◆ instagram.com/yenpress

First Yen On Edition: May 2023
Edited by Yen On Editorial: Payton Campbell
Designed by Yen Press Design: Andy Swist

Yen On is an imprint of Yen Press, LLC.
The Yen On name and logo are trademarks of Yen Press, LLC.

The publisher is not responsible for websites (or their content) that are not owned by the publisher.

Library of Congress Cataloging-in-Publication Data
Names: Rakuzan, author. | Miyuu, illustrator.
Title: My summoned beast is dead / Rakuzan ; illustration by Miyuu.
Other titles: Ore no shokanju, shinderu. English
Description: First Yen On edition. | New York : Yen On, 2023–
Identifiers: LCCN 2022057642 | ISBN 9781975361600 (v. 1 ; trade paperback)
Subjects: CYAC: Fantasy. | Magic—Fiction. | Schools—Fiction. | LCGFT: Fantasy fiction. | Light novels.
Classification: LCC PZ7.1.R347 My 2023 | DDC [Fic]—dc23
LC record available at https://lccn.loc.gov/2022057642

ISBNs: 978-1-9753-6160-0 (paperback)
       978-1-9753-6161-7 (ebook)

10 9 8 7 6 5 4 3 2 1

LSC-C

Printed in the United States of America

CONTENTS

1.

The Summoner Struggles Against the Archangel

When I turned to look at the sky over the wreckage, everything I beheld was beautiful. The azure expanse that seemed like it would swallow me into its depths, the dazzling contrast of light and dark as the sun illuminated the scattered clouds—and more than anything, the archangel whose six pure-white wings were outstretched across it all. To be frank, the sight left me so emotional, so awestruck, I almost forgot to breathe.

That was when I realized there were phenomena in this world more beautiful and more glorious than I'd ever be able to imagine—and that, in *this* particular instance, *this* particular phenomenon was trying to kill me.

The absurdity caught me off guard, and I ended up letting out an incredulous chuckle.

The archangel was just *that* impressive. She was way up in the sky, floating just below the clouds. She was likely the same size as the clouds, considering she was easily taller than ten full-grown men. Her long, golden hair fluttered in the westerly winds, her eyes hidden behind a silver mask.

There was also the fact that she was quite underdressed. While her arms and shins were properly covered by silver armor, the rest of her bodily contours were left unprotected. Both her shoulders were bare, and her intricately decorated breastplate was cut so low, it wasn't even protecting the body part its name referred to. The apron dangling over her pelvis seemed to invite rather than conceal, and the little armor that accompanied it only protected the sides of her hips. A single long stretch of pure-white cloth fell from behind the angel, fluttering in the wind like a tail.

It was said that many men fell in love with angels.

That seemed likely. Considering their humanoid shape and their elegance—their grandeur—it felt only natural that most humans would let their hearts be stolen away. Naturally, the same applied to me. It wasn't like I didn't appreciate them—even if one was currently after my life.

"Gah! Agh!!"

I squeezed out all the strength I had to push aside the rubble and sit myself upright. I slapped myself in the face, trying to remind myself of the danger we were in after I'd been entranced by the archangel for so long.

"Hey, you two! Y'all alive?!" I yelled between coughs. "Dammit, this is ridiculous. It's like she's *tryin'* to kill us."

I patted down my long conjurer's robes—which looked a lot like a clergyman's garb—as I stood up.

But dusting myself off ended up proving pointless when I was showered with rubble from a nearby pile as another person appeared next to me—they were tall, dark, and handsome.

"This only happened because you decided to step on the tiger's tail, Feil," my teammate said, brushing aside his blond braid. Then he extended a hand to the rubble pile he'd been buried under a moment ago and said, "Are you all right, Myfila? You're not hurt, are you?" He pulled up a small girl whose arm barely poked out of the sleeve of her own conjurer's robe. She looked no older than sixteen. "Anyone could have told you that we can't stop Sasha by *melting off* her clothes with a slime."

That was Cyril Ojlock—a first-year at the summoner's training school, also called the Academy. He was one of my teammates for the Academy's ranking matches. The guy's deep-set features and jewel-like blue eyes were popular with the Academy girls, and he was about half a head taller than me, not to mention physically fit. I was also pretty sure he was one of the most athletic Academy students.

Some people made fun of him for having a braid, claiming it made him look effeminate, but he was super popular with the ladies, and they all found it endearing. Just went to show what a specimen Cyril was.

He was the heir to the great Ojlock aristocracy, after all. The words *dignity*, *grace*, and *pride* seemed to exist solely for him, and he put in the effort and had the talent to play the part. His composed demeanor made him seem older than sixteen. Plus, even though he was a summoner just like me, he was also known for his prowess with the sword and the lance. Even today, he wore an aristocratic military uniform with a stiff collar under his Academy robes. A large empty scabbard was also strapped to his side.

"Seriously. We never should've gone with your plan, Feil."

Cyril picked his large sword off the ground. "The angel took out my summon with one blow," he said. "It's a wonder we're all alive." Then he plunged his drawn blade deep into the ground. With his hands now free, he quickly dusted off the girl standing next to him.

"Wait, Myfila. A girl like you shouldn't walk around covered in so much dust." The guy was starting to sound like an overprotective dad.

He ignored me when I told him, "Myfila can handle herself, y'know."

"The two of you should care more about these things. The Academy allowed for an audience, and I'd think our duties as students include looking the part," he said, quickly fixing even Myfila's hair now. Then he looked into a winged round mirror that had been hanging out near us and gave it a tender smile. He even went as far as to wave a hand.

The mirror broadcasted all it saw to a screen in front of an audience of about a thousand. The women and children who had come to see Cyril were probably screaming and swooning in the Academy's great hall right around now.

...Meanwhile, we were out in the Academy's expansive rear yard on the verge of death.

"The princess didn't even seem embarrassed," Myfila muttered as she turned to me. Just then, her cowlick sprung right back up at the top of her head. Despite all of Cyril's attempts to fix her hair, it was always an untamable, explosive force. That was Myfila. She didn't even have a last name. Just Myfila.

She was so small that her robes dragged even when she wore the smallest size available. At times, she'd even get mistaken for a ten-year-old when she ran errands at the market.

Despite that, everyone at the Academy likely knew of her, considering she was supposed to be a genius who'd deciphered the *Arcane Autogram* even before entering the Academy. She was also an odd one—her favorite things in the world were corpses possessed by necrospecters, the elementals that were supposedly the observers of death and fate.

She spoke in a monotone, so it was difficult to read her, especially with how her bangs hid half her face. There weren't a lot of guys who'd notice her, but if they just bothered to look, they'd find a small, beautiful girl with golden eyes staring back up at them.

"Yeah, she really didn't," I said. "But *I* sure thought it was a good idea."

I tousled Myfila's hair and surveyed the area around us, which was almost unrecognizable from just barely ten seconds ago. I let out a sigh. A strained smile had worked its way onto my face before I'd even realized it.

The angel's spear of light had overturned the terrain with its supernatural destructive force. She'd transformed the vast field that was normally peppered with rocks—now the ground was split and heaved up to expose even the bedrock underneath. It looked almost apocalyptic.

I was surprised we'd all even survived.

One misstep, and we would've been crushed under some shattered boulder or nose-diving into the deep chasm.

This destruction had been wrought by none other than one of my own classmates. One Sasha Shidoh Zultania.

I couldn't even hold a match to her when it came to summoning ability. No matter how I worked and struggled, catching up to her seemed impossible—and right as I thought that, I let my guard down for just a wink.

"Shadow Shield."

Amethyst light shone toward the sky from Myfila's extended hand. It was beautiful, like the sky before sunset, but instead of immediately fading, traces of it hovered just where Myfila's fingertips had been.

She drew a simple summoning circle with a single stroke, and my shadow on the ground came alive, abruptly standing up to shield me from a lightning bolt coming in from my blind spot.

When I saw the attack burst right in front of my eyes, my heart nearly leaped out of my chest.

"Dammit! Wasn't payin' any attention just now!" I chided myself, then broke right out into a run. "Do you *have* to take everything so seriously?! At least give us a chance to catch our breath!"

I scrambled over the uneven boulders stacked on top of one another and ran across the cracked ground with everything I had.

When I looked back up at the sky, I saw two pegasi and Sasha Shidoh Zultania's teammates riding atop them. I could already tell her two summoner teammates (who were good-looking themselves) were prepping to cast their next electromagic spell. That was obvious, though. I didn't have to check to know.

I mean, see. Just as I was wondering when the blitz would come, a bunch of lightning bolts touched down right behind me.

Cyril was huffing and puffing as he carried Myfila out of there, running right alongside me.

"Sasha's teammates are her number one worshippers! Of course she would go all out after you teased her with your little slime stunt!" he yelled.

"What teasing?! And who kills someone over a difference of opinion?!"

Lightning bolts were raining down on us one after another in rapid succession.

They might not have been lethal, but they sure would've knocked any of us out if we were hit. We both knew exactly what would happen if we slowed down even in the slightest, so Cyril and I had cast aside any hopes of looking respectable and just made a break for it.

"Stop right there, Feil Fonaf!"

"How dare you resort to such vulgar ploys! Have you no pride?!"

The girls were bellowing at me from above. I shouted right back at them, facing them head-on. "Sasha's the slowpoke who let a slime hop onto her, ya nitwits!"

That earned us double the number of electrical spells, but their aim got a whole lot messier. No, wait, scratch that. They were just striking at random, like they were playing with us.

I scrambled over a pile of rubble as fast as I could. "They're not even breakin' a sweat. They're toying with us…!" Sure, we were being driven into a corner, but now things were getting interesting. I smirked as I asked Cyril and Myfila, "Okay, what's next?! What's our play?! What can we do?! Whaddaya wanna go for now?!"

Then Cyril shouted, loud enough to rival the thunderclaps ringing out right next to us, "You haven't given up yet?! We're lucky the three of us managed to survive this long against Sasha and her entourage! How about we throw in the towel before we end up dead?!"

Then I shouted back at him *just* as loudly, "You're joking! They got a warning for using an unblockable attack just now! Next warning they get, they'll lose on a technicality! This is the perfect opportunity!"

I pointed at the horizon, at the archangel right below the scattered clouds. There was a guy on top of a creature with the upper body of an eagle and the lower quarters of a lion—a griffin—who'd appeared barely a second ago. It looked like the summoner guy was saying something to the archangel.

Cyril immediately followed my finger. His handsome features screwed up as he replied, "You're serious about winning against Sasha?!"

"'Course I am! I wouldn't go into a battle expectin' to lose! Same as always!"

"I've never heard of Sasha ever being upset before, you know!"

"Then if it's a first for her, maybe she's gotten weaker! Not everyone gets more powerful just 'cause they're mad!"

We'd been pursued by the onslaught of thunderbolts and running for our lives for a whole minute.

My blood was pumping so fast to my muscles, it didn't feel like any of it was reaching my brain. I pummeled the side of my head just to see if that'd help, but I still wasn't coming up with any ideas for a counterattack.

My lungs burned. I needed more air.

Then right as I was on the verge of surrendering to helplessness, Myfila whispered to me, "Feil, let's try *that*."

"'*That*'?"

I didn't know exactly what Myfila meant in my oxygen-deprived state...and then, three seconds in, I finally laughed. "Ya mean the combo summon."

I dug the heels of my boots into the ground.

Before I could fully stop, I used my momentum to flip around onto one knee. I concentrated my spirit into my fingertips until blue light flickered into existence on my index and middle fingers, then I began tracing a summoning circle directly on the ground.

It only took me two seconds to finish drawing it.

Right as I finished etching the two squares contained within a circle, I declared the magic words: "Land Rising!!"

"Feil Fonaf!"

"Now you resort to sly tricks!"

The next moment, a gigantic pillar of stone flew out from the ground and created a thick wall to shield us from the lightning bolts hailing down from the pegasi overhead. Since they couldn't stop quickly enough, they speedily flew away from us. That probably bought us some time since they'd need to do a one-eighty to get to us.

And that was also our opportunity to attack.

I pulled out a small leather-bound book from the inner pocket of my summoner's robes and started to recite an arcane verse.

"Ye that writhe nocturnal, spirits entombed of the land internal. A gale gloomy spied by eyes of many, they who leave the Great Woods Vanuka empty. The flowers of yore now abloom, the time long bided for glory thy shall assume."

When I looked over, I saw Myfila open a book much like my own as Cyril held her in his arms.

"God Croaka of the lachrymal, begotten children of the tranquil. The titan falls as night of moonlight breaks. Dawn shall come as thine corpse awaits. A tranquil cloak keeps the wind at bay for the corpse in the chill of morning day. Anon, the time has come without delay for thine silence to be cast away."

Cyril started to panic. "Wait, wait, wait, wait!"

He ran over to me (still carrying Myfila) with an eyebrow raised. "Stop, you two! By 'combo summon,' do you mean that *thing* you did earlier? That's not allowed!"

But I replied, "It's not? We ain't breakin' any rules. We're just bein' 'inventive' is all." I overruled Cyril's attempt at stopping us. Anyway, I'd already found the page I needed from my book, so I was too busy tracing the line of verse I'd recited from memory just now with my finger.

Then I let out a forced laugh—it didn't benefit anyone to think too closely about things now that we'd gotten this far into the battle.

"You're definitely going to get in trouble!"

"Fine by me. If I'm goin' to do it, might as well do it right."

Then Myfila and I simultaneously closed our books.

The effects were immediate. A gigantic blue summoning circle rose from behind me as a purple circle appeared on the ground under Myfila, where she was still in Cyril's arms.

"I'm gonna make *the* Sasha Shidoh Zultania scream."

Just as I grinned, I heard a loud crash, like a bunch of glass breaking.

I searched for the source of the sound and realized a gigantic arm was reaching toward us from overhead. It was pale but muscular and gargantuan. So far, it was elbow deep into our world.

The arm had ripped through the barrier of worlds to appear in our own realm. I caught glimpses of starlike lights twinkling in the indigo beyond. We didn't just have an arm. Eventually, the rest of the giant broke through the barrier and appeared, its form so large that it could have easily had an overhead view of any two-story building.

Its brown hair was long, and its thick torso was covered only by a single loincloth.

Instead of a sense of gallantry, it seemed to give off an unearthly air, which was likely because the gigantic body was just that—a carcass no longer of this world. Its eyes were empty, its long tongue lolling out of its half-open mouth and its blue skin showing no sign of blood flow. Though it was large enough to brawl with a dragon, instead of moving of its own volition, the giant was being manipulated by the necrospecter within it.

The peculiar and powerful elementals, which ranked after the four elements of fire, water, earth, and wind, had a penchant for putrefaction and could even control the smell coming from rotting corpses. Many people were even devoted to them, believing they were the messengers of the god of death, Croaka.

Myfila had summoned a necrospecter in the corpse of a giant that had lived long ago. But…which era had she summoned the monster from?

Though the necrospecters controlled decay, there was no way any giant corpses existed in the human age, and any giants from the age of gods wouldn't have commanded much grandeur. She'd probably summoned it from between those eras—during the age of elementals and beasts.

If I were a gambling man, I'd say the giant came from the time when elementals and beasts were glorified the world over, after all the gods had decided to withdraw into seclusion. So it was one of the great titan's descendants. The last generation of their race, which had fought against the gods.

In terms of difficulty, it was one of the lower upper-class summons.

It was already unusual enough that the necrospecters were responding to her summons, and even though the giant was only a descendant of a titan, the fact that she'd summoned its body increased the complexity of the feat by leaps and bounds.

It had only looked easy because Myfila was a prodigy.

The titan knelt for her, and Myfila wasted no time slipping out from under Cyril's arm. "I don't need you anymore, Cyril. I'll stand on my own," she told him as she stepped onto the outstretched right hand of the giant.

"Myfila, I'll ride, too. Let me ride it, will ya?"

I got onto the hand right after her.

Then the titan stood back up, straightening to its full height, and the scenery swept down around me as I rose to an elevation twice my height, then three times, on and on. It felt precarious so high up, like even a slight breeze would make me lose my footing.

"I'm not getting involved in this," Cyril said from down below, where his voice came up to us as hardly a whisper. He looked pretty grouchy.

I gave him a toothy smile before replying, "We'll find an openin'. We're expectin' a real big attack from you, Mr. Hero."

However, all he replied with was another irritated "I'm not getting involved in this!"

But this was Cyril, and Cyril wasn't the type to abandon anyone. Even though he was angry and making a big show of it, I was pretty sure he'd be there when we needed him for the final blow. And if he wasn't, we'd have a huge problem. If we wanted to win, Cyril Ojlock's offensive capabilities were absolutely essential to us.

The giant lifted us to its right shoulder, and Myfila hopped on board.

I stood directly across its gigantic head on the left shoulder, taking a firm hold of a long lock of hair to act as a safety tether, then pointed at the archangel above and laughed loudly. "Dah-ha-haaa!! Come an' get us, archangel!"

Then Myfila pointed up just like me and hollered, "Archangel!"

Normally, no one would've heard our jabs from so far up in the sky, but we were fighting a legendary archangel. Her ears couldn't miss even the tiniest of prayers, which naturally meant she wouldn't miss any blasphemy targeting her, either.

She didn't even need to flap her wings to begin her descent toward us.

With the sun directly behind her, she was blinding to behold. I hoped the clouds sweeping across the skies would block out the light.

Eventually, the archangel stopped at about five times the giant's height—which was just perfect. Her long hair fluttered in the strong westerly wind as she watched us from beyond her mask.

"Ha-ha-ha! 'Course you're still lookin' down on us," I snorted as I stared at the archangel's stomach.

Instead of holding a sword or shield in her hands, both were occupied by a single girl. Her platinum hair was less brilliant than the archangel's golden locks as it whipped in the wind around her cool yet pretty face.

Her nose was beautiful enough that I was tempted to trace its slope. Her alabaster skin was accentuated by her pink lips. And then there were her purple eyes, which were more captivating than any I had ever seen.

They weren't just an unusual color, either. They were the perfect size and shape, too. Her delicately sloped eyes were draped by folded eyelids. There was something enigmatic about them, though they still gave off a tender impression. Even the bottoms of her eyes were shapely and adorned with long, gorgeous lashes.

Anyone would fall in love upon meeting those eyes, whether they were a demon from hell or a god from the heavens above. Supposedly, the goddess of love and trickery, Pearla, had once stopped the berserk mythical beast with a single glance. If anyone in this day and age could do the same, I was sure it was her.

Sasha Shidoh Zultania.

Everybody at the Academy knew her name, and I'd bet you'd be hard-pressed to find anyone within four mountain ranges of here who hadn't heard of her.

She was the third princess of the land of Shidoh, which was one of the eight kingdoms reigning over the world. As in a genuine princess. Like *wave from the terrace of the palace* kind-of-princess princess.

"Sheesh... She could've acted a *little* embarrassed. We went through all that work tryin' to get the slime on her for the audience... What a pity."

There were giant holes in her robe, reducing it to little more than rags that barely covered her chest and hips, but Princess Sasha still proudly held herself at her full height, her feet a shoulder's width apart.

The beautiful (albeit half-dressed) princess was standing on the (also) beautiful archangel's hands because she was the angel's summoner, of course.

They were both bursting with dignity, and the moment the angel had responded to the call, their hearts had beat as one. When their souls were tied together, their very senses and emotions would also be shared.

In other words, summoners and summons were essentially one being.

"You have no chance of winning, Feil Fonaf. You should surrender quietly."

...So it was no surprise when the archangel answered in exactly the way I would have expected Sasha to.

Instead of being whisked away by the wind, the angel's voice seemed to come down on us like a tempest, like rain, drenching the earth from above. Her voice was clear and beautiful without the faintest hint of a rasp.

And as for me, I looked up at the heavens and laughed. "Ah-ha-ha-ha-ha-ha!

"Sorry! I ain't just some pushover who'll roll over 'cause somebody suggested surrenderin'!" I yelled up at the sky as I drew a summoning circle.

"Flame Bullet!"

Once I chanted the quick spell, three hundred gigantic flames leaped out of my magic circle, tearing through the air faster than a military-grade arrow at the archangel. One of the fist-sized flames of hellfire alone would have been enough to reduce a person to ashes.

"Lady Sasha!"

"We will protect you! Holy Shield!"

However, a gigantic shield of light blocked my spell. The two summoners straddling the pegasi at the angel's feet had cast the spell.

"You always gotta show off! That gets on a person's nerves after a while! Myfila, cover me!"

"You've got it, Feil. Don't stop till you drop."

After that, I had a battle of the wills—and magic—with the summoners on the pegasi. A crimson spear of flames. Purple lightning. A deluge of cerulean water. Inorganic boulder bullets. Blades of verdure wind.

I devoted myself to unleashing every kind of offensive spell I could think of as the two summoners blocked it all with their shields of light and countered with rays of light that held their own destructive power.

"Dammit. Karma Light is such an annoyin' spell to deal with."

Though Myfila blocked all direct attacks at me by shouting, "Ice Shield," and creating a thick wall for me, the stray rays that missed the giant would hit the ground and burst.

"Damn! So they *are* just toyin' with us."

I shielded my head from the clumps of dirt raining over me and poured all my focus into drawing more summoning circles. My whole mind was devoted to the sigils at my fingertips as the blue light of the spells continued to glow.

Then suddenly, I felt my head throb, but I knew I should have been far from depleting my magic supply. I was supposed to have more magical reserves than the average summoner. Even within the

Academy, I was in the upper ranks when it came to that. A little bit of reckless spellcasting wasn't going to make me keel over.

"What's wrong, Sasha?! Must be nice bein' a princess who watches from on high without havin' to lift a finger, huh?!"

Past the giant shield of light that stubbornly refused to break under my barrage of spells, Sasha silently stared as I made a funny face and blew a raspberry at her.

Finally, my dedication to provoking her seemed to have gotten through. The archangel beat her giant wings.

"You fool. I was simply giving you the chance to show off. If you'd really like me to end it, then I will without delay," the archangel said coldly without even the slightest hint of a grin or smirk as the two pegasi obediently made way for her.

In the next moment, the shield of light disappeared, and the flame spell I'd unleashed collided directly with the descending angel, but it wasn't as though my human magic would have any effect on a creature of fables. The bright-red eddy of flames crashed into her abdomen and simply poofed into white smoke.

"I suppose that thing that used to be a giant is meant to be your secret weapon? Or do you have another trick to delay the inevitable?"

"Heh! We summoned this lug to have a brawl with your archangel! I'm gettin' a punch or two in, you'll see!"

"A brawl, you say? This is rather small for a descendant of a giant, if you could even call it that. You have some nerve making such large claims when this thing isn't even half the size of Cecelia."

"Ha-ha-ha-ha! You've got a point! But height ain't what decides who wins in a fight!"

"Supposedly, the weaker the dog, the more it yaps... I see. Feil Fonaf, it sounds like you underdogs are ready to lose. All right, then. I think it's time to put my foot down and bring an end to this."

Right as I was wondering what she meant by "put her foot down," I realized everything in my vision had suddenly gone dark. I lifted my eyes, trying to find the source. Only then did I realize that towering above Myfila, the giant's corpse, and me was the archangel.

The sunlight had been blocked by her gigantic form and the six wings that stretched from her back.

Apparently, she was even faster than the human eye could perceive.

All I could do was watch as she produced a blade of light from her armor-ensconced right heel and pierced straight through the crown of the giant's head. As the archangel descended to the ground, she sliced the giant's corpse right in half.

It tumbled to the ground. I held on to the giant's hair, but that was no use anymore, seeing as the whole thing was coming down and I was being dragged with it. I watched as the scenery rushed up in what suddenly seemed like slow motion.

As the world seemed to lag around me, I saw Sasha's beautiful but cold face watching me from the solar plexus of the archangel.

Then I pointed at her with all I had and shouted, "Ya fell for it, Sashaaa!!"

Right at that moment, Sasha and the archangel were both covered in a black mist that flowed out of the giant's corpse before my eyes.

The black "fog" was my summon, a swarm of winged insects and beetles—hundreds of thousands of them, to be exact.

This was the epitome of a combo summon. We'd set up a surprise attack. After Myfila had performed her summon, I'd called forth bugs to embed themselves in the corpse so that the person who attacked the giant would be countered with the creepy-crawlies.

"Ha-ha-ha-haaaa!! Must feel terrible with all those bugs crawlin' over your bare skin, Sasha!"

Right before I was about to hit the ground, the giant's corpse moved to catch me.

Bisected or not, the corpse was still home to the necrospecters. The thing could've been torn limb from limb, but it'd still move because it was Myfila's summon. Gross but reliable.

I tumbled off the hand, and the giant quickly crawled along the ground even as its own viscera sloughed out of it. Then it latched itself onto the archangel's leg. In fact, each half of its body had laid claim to one.

Meanwhile, the archangel's upper half was still surrounded by the pitch-black swarm of insects, which was in a layer so thick that I could no longer make out the angel's masked face, her large chest, toned abs, or even her stomach, where Sasha should have been.

I could hear the sound of beating wings and cracking insect shells as the black swarm writhed.

Then in the next moment, I heard the loud roar of a beast.

The Tiger-Saber King, Zylgar—a gigantic beast—had bolted along the ground and leaped onto the archangel.

The four-legged beast wasn't *tall* in comparison to Myfila's summon, but it was larger all around and incomparably stronger. It was monstrous—four times the size of any normal tiger or lion.

Its fur was ashen gray, but other than the horns, which were sharp as swords and protruded at random from the center of its head, it sure looked like a normal tiger. Its thick front paws were capped with frightening claws.

I saw Cyril with it.

"Is this good enough for you, Feil?!"

The handsome dude in his military uniform was mounted on top of Zylgar and using the beast's fur in place of reins. In his other hand, he brandished a large sword in the air.

In the same instant, both the sword and the beast's claws came sailing down. Though we were up against an archangel, she couldn't block Cyril and Zylgar's attack if she couldn't see them.

My lips twisted as the assumption that we'd won wormed its way into my mind, but then a pure-white flame flared from the angel's entire form. She burned away my insects instantly, even reducing the corpse of the giant still grasping her legs to ash.

While I was left dumbstruck, Zylgar's claws bounced off her, too, in a shocking turn of events.

With a longsword of pure-white flames, she had blocked the claws of a beast known to make sport of hunting dragons. Though she'd just been holding Sasha on top of her overlaid hands, she now gripped the sword in her right. Then her left hand went on the move as she removed the silver mask covering her face.

The next thing Myfila, myself, and Cyril, who was balancing on top of Zylgar after they made their landing, realized was that the archangel's uncovered face was actually an exact copy of Sasha's.

"Thank you. That was a rather quaint trick."

We could only murmur to ourselves in disbelief.

"A Volte-face..."

"I heard Sasha could do it, but still," I said, "we're up against an archangel and a Volte-face..."

"This isn't even funny," Cyril said. "We were doomed from the start..."

To merge with one's summon in both body and mind was to perform a Volte-face. It was supposed to be the ultimate secret for summoners. In this day and age, you probably couldn't find many summoners who could perform one. I estimated there had to be no more than thirty at most.

"Ahh, what a nice breeze."

The angel with Sasha's face whipped her wings, buffeting us with a gust of wind that sent the pure-white flames along with it.

Though our robes whipped up in the wind, we all braced ourselves and held out against the tempest. Myfila and I were both gripping the front of our robes hard as the pain of losing our summons assaulted our hearts.

Eventually, Sasha addressed me. "Now, Feil Fonaf," she said, her gaze dropping to me and only me as she pinned me with an icy glare. Still an archangel, she thrust her longsword—large enough to slice a castle in half—into the ground.

"Will you forfeit?"

I simply glared right back at her beautiful face and didn't give her the satisfaction of a reply. Still gripping my chest, I tsked in frustration, gritting my teeth to hold back the chagrin of my surprise attack failing and the pang in my chest from losing my summons.

From a distance, I heard the bell ring out to call the match.

The professors presiding over us as judges must have determined there was no point in continuing. In other words, they'd decided that my friends and I had no chance of winning at all.

2.

The Summoner Has a Squabble in the Dining Hall

"You put on quite a show out there, you three."

"Yeah, not everyone's tenacious enough to survive a match against Princess Sasha."

"And that ending—whew! I was nearly convinced you'd actually win against her!"

We were in the Academy's dining hall, a building with such high rafters, anyone would've mistaken it for a chapel.

Long, massive tables filled the large space in neat rows, and though I'd never bothered to count, I knew it was big enough to seat at least three hundred, if not more. Everyone in the Academy could gather in the space, so it was usually used for ceremonies, like commencement and graduations.

"Huh?"

The students who'd come to chat as we ate in front of the wall sporting the *Saint Marianne's Affection for the Young Dragon* mural were three of the strongest first-years. They were all neatly dressed in the black summoner's robes mandated by the Academy.

Cyril paused just as he'd been about to slice into his thick serving of steak. "What a pleasant surprise," he replied as he dabbed at his mouth with a paper napkin on the table.

He delivered his usual aristocratic smile at the brown-haired girl who seemed to be leading the group.

"It's an honor, Lulua. I'm pleased to hear a team of your caliber was watching our match."

Though Myfila and I glanced over at them, we left the conversation and visitors to Cyril and turned our attention back to our meals. It was already past three in the afternoon, and we couldn't help being famished.

"How couldn't we watch it? There's no way we would have missed it for the world. You're full of surprises every match you enter. Since we never know what to expect, it's always a learning experience. Why, even today was several times more shocking than normal."

"Our leader is quite enthusiastic about improvising, after all," Cyril said.

"Ah-ha-ha! Well, he did seem dead set on disrobing the princess and even managed to use the giant in a surprise attack. You're the first group ever to have held out for a whole hour against her. Why shouldn't you be proud of that?"

"Should we be? I think some less sympathetic people might tease us for an hour of disgraceful behavior."

"I'm not so sure. If anyone thinks that was disgraceful, I don't think we'll ever have a team at the Academy who could win against the princess. Right, everyone? Don't you agree, Feil Fonaf?"

When they started to suddenly address me, I didn't even bother swallowing the food in my mouth as I replied, "Dunno. We just fought the way we could.

"I think we can each decide for ourselves what counts as embarrassin' or not," I said.

A short-haired, large-built guy next to the brunette slapped me on the back. "My buddy Feil's got a different take from everyone else! Guess that's the wisdom you get being an eighteen-year-old."

"What—? Gh-Ghol, what's gotten into you? His age isn't relevant..."

"Oh, sorry. My bad, Feil," Ghol said.

"Don't sweat it," I said. "Doesn't bother me at all. It's the truth. I got into the Academy two years later than everybody else."

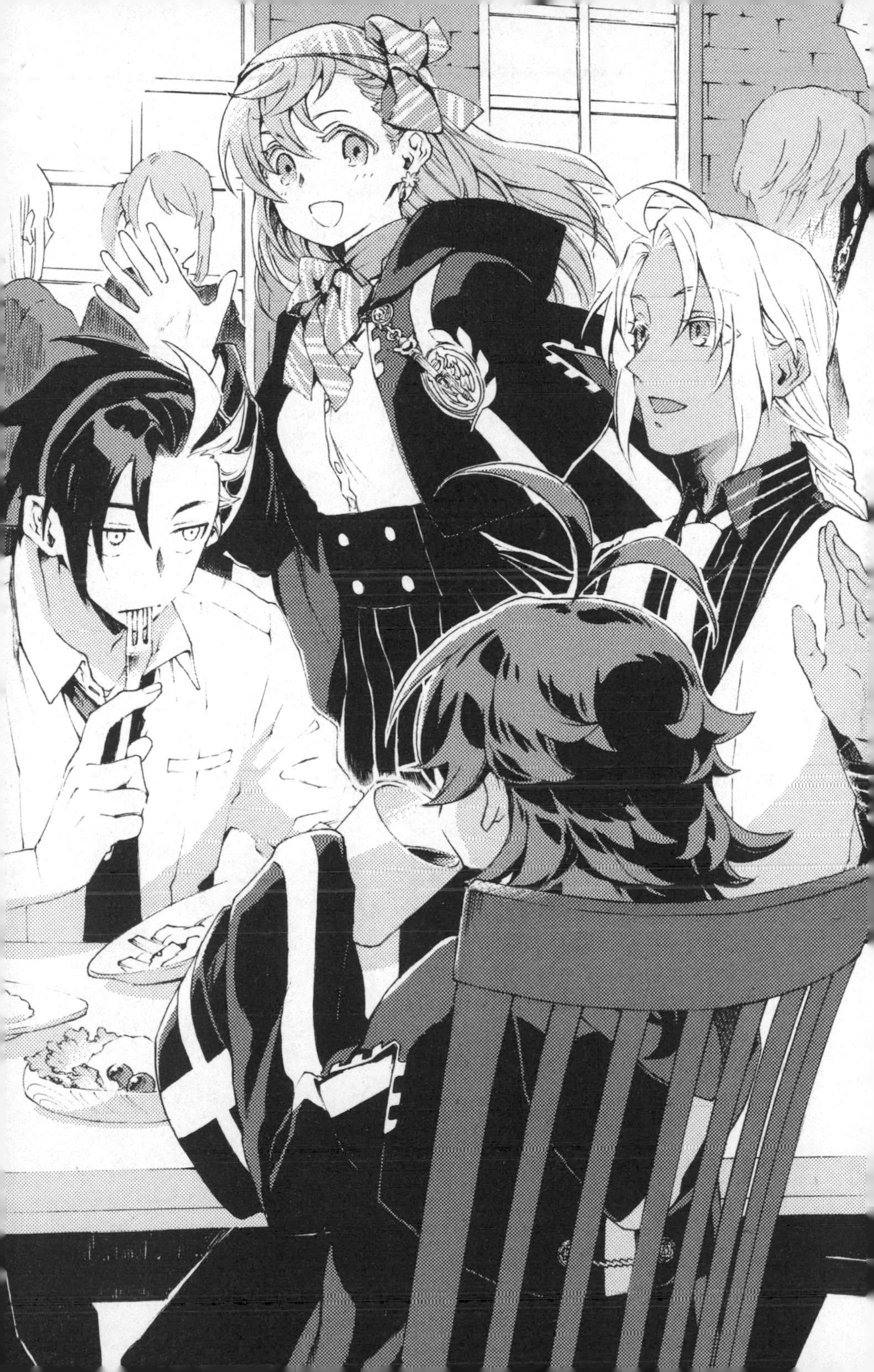

Myfila, who'd been sitting pretty and sipping away at her hearty beef stew, muttered right after me in an attempt to smooth things over. "Being older hasn't made him any less unmanageable anyway."

I just shrugged, since I didn't have a good reply. Cyril followed up with a sigh and said, "Yes, he's three times as much trouble as any of our other classmates." The other three could only stand there and awkwardly smile back.

Once she pulled herself together, the brunette gave us a genuine smile and looked us over again. "We don't have any other lectures today, so you'll be here having your meal for a while, right? How about we treat you to drinks?"

"Really?"

"Sure, as thanks for showing us we've got potential to grow, too."

"Ha-ha-ha. You'd put us in a sorry situation if you improved more, considering you're second rank in our year, but well, I'll take you up on it. Could I have another glass of wine?"

Cyril traced the tip of his finger around the rim of the wine glass in front of him. I realized the three had probably made their offer because they'd noticed only a mouthful of the red liquid remained in the glass.

"What kind?"

"The Yorand red, please."

"Oh, I never took the son of Ojlock for someone who'd drink such reasonably priced liquor."

"The price tag isn't what determines the taste. Even wines served at cheap pubs can have their flavor."

As she thrust her empty glass at them with both hands, Myfila only said, "Orange juice."

Then finally, the brunette's eyes landed on me just as I was picking at the sautéed vegetables on my half-cleared plate.

"And you, Feil Fonaf?"

I deliberately gave her an indifferent look and turned away before replying, "I'm good. Still got some water."

In order to distract myself from the awkwardness that came with turning down her kindness, I stuffed the vegetables into my mouth.

"You don't have to be so polite, Feil, my man! Isn't this the perfect opportunity for you to try some ale after suffering through only water all this time?!"

"Ghol, seriously, stop! Can't you have some tact for once?"

Cyril then chided the one who'd suddenly been rude—not the brunette's teammate but me instead. "I know you hate people doing you favors, but it's only polite to accept an offer from a classmate."

"I know that...," I said. "But I really am fine with just water."

I knew I was at fault for my own stubbornness in this situation.

I knew the brunette had no ulterior motives and that, to her, offering to buy someone a drink at the dining hall just came naturally.

Her name was Lulua Folicker. I'm pretty sure that made her part of one of the famous conjurer families. She'd likely grown up pampered and never had to worry about money. A lady through and through, and probably brought up like a princess herself.

On the other hand, I just couldn't stand handouts. If I accepted a drink from her now, I knew I'd never have a means of reciprocating later, and that weighed too heavily on my mind to take her up on the offer.

Lulua was already replying. "W-well, it's all right. I'm not going to force you to accept," she said, trying to tide things over.

"Get a load of this! The commoner's son is eating the veg-scrap special again!"

A group of conspicuously less-considerate classmates had filed into the dining hall then. I saw Duck-Head was taking the lead with a detestable grin on his face as he brought all six jokers over to us. His bangs were slicked back sky-high, and the sides were close cropped. This guy—the one I'd christened the duck-head summoner—was more commonly known as "Bernhart Hadcheck" by others.

He came from a family famous enough to rival Cyril's, but unlike my friend, he was infamous for being a moneyed hack. The guy was wearing his usual uniform of garish and expensive necklaces and bracelets, which only served to flaunt his buffoonery. The henchmen trailing after him were decked out in gold, too—likely a gift from their boss, Lord Bernhart, himself.

"Yo, Cyril, must be tuckered out from all that running away."

"Yes, I'm quite tired, so if you have no business here, I'd appreciate it if you could go on your merry way. Simply hearing your voice makes me break out in hives."

"Don't be like that, bud. Don't you want to know what happened in the matches after yours?"

"Nope. In fact, I have no interest in them."

"It was a sweep! For *me*! It was such a piece of cake, I didn't even have the chance to work up an appetite, but you know we gotta celebrate three conquests in a row!" Bernhart took a look at the food I'd ordered and snorted. "Do you ever eat meals that don't stink, pauper?"

Then one of the henchmen behind him piped up, "He's got a boor's palate! The only thing he's ever eaten is the veggie-scrap special, after all!"

In that moment, as those idiots spewed nonsense, I felt indignation bubbling up to the forefront of my mind. I wasn't the kind of person who could stand idly by while people were making a fool out of me. There are some fights worth getting into.

I gave in to my emotions, bringing my fist up to slam it down on the table, but right then, someone beat me to the punch. Cyril stood up without a word. His usual nobility was nowhere to be seen. His muscular body, more fit than anyone else's around, was oozing frigidity as he looked down on Bernhart and the henchmen.

"Bold of you to make a mockery of the Ojlock family, which prides itself on bravery and tactical skills... You seem intent on starting a war with me."

They say that serene people are frightening when angered. Seeing Cyril's quiet fury, I quickly forgot my own.

That put the miscreants, who'd only been running their mouths because they were with their leader, in a much more frightening position than if I'd yelled at them myself.

One of the henchmen looked terrified as he started to blabber excuses. "W-we weren't— We were just making fun of Feil Fonaf—"

"That's exactly why you're at fault. Do I seem like the type to laugh off your making a mockery of my friend?"

And then…no one could work up the nerve to say anything in the awkward atmosphere.

Bernhart was the first to break the silence—by punching the daylights out of the henchman who'd teased me.

"Let's go! You've got a lot of nerve putting a damper on my victories!"

After spitting that out, he stalked off into the large dining hall. The kid he'd punched got off his rear end and followed right after, howling, "W-wait for me! Bernhart!"

Cyril sat right down without a word as though nothing had happened at all. He swigged the remainder of his wine and talked Myfila down, saying, "If you use lightning spells at this range, someone's going to end up dead, so cool it." Apparently, she'd been planning to cast a spell the moment the bullying had begun.

Lulua, who'd seen it all, said to me, "You've got great teammates."

"It ain't exactly a good thing they're more hot-blooded than me."

"Pfft! Ha-ha! That's a riot considering you're the most off-kilter maverick in your grade! Okay, just give me a sec. I'll get drinks for Cyril and Myfila."

The order counter was right next to the entrance. As I watched her head off with her two friends, I murmured to myself as a thought occurred to me. "Wonder if Sasha's hungry. I'm pretty sure she used plenty of her magic, too."

It wasn't like I was looking for anyone to answer, but Cyril obliged me with one anyway. "You haven't heard? Sasha's team has another match today."

"You kidding me? Normal people would die havin' two in one day."

"It can't be easy being the top of her year and the top of the Academy, too. Actually, she's probably giving the third-years a run for their money like usual right around now. It's Agnika Aluka. Sasha wouldn't let anyone like that beat her."

"Huh...?"

At the Academy, we had matches between the summoner teams every day in the afternoon. They were straightforward mock battles—two teams of three per Academy ranking match. Who lost and who won would determine our grades for practical skills.

Our team just so happened to be fifth out of the first-years and twenty-second out of the whole Academy ranking. We'd been putting in the work. We were average, but greedy.

"Feil, want to head back to the dorms after eating? I want to ask you and Myfila something about the interpretation of the tome you showed me yesterday—*The Warrior's Last Teaching of Suspicion*."

"Sorry. I've got overnight work today."

"Can't you get a day off considering you fought Sasha? I think you're going to work yourself to death at this rate."

"Dude, I'm poor. If I don't work, I can't afford to eat."

"I've been telling you that I can help you out with your monthly living expenses..."

"I'm fine. Bein' alone in life makes things easy, but it comes with its fair share of hardships, too."

The Summoner Accidentally Sees the Princess Undressed

"Get it together, Dad! You better not die on me!"

The spark of life was disappearing right in my arms. His breathing was growing shallower by the second. I wanted to keep him awake, even for a second longer, so I slapped my old man across the face.

"I cast a spell! Your wounds are all closed up now! Ya just gotta hold on a little longer! C'mon!"

My hand, sticky with blood, had left a red print across my father's pale face.

"God…!"

I'd never in my life, in all my memory, genuinely begged a god for anything.

But now the only hope I had left was a prayer for a miracle that would save my dad's life. If any god could only grant me that, I'd dedicate all my worldly possessions, everything in my ability, my whole future to them. If my dad could live, I would have given up on my goal of becoming a summoner and made myself a disciple.

"Why…? Why did it come to this? Dad, what did you do?!"

The flimsy front door had been left open, letting the unseasonal gusts from a blizzard whip at us mercilessly. Farther down the entryway, it was pitch-black, as though life had been breathed into the shadows themselves, which were buffeting us with unforgiving snow.

"Who'd stab a penniless farmer?!"

The light of the candles hanging from the ceiling heartlessly illuminated the pool of blood that had gathered on my father's torso.

I had no idea how many attempts I'd made at a healing spell.

If I'd only been there when my dad had been struck, I never would have broken down like this. The stab wound, which had reached deep enough to hit his liver, would have sent me reeling even then, but I would've held out a faint line of hope and been able to concentrate on healing him.

"Keep your eyes open, Pa! You've...you've gotta live! Are ya gonna leave me all alone?!"

This was the limitation of healing magic. Through the manipulation of time, a wound could be recuperated, but the blood lost could not. When I came home to find my dad unresponsive on the ground, I thought for a second that it was all over. That he'd lost too much blood. That a healing spell would be too late for him.

"Say something, man! Wake up and talk to me!"

Even if I averted my eyes from the ghastly sight I didn't want to see, the warm liquid flowing from the wound on his torso and onto my hands, my own stomach, and my thighs whispered the fate of the only blood relative I had left.

"Fe...il..."

As he rested in my arms, my dad's right hand slowly stirred. Even as his hand weakly trembled, he managed to bring it to the inner pocket of his coat and produced a small hemp bag, telling me, "Th-this... Take this... You can...go to school...when you're sixteen, right...?"

The bag clinked, revealing its contents to be coins.

In that moment when I realized what had happened, I clasped my dad's hand over the bag. "Who cares 'bout money?! Who cares?! If you're not here, what does it matter if I become a summoner if no one's there to see it?!" My face crumpled.

He seemed startled by that, but he didn't have the time or energy to even give me a strained smile. "It wasn't supposed to be like this."

At the very end, he looked regretful. He looked pained, as though he could have broken out into tears at any moment. "It wasn't supposed to—"

I gritted my teeth so hard, they felt as if they were about to crack. "I can't believe you. I can't believe you, dammit." I couldn't stop the tears streaming down my face, and I didn't even bother to wipe the snot from my nose.

Then, suddenly, all the strength left my body, and my entire mind was overtaken by lethargy.

With my dad still in my arms, the tears and snot still running down my face, I had frozen.

Eventually, I tried to wipe my wet face with my bloodied left hand, and that was when I awoke from my dream.

"That was...awful."

When I opened my eyelids, I found that I was lying on top of a rock. Because of how heart-wrenching my dream had been, waking up was rough, to say the least. My back was fully exposed, and both my shoulders felt cold as ice.

Where was I? And how had I fallen asleep?

I tried setting aside the memories of my dream as I grasped for anything familiar, but that got me no closer to my answers. I'd been working late into the night—at least until one o'clock—and made a hasty retreat back to the dorms, where I'd drawn out the last of my strength to get into the communal baths...and that was where my memories puttered off. It was almost as though everything after soaking into the water had been wiped clean.

"That was close... I was almost a goner..."

I groaned from relief as I realized I'd avoided drowning, then I slapped a hand on the rock floor to heave myself up. Apparently, I'd lost consciousness at the edge of the bath and collapsed facedown with my upper half clear out of the water. The rest of me was still soaking.

Thanks to the enchanted lights lining the ceiling, the bath was lit bright as daylight.

Seeing as I worked late nights, I was grateful the baths were generously open twenty-four seven, but the prospect of falling asleep in them frightened me. If I died like that, well, I'd never be able to live with myself.

"Ahh..."

I leaned along the side of the bath and sunk down to my neck. Once my back and shoulders got warm again, I needed to scram. What time was it anyway?

As I was thinking that, I looked up.

"What the…?!"

As I lifted my face, I saw someone standing right in front of me, legs in a wide, imposing stance. The shock nearly killed me all over again, and I couldn't back away because I was at the edge of the bath.

"So you're finally awake."

A beautiful girl with platinum-blond hair looked down at me. Through the thin layer of steam, I could see she was wearing a pure-white robe.

I realized who was towering before me, her arms crossed—it was Sasha Shidoh Zultania.

But wait…the robe itself was already thin, and wet as it was, it clung to her so closely that she might as well have been wearing nothing at all. She also had her arms crossed right below her heaving bust. Her cinched waist made her hips look even more alluring.

She was as radiant as a goddess, so much so that she could've seduced a saint, or a dragon of yore, or other such mythical figures.

"You scared me half to death! …Can't believe I'm in the bath with a princess."

"No, *you* scared me. The moment I get in, I run into Feil Fonaf himself hanging off the edge of the tub."

"Ya should've just woken me up."

"I did, in fact, make an attempt to shake you awake, but you didn't even stir. So I decided to observe you for a while instead. You were very quiet… A first for you."

She was still looking straight down at me without batting an eye. I started to wonder if she felt even an ounce of shyness over the fact that I was staring right back at her.

From midnight to dawn, the bath hardly got any visitors, so it was open to everyone during that time, meaning that anyone living in the dorms—male or female—could use it. But it was common courtesy

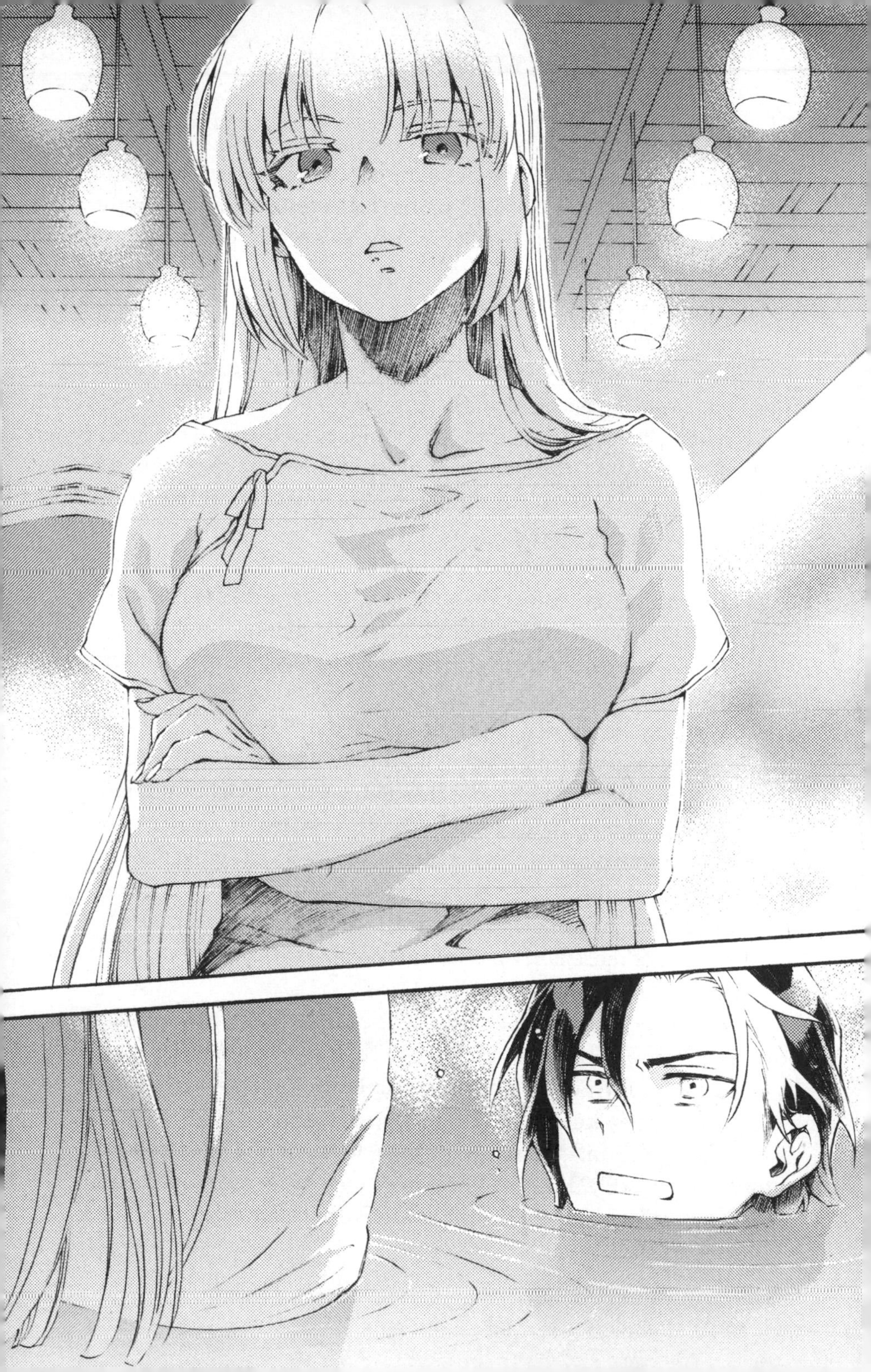

not to use the bath when someone of the opposite sex was already in it. Besides, I was pretty sure Sasha's room had a private bath anyway. The highest-ranking students in their respective years were all assigned special luxury rooms.

"What time is it?"

"Almost morning."

"Shoot. How long was I out? Also…Sasha, could ya quit standing there like…*that*? I have no idea where to look."

Sasha finally sat down in the bath when she saw the flustered look on my face. She didn't take her eyes off me the entire time, though, and went right back to interrogating me. "Are you still working?" she asked without any hesitation.

I couldn't get out of the bath.

I was burning up beneath the water, and it was Sasha's fault. Also, since I had no interest in being labeled an exhibitionist, I was gonna to have to stay put until the silver-haired maiden decided to go on her merry way.

"They didn't have enough people to help out. Besides, business is booming. I've been working overnight shifts for the past month. Working the kitchen's pretty rough, and it's not worth the eight hundred 'n' sixty gants an hour, quite frankly."

"Eight hundred and sixty? Is that normal for a tavern the masses frequent?"

"Yep, sure is. A glass of beer's a cheap two hundred gants, y'know. This isn't one of those fancy restaurants on Main Street."

"I see… It seems I have much to learn."

I willed her to get out of the bath already, but for whatever reason, Sasha showed no sign of budging. Then a newfound suspicion took root in me. "Wait…," I murmured as I tilted my head to the side.

"…How'd you know I work at a tavern?"

Sasha replied unassumingly, as though it were the most natural thing in the world, "Because I approved your labor petition. We're classmates, but as a member of the Shidoh royalty, I'm also one of the Academy trustees."

That was the first I'd heard of it. I couldn't stop my eyes from going wide.

"Whoa. I had no idea."

"You didn't even suspect that might be the case? I'm both a top-ranked summoner and part of the Academy's administration, after all."

"Nahhh, no one who saw you summon an archangel, of all things, would doubt that you're at the top of the class. But I dunno how to put this... Being both a student *and* a princess seems like a lot."

"It's nothing as difficult as what you're doing, Feil Fonaf," she said.

"Huh?"

"You're the only student employed in town right now. Most students would already lose their entire day to spell research and combat practice, yet here you are working a part-time job as well. You do understand that at this rate, you'll quite literally work yourself to death, don't you?"

Sasha was never one to sugarcoat anything...

I let out a gut laugh before I realized it. I braced myself against the edge of the bath and stared up at the enchanted lights lining the ceiling. I squinted at the incandescent lamps, which had supposedly been invented a century ago.

"Senior conjurer and summoner jobs are burstin' to the seams with filthy rich kids, and the Academy tuition is too damn high."

In her eyes, I probably looked like I was on my last leg. Sasha's voice was quiet as she asked, "Then why do you work so hard?"

Exhausted as I was, I let a weak smile form on my face and answered, "'Cause I don't have time *or* money." I scooped a handful of the bathwater and rinsed my face. "Unlike other first-years, I'm already eighteen."

I let out an exhausted sigh that disappeared into the vapor. Once I was out of the bath, I was planning on reading over a spellbook I'd checked out from the library until first-period Morphological Theory of Elemental Summons started.

"Since I made it here by the skin of my teeth, I've gotta over-compensate and work my ass off, or I'll never achieve anything."

"But…I heard you applied to the Academy three years ago, when you were still fifteen."

"Well…I had a hard time comin' up with the enrollment fees."

"I see…"

She probably realized continuing the conversation down that route would be as good as stepping on a land mine. Instead of prying, Sasha changed the topic entirely. "Come to think of it, you severely underestimated me during yesterday's match."

"What, you thought we were just having fun and teasing you?"

"No, not that. I don't care about you targeting my clothes or even the swarm of insects. But, Feil Fonaf, you were up against me and never bothered to summon your Counterpart."

"Oh…that."

"I called Cecelia; she's mine."

"Well, Cyril summoned Zylgar on our side. And you know about Zylgar—that monster could've faced any of those teams solo an' come out uncontested."

"But that wasn't nearly enough. I understand why Myfila didn't summon her Counterpart, since hers isn't fit for combat, but how long will I have to wait until you produce your ultimate summon? You've kept it a secret all this time."

I couldn't answer her.

She'd called me out without any idea what kind of situation I was in.

Cyril had the Tiger-Saber King, Zylgar, and Myfila had the Starry-Sky Whistler, Parol. Every summoner, without exception, had a Counterpart to their soul—a summon they could call on.

We summoners borrowed the powers of a partner who would cross time and space to unconditionally answer our call, and through that, we would gain the intuition to summon others. But those without the experience couldn't become summoners no matter how great a conjurer they were. In fact, I'd only performed my first summon the day before the entrance ceremony.

The first summon that answers a conjurer's call is called their Counterpart. And more often than not, that Counterpart is supposed to be the summoner's strongest and best summon.

"Mine's as uncooperative as I am," I told her. "Haven't prepared enough to summon my Counterpart in a match."

"So you mean to say that slimes and swarms of insects are not your specialty?"

"'Course not. I like comin' up with strategies as much as anyone, but I'll show ya what I can do head-on, too—next time, all right?"

Then Sasha giggled. "Ha-ha-ha, next time. I see." Finally, she got up from the bath. Droplets dribbled off her robe as it clung to her skin, making her look entirely too captivating.

"I do get the feeling I'll be fighting against your team again," she said. "Soon, I believe."

As I looked up at Sasha, fresh from the bath, the corner of my mouth lifted.

She was so unfazed by a male gaze on her, and the deep valley of her breasts and striking curve of her hips were so out of place for her sixteen-year-old frame that I couldn't help but want to laugh.

I was so focused on not letting her overpower me with her charm that I blustered out...

"Just wait for the summons festival." "I'll be waiting for the summons festival."

We both ended up speaking at the same time.

4.

The Summoner Clambers Up
His Counterpart

"Feil, are you *sure* you wouldn't be better off giving up? That's not going to get it to move."

I heard Cyril rasping from somewhere far below.

I yelled back, half out of desperation, "The verses take up a whole ninety percent! It's basically life-and-death!"

When I looked down at the bare bedrock below, I could see Cyril and Myfila, though from where I was standing, they looked like grains of rice.

This was what you'd call "towering heights." I was pretty sure my current elevation was on par with Sedra Cathedral, which was the tallest building in town—a structure with breathtaking spires that towered over the region. If I fell from this height, I'd probably plummet for a good five seconds before becoming a pancake on the ground below.

A gust of wind from the wildlands whipped past me, billowing the hem of my robe.

"Ugh…"

I felt like I'd almost been whisked away along with the zephyr, which sent shivers down my spine. I'd buttoned my robe up, but there was a whole lotta fabric to catch in the wind. I started to really regret not dressing for the occasion before heading up.

"C'mon… Move, Pandora…"

I'd found purchase on a protrusion and used a strengthening spell to help with my grip.

"If you could just move...that'd be a miracle..."

I nimbly worked my way up, grabbing hold of the bluish-black wall before me.

But no matter how far I climbed, I still hadn't caught sight of the peak. Even after strengthening myself three times over, scaling the wall was rapidly draining my stamina. I had no lifeline, and the sheer terror of the drop below was enough to make my heart plunge.

"Pandora, what's your problem?! Seriously! I'm puttin' my life on the line. Would it kill you to give me a sign of life or *anything*?!"

I huffed and puffed as I grumbled at the wall. I felt like I was dressing down a family member who had gotten out of control.

I suddenly stopped my ascent. "Pandora...," I whined and set my forehead against the bluish-black surface. There was a strangeness to the texture. It was hard as steel yet felt weirdly moist. It was also smooth, kind of like skin.

"You're so stubborn! You're an even bigger problem child than I am!"

As I grumbled and turned up to the sky overhead, the afternoon light illuminated the gigantic form from behind.

It was like a steep cliff. Well, if the top of a cliff were rounded and looked a little like human shoulders.

"Sheesh..."

I tried to restart my climb and stuck my hand into the chalk bag on my belt to keep my hands from getting slippery.

Right at the perfect time, the strongest gust of all swept past me. I couldn't hold on with just my right hand and watched as my fingertips were pried away from the part of the structure I was gripping. A moment later, I was blown high into the air.

Welp...I'm dead.

When I felt the chilly air on every inch of my body, I was convinced that this was the end for me. I reached toward the wall instinctively, but I was too far away no matter how I flailed my legs. I was consumed by fear. All the blood rushed to my head, and the back of my eye sockets throbbed.

I dropped from a dizzying height.

"Guh!"

...And suddenly, I felt my body hit something—the impact stole all the air from my lungs.

I coughed and looked down, realizing the scenery was traveling sideways instead of toward me. Everything around me seemed much darker, too.

I looked up to find the source of the shadow above me... My midriff was in the talons of a monstrous bird with what looked to be a wingspan of a whopping 10 mejals—1.7 mejals being the average height of a full-grown man.

The rainbow-winged bird had the gigantic face of a Steller's sea eagle.

Black scales covered its claws, which were large enough to carry a calf, and continued all the way up to the bird's torso, acting as fortification around the bird's neck. It had the effect of making the bird look like it was wearing armor.

It wasn't like I'd gotten lucky and a marvel of a monster bird happened to just pass by right when I needed one.

Obviously, this was one of Cyril's summons.

As if to confirm my thought, I heard Cyril's soothing voice come from the bird's yellow beak.

"See? This is what happens when you're reckless."

Though the bird didn't have human vocal cords, an ancient bird like this possessed enough magical ability to make such a feat seem trivial.

He must have summoned the bird to help as soon as he saw me lose my grip.

"Thanks, Cyril... You seriously saved my ass just now."

"Don't mention it. I understand why you're so worked up. If Zylgar were in the same state, I probably would have tried everything I could, too."

With a single flutter of its wings, the gigantic bird sailed along the air current. It was rising up in a large arc. Its rugged talons were giving me the creeps, but now that it was carrying me, I had a bird's-eye view of the rocky terrain.

We were at the base of the barren Agona Mountain and right next to the sprawling desolate wildlands that stretched before it.

The land was to the south of the Academy, after crossing a mountain range. Some students would apparently use the area to test out spells that could result in wide-scale destruction, but it was generally free from prying eyes. Since the only way to get to it was with the aid of a winged summon, it was just the perfect place to handle a "big" secret on a day off like the weekend.

"Pandora looks as huge as ever…," Cyril commented.

"Too huge, if you ask me. How the hell did *I* summon something like *this*…?"

Yes… This desolate area was the perfect stage to summon *my Counterpart*…

Cyril's bird flew high into the air, easily achieving an altitude of over five hundred mejals.

At first glance, it seemed as though a bluish-black mountain had suddenly appeared to tower over the middle of the red bedrock. However, it was too smooth to be an actual mountain and too complex a shape to seem like a natural rock formation.

But who would have realized it was actually a gigantic humanoid life-form that had plopped itself down to sit in the middle of nowhere?

You couldn't call this thing a *mere* giant, either. The creature's entire body was covered by some exoskeleton composed of who-knows-what material.

It also wasn't a god. With its head that looked something like a cross between an extravagant knight's helmet and a dragon head; its torso, which perilously tapered in like some sort of upside-down triangle; and the forked tail that was too large and too long for its body, there was something sinister about every part of it.

It wasn't a devil, either. I knew that because my Counterpart had ten misshapen wings that looked like gouts of black-and-blue flames along its back. Devils never had more than four wings.

"Well…it *is* Pandora, Legendary Beast of the Last Realm…," Cyril came in again.

"I drew the short straw. I didn't think somebody who'd pick a fight with the *gods* would answer my call… Honestly, I never even wanted this. There's such a thing as too much, ya know. There's only so much one person can take on."

Standing up, Pandora could have been over three hundred mejals tall. Even sitting with his head drooping as it was now, he was still nearly a hundred and fifty. And just earlier, I'd been scaling the right arm of my Counterpart, the Legendary Beast of the Last Realm, Pandora.

I figured that if my life was in danger, he'd have to react… At least, that was the plan.

"He didn't even flinch when you fell, Feil."

"So I noticed…," I said.

"Looks like another failed attempt."

"I gathered that, too," I said.

"I didn't want to say this, but sometimes, you get to a point when you just have to cut your losses."

"……I've realized that," I said.

Cyril's summon leisurely circled the top of Pandora's head. When the head came into view, I almost averted my eyes. Pandora stayed seated, not moving an inch.

There hadn't been any decisive battle with an all-powerful god and legendary beast here today. My Counterpart was in the same exact shape he'd been in since I summoned him in the morning…yet in spite of that, the left half of my summon's head had been crushed to a pulp.

His thick exoskeleton had been crushed, too, and cracks spread far along his outer skin. It was almost as though someone had brought down a blunt weapon over his head. The deepest fissure in his exoskeleton armor reached all the way around to the back of his skull, exposing his brain matter for anyone to touch.

This had apparently happened a long, long time ago during some sort of conflict, when the elementals were still nobodies during the age of gods.

The legendary beast Pandora had challenged the gods above to a battle. After tearing several of them limb from limb, he'd finally succumbed to the Supreme God Zen's thunderous hammer, which obliterated part of his head. After that, the surviving gods had entrusted all things in the world to the elementals, powerful beasts, and angels in order to spirit themselves away into retirement at the Garden of the Edge.

Every kid knew the famous legend, no matter what country they were raised in. Even I'd heard it time and again at the village temple. But still…

…I didn't understand why my Counterpart was Pandora *after* he had been defeated by Zen.

Summoning was supposed to be a marvel that crossed time and space, so why was it that my partner had been summoned from *that* exact time?

This was a huge pain in the ass to deal with. In his current state, he was absolutely useless…but that wasn't even the start of my actual problems.

"Come back, Feil."

"You tried your best, Feil."

Eventually, I landed on the ground with Cyril's bird. For a while, I just stood there.

At the foot of Pandora's body, they'd laid out a picnic blanket. The scent of coffee wafted toward me. Cyril and Myfila each nursed mugs as they read tomes to pass the time.

"How about a cup of coffee? It'll help you unwind."

"Nah, I'm fine," I said. "Um, have you seen my— Ah, here we go."

I took a swig from my leather canteen to quench my thirst. Then I flopped right onto the edge of the picnic blanket. With my legs splayed out across the ground, I looked up at the majestic view of Pandora.

"I thought it was a good idea, though…," I murmured to myself.

"You shouldn't have attempted it," Cyril said to me after hearing me talk under my breath. "You shouldn't put yourself in danger just to get the attention of a summon."

I snorted before I could stop myself—the scoff was aimed at me, of course.

"Well, normally, summoners aren't ignored by their Counterparts."

I said it nonchalantly, but neither of my friends spared me a laugh. Actually, they were looking pretty serious as they stared me down. That was the look they'd probably naturally ended up with after trying to hide their pity for me.

"Just listen, you two," I said.

I faced Cyril and Myfila, who were both sitting cross-legged and seemed to be leaning in toward me. With a sigh, I continued, "I'm sure of this now. Pandora's dead as a doorknob."

That earned me two sincere looks from them and their silent companionship.

This didn't feel like any chat over coffee, and every single word took me effort to get out.

"Even after I was in mortal peril right next to him, I never even felt Pandora's heartbeat. He didn't acknowledge me in the slightest. So my Counterpart isn't the Legendary Beast of the Last Realm, Pandora; it's Pandora's corpse. Who's even heard of somebody with a corpse for a partner? It's unprecedented."

I tried to keep things upbeat, but I was only met with more silence. Cyril seemed like he wanted to say something, but in the end, all he managed was a slight quiver of his lip. He was speechless.

And naturally so. This was essentially the moment a dark cloud had formed over my future as a summoner. Half-hearted consolation from my friends wouldn't do anything here. It wasn't their fault, though. Had the roles been reversed, I don't think I would've been able to find the words, either. I probably would've stared with the same grim look on my face, just like the ones they were wearing.

So all I could do was put on a brave face and tell them, "Anyway, there's no point in me wallowin' over it. It took me half a year since starting at the Academy, but now I finally know who my Counterpart is. In a way, that's a win. I have no clue why an inanimate corpse answered my summon, but first things first: I've gotta figure out a practical use for it."

Once I'd rambled on to that point, Cyril's lip finally twisted up. It was a subtle expression. I couldn't tell whether his smile was one of admiration or one of pity.

"You don't let anything bring you down, Feil."

"That's just how I am. I gotta make the best of the hand I'm dealt."

Then Myfila had something interesting to say. "Pandora's still the strongest summon, even dead."

I thought over the meaning of those words. "Well...," I said, producing a small, leather-bound book from my conjurer's robes and starting to thumb through it. I pinched pages one through one hundred ten between my fingers, showing the two how thick it was.

"He's dead, but look how many pages he's filled with his verses. I reckon Sasha's archangel only takes twenty pages at most."

A summoner would create one book of *Summoner Incantations* in their lifetime.

Each summon would leave behind a verse. Or rather, it was more like the words would spontaneously appear in the book once the summon was contracted.

Slimes and fiends would get a few lines at most, and something as powerful as a dragon would claim multiple pages. Anything that took up more than ten pages was basically a monster from myth or legend. Only a few summoners in all recorded history had contracted with summons that took up more than twenty pages.

No matter how great a summoner was, they were limited to what their single volume of incantations could contain. Yet here was my book, already 90 percent filled just by Pandora's description.

Once summoned, it was over. There was no way to erase the words already documented. Even though the Pandora summon was a bust, because of the way that the summoner world worked, I couldn't just go and find another powerful beast to take on as my partner.

My only option was to make the best of the few pages I had left.

"What do those hundred pages say?"

"That's what I wanna know," I said. "The language either predates Catagmark civilization or was never a writing system used in this world to begin with... All I've got is the introduction for summoning him. If I focus until I feel like I'm gonna die, that's when those words appear in my mind, but that's it."

"*Arise, O beast that thwarts despair, over darkened sea your wings claim the air...* Was that it?"

"Yeah, and *I'm* the one despairin' here."

I rested my chin in my palm as I slouched over crossed legs. But then it occurred to me that there was no point to being bummed about it again so soon. "Well, anyway, puttin' that aside, I need to figure out how to use Pandora," I said, bringing us back on topic. "If he's dead, he can stay dead. But is there a way to get him to move?"

Cyril looked dubious. "You want to treat him like a puppet?"

I snapped my fingers and pointed right at Cyril with the same hand. "The issue is how big and heavy he is. I could use a fettering spell to manipulate his limbs, but human and beast spells aren't even gonna work on his fingertips."

"How about botanical spells? If you just keep feeding them magic, you can grow as much ivy as you need."

"But all they'll do is grow. A vine's resilience is proportionate to how thick its stalk is. First, I'd need to find a plant that can lift Pandora."

I crossed my arms, and Myfila matter-of-factly offered a suggestion. "Then just summon the World Tree. It's bigger than Pandora and wouldn't collapse under his weight."

Cyril and I both forced smiles for her.

"That's basically summoning a piece of the world. If I could summon the World Tree, I wouldn't be worryin' about Pandora in the first place."

"But you might be able to summon a branch. There's a slim chance."

Myfila might have actually been earnest about her suggestion. Since Cyril and I hadn't taken her seriously, she pouted (rather cutely) and let out a sulky "Hmph."

I wasn't trying to get on her good side by saying it, but I asked her, "Actually, thinkin' about it, since we've got a corpse, this seems like the perfect time for necrospecters. What does our resident genius necromancer have to say to that?"

"No can do," she said without missing a beat. Even after Myfila crushed all hopes of the most practically feasible method I could think of, I still couldn't back down. I couldn't just accept Myfila's assessment right then.

"How about if four or five of 'em worked together? I know it'd be rough for one to move Pandora on its own, but if each of 'em took a limb or somethin'..." My words were naturally speeding up as I went.

Myfila looked up at Pandora's giant body, then said, "Even if Pandora's soul is gone, I'm pretty sure you summoned him immediately after he died. He has too much vitality left in him for a necrospecter to enter the body. They'd die the moment they touched him."

"So what you're tellin' me is that I've gotta let his body rot completely first?"

"If his insides completely liquefy, then they might be able to manage possession of a finger."

"I see. So basically, that's a dead end, too. Summons compulsorily disappear when their summoner passes out. And Pandora isn't gonna rot in one or two days, no matter what kind of spell I use. Even I'd probably die after four all-nighters."

"I doubt Pandora would rot even if you waited a whole century."

I looked over at Cyril and said, "If only we had time-manipulation magic." Suddenly, he burst into laughter.

"I think it'd be easier for you to do a hundred years of all-nighters, Feil."

"You could summon the origin elemental of death. An origin elemental would be able to enter Pandora."

"Don't be ridiculous. They're as legendary as the World Tree, if not more so," I said.

I was fresh out of options. When Cyril saw me hold my head in my hands, he couldn't help but try to pitch yet another idea. "Uh, right.

How about you treat summoning him like a spell, instead of forcing him to move?"

"So, like, summon him in midair and let him fall or somethin'?"

"Well…is that something you've considered already?"

"Well, I can't do that around other students. If Pandora's giant body came falling from the sky, I'm pretty sure we'd end up with more corpses than just his. Not exactly a strat for Academy ranking matches."

"Yeah, you're right. They're just academic duels in the end."

I really felt backed into a corner now. Three heads were better than one, but it wasn't like putting our heads together would make us geniuses. We couldn't come up with any better ideas as the dry winds of the wildlands filled the silence.

Eventually, Myfila sipped from her mug of coffee and murmured, "It won't be an origin elemental, but would you like one of the greater necrospecters to take a look at Pandora?"

Cyril and I had no idea what she meant at all.

Myfila just pointed up at the blue sky and squinted at the expansive emptiness and glare of the sun.

The Summoner Finishes Work

After another day of shaking iron pans, my arms were trembling. I worked the night shift for seven hours straight, starting at six PM. I was used to working in the kitchens after my dad, a farmer, died when I was only fifteen and one of the cooks in my hometown employed me. But I was still dead tired after my shift.

"Wheeew…"

I pulled off the sweat-soaked handkerchief I'd tied over my hair and headed out of the scorching hot kitchen into the large hall.

The dozen or so oil lanterns fastened to the wall painted the entire hall orange.

The drunkard regulars who'd been drinking until not too long ago had left the chairs in disarray. A few of the thirty-eight round stools had been knocked over, and the rectangular tables were misaligned. All I could do was smile wanly at the ruckus they'd managed while I was stuck in the back.

"I'm exhausted…" I righted a stool at my feet and sat myself down on it, almost falling into the seat.

"Good work today. There sure were a whole lotta customers again." A young girl's voice addressed me.

I looked up to find a brunette. The apron-style dress she wore was wide-open at the front. She had a smile that seemed immune to fatigue as she thrust a stein at me. It was filled with ordinary cold water.

"Sorry, Ilecia."

I bobbed my head at her as I took the stein and drained the water in one go. "I was so busy today that I didn't even have time for a sip of water." I laughed and let out a languid sigh.

Ilecia tilted her head to the side and smiled, her long loose curls fluttering down as she did. She perched herself on the edge of the table and started to chat with me.

"You better not faint on us. If you do, the boss is going to give us a hell of a time now that he's feeling so rushed."

"Seriously, though, what the heck happened this month? I feel like we've been serving up all the expensive booze we rarely ever bring out..."

"Oh, that. There have been reports of this mysterious group of people handing out money."

"They're handing out money? Did the trade city get their own Robin Hood or something?"

"I just heard about it today from old Mr. Coulon. Apparently, someone's been visiting the poorer neighborhoods and using people there for a search party or something. I think they're a scholar of some sort? Maybe a government official? I don't really know for sure, but apparently, someone with a whole lot of personal baggage drifted into Raddermark."

"A scholar, huh...? I wonder if they stole an old relic or something."

"As a result, some of our regulars are a lot more well-off now, and some of that cash flow's trickling to us, too. I'm sure it'll settle down eventually. I mean, they've been guzzling booze without sparing a thought for anything else, after all."

Raddermark was a trading city of three hundred thousand that had been developed on a major road connecting the land of Shidoh and the land of Rodoh.

The north was occupied by the Academy, which produced summoners, while the east was where the large marketplace was situated, where you could find anything from ingredients for dinner to magical tomes. The sprawling land was unencumbered by outer walls, so the place had developed aristocratic manors, slum streets, cathedrals, a red-light district, a library, theaters, sewage systems, and even an underground cemetery. The large city was only outmatched by the land of Shidoh's capital.

And this place that I worked at, the Horse's Drool Pavilion, was right on the border of the great market and the red-light district. The clientele tended to be upper-lower class. Our regulars were the laborers with small salaries—so people like the assistants at the markets or the manservants at the red-light district.

"Someone touched my butt again today. Don't they know that's a terribly rude thing to do to a future star?" Ilecia complained.

"Well, they're all a bunch of good-for-nothing drunks. Hey, maybe we could add that to the menu. Cop a feel for just fifty thousand."

"Ah-ha-ha-ha! That's way overpriced! They'd only be touching, right? I think the going rate for that kinda service is around ten thousand. If I debut on stage and make a name for myself playing a dashing heroine, then we can bump it up it to fifty."

As I was chatting with Ilecia, a twenty-one-year-old future actress, a giant dish appeared on the table right in front of my eyes. It was piled high with fried chicken and fried veggies.

"Oh, Feil, you have school in the morning, don'cha? After you eat, hurry up and head home."

"Oh, geez, boss," Ilecia said. "You can't serve someone fried food this late at night."

"It's fine. Being a summoner drains the stamina like nothin' else. So meats, veggies, and fats are the best thing for us."

The meal had been provided by a bald bodybuilder.

He was shorter than me, but the muscles bulging from his short sleeves were nothing to scoff at. His eyes, with their folded lids, glinted like a hawk's. If someone had told me he used to be a knight captain or something, I would've believed it just based on how intimidating he looked.

"Thanks for the food, boss. I appreciate it."

He was also my direct supervisor as the Horse's Drool Pavilion's head chef. I stood up and bowed.

"By the way, the owner said he's uppin' both o' yer hourly wages by a whole hundred gants."

Ilecia leaned forward immediately when she heard that, and she was already shouting, "Are you for real?! Boss, you're not pulling my leg?!" Then she thrust her fist in the air and said, "All right! I can buy makeup now!"

I'd also clenched my hand into a fist before I'd realized it. A hundred-gant raise was enormous, especially sprung on us like that.

"This pub wouldn't function without the two of ya around. Every one of our floor employees is out the door by eleven—everyone except you, Ilecia. And, Feil, you've pretty much got the taste of our grub down perfect."

"Can't believe that stingy owner's finally recognizin' how much we're worth. I gotta hand it to you, boss," I said.

"That reminds me. What do you two wanna do about next week's shift? Think you can stay till closing like you did this week?"

"Oh, sure," Ilecia said. "Especially with the raise."

Next was my turn. "Sorry, boss, could I get a day off next week on Saturday?" I bowed my head real low when I said that.

He looked a little put on the spot as he rubbed his bald head, but he didn't say no.

"Well, sure ya can, but… Somethin' happenin' at school?"

"I'm going with my teammates to the floating cemetery. It's gonna pass by just next week. Sorry, don't mean to cause any trouble."

Ilecia, who was from the countryside, seemed kind of puzzled, but the boss got it.

"I got ya. Didn't realize it was that time of year already. Well, you *are* a summoner."

He growled out a laugh and headed back to the kitchen.

The Summoner Flies at Dawn

Our world has tons of incredible things floating in the sky just overhead.

Things like pure-white castles built on top of giant, fluffy clouds. Or long and stout dragons that have curled up for a slumber. Or the giant statue of the goddess Talia that miraculously floated up there one day.

The floating cemetery was just another one of those oddities.

These phenomena dated all the way back to around twelve hundred years ago, during the battle of the summoner of ruin, Oldenier Gallow. Oldenier had summoned seven wyverns and bathed the lands in fire, but the summoner's collective gathered, overcoming national borders to defeat him. After that, the geniuses of the collective constructed a cemetery in the sky.

The floating cemetery's purpose was to act as a resting place for the departed souls, but it had a second goal of acting as a deterrent, too. It'd circle the skies of the world as a reminder for the summoners who looked up and saw it to not become a second Oldenier. It basically served as a lesson in self-restraint and a warning that pulling a similar stunt would inevitably lead to ruin.

To us, however, the whole battle between Oldenier Gallow and the collective is ancient history. It basically sounds as ridiculous as an actual fairy tale.

But the important point here is that the floating cemetery still flies.

They say the place is chock-full of treasures that could even re-create the gods' miracles. Supposedly, the great necrospecter Tory watches over the slumbering dead, too.

Tory was this greater elemental who lived through the age of gods, spirits, and humans—basically, she'd lived a helluva long time. The origin elemental of death, which was rumored to be the reason for the concept of death in this world, had given birth to her. It's said she even killed one of Oldenier's wyverns with a curse.

"Looks like there's a whole lotta people. There's a hundred already, even before dawn..."

"The cemetery's full of rare artifacts. I'd guess ninety percent of them are looking for relics of the summoners famous enough to go down in history books."

Right before the face of dawn peeked over the distant mountain range, Cyril, Myfila, and I mingled with the crowd of students on the school roof, clad in our cloaks.

"So sleepy... Cyril...carry me... Cyril..."

Myfila, who was vehemently not a morning person, was holding hands with Cyril and seemed like a marionette whose strings would be cut at any moment. He was barely keeping her up by the right arm.

"That's Agnika Aluka, and that's Socie Record over there. Looks like some of the more well-known third-years are here, too."

"This only comes around once every five years, after all. It might be worthwhile to attempt, even with the risk of serious injury right before graduation. Maybe they need some ancient artifact to stand a chance against Sasha's invincibility or something."

People made a concerted effort to keep the volume level low.

Then again...we were still making a commotion for our surroundings to a certain extent, considering over a hundred of us were gathered on a wall-less, fenceless roof and speaking to one another in hushed voices. It felt like the morning of a festival.

"Good morning, Feil Fonaf, Cyril. So you're planning to fly, too?"

I turned around to find a brunette being accompanied by two other guys. It was Lulua Folicker. Their team was second rank in the first-year Academy matches and sixth overall.

The loose and soft curls of her long hair were held back by a scarf, and her expensive-looking coat, which made lavish use of lamb pelts, guarded against the early November chill of the morning.

"Who would have expected it? And here I was convinced you had no interest in treasure hunts. Especially you, Feil."

Her smile was bright, not even showing a hint of drowsiness or lethargy.

I had to hold back a yawn when I replied to her, "I'm not gonna go diggin' up peoples' graves. I'm here to have a chat with the gravekeeper."

"You mean Tory, the necrospecter?"

"Heard she's a temperamental greater elemental, so we'll see if she's interested in what we have to say first."

"Well, isn't that intriguing? Will you let us know if you hear anything interesting, then?"

"Sorry, it's kinda complicated… Actually, you guys are already second rank. You could sleep in on the weekends, y'know. What's the point of rootin' through a cemetery just to get even stronger?"

"Ah-ha-ha-ha. I might be greedier than you think."

"Who likes a prodigy who doesn't care about appearances? Just makes 'em unmanageable."

I gave her a strained smile, and the crowd around us suddenly began to stir.

I was trying to figure out the source of the commotion, and that's when I saw it—three pure-white pegasi had appeared on the roof, the sun rising against their backs.

Their great white wings beat against the air, allowing them to hover in place as they carried their riders—three beautiful girls who were instantly recognizable as the top team in the Academy. At their center was the Princess-Knight Sasha Shidoh Zultania, wearing light armor in the colors of the devout.

I had no idea who the hell designed her armor, but her helmet was just a headband that protected her forehead, like the outstretched wings of a bird, and her breast plate was wide-open at the front. Because of her short skirt and the shin guards, which only came to the tops of her knees, her unblemished thighs were in direct contact with her pegasus's white coat.

The girls on either side of her wore heavier equipment, their feminine silhouettes fully ensconced in armor without a hint of thigh. Their chests were covered with plates of metal. It occurred to me that the imperial knights who protected the palace of the land of Shidoh probably wore armor like that.

The commotion from the summoners gathered on the Academy's roof immediately died down.

There were some dudes who yelled, "Princess Sasha's here!!" "Her Highness's boobs are huge!!" "C'mon, show off more of those thighs!!"

"Quiet, you fools!!" A single shout from Sasha's teammate was all it took to silence the riffraff.

A hush fell over the morning crowd.

"My name is Sasha Shidoh Zultania. I am here today to represent my father, the successor of the throne, Jikfrit Shidoh Zultania." As she drew the sword at her side, Sasha's melodic voice declared her name. Then she pointed the tip of her sword directly at the more than hundred summoners below her feet. "Students who seek the wisdom of yore, and the youth who trample upon the resting dead for knowledge."

As we fell into silence, our meekness showing on our faces, we listened to the words of the third princess of the land of Shidoh.

No summoner here was unaware of what would happen in this place.

"The floating cemetery was originally the resting place of the dead, and because of the great power the land holds, the eight great royal families are in agreement that entry shall be rigorously restricted. It would be a nicety to call a grave robber shameless."

This was the long-standing Ceremony of Rebuke and Permission.

In order to enter the forbidden domain under the management of His Majesty, everyone had to go through the appropriate procedures, no matter where they hailed from or what age it was.

"However...the sages who rest in this cemetery were once pupils of this very Academy. It stands to reason that the forebears entrust the future generations with their knowledge."

The floating cemetery we were all headed to right now was one of those forbidden grounds, appearing above the Academy's skies once every five years. It was established that the only way to enter was to gather on the Academy's roof on the morning it appeared, then receive the rebuke and permission of the royal family.

"And for that reason!" Sasha brandished her sword, raising it toward the sky as she also raised her voice.

In that moment, the thought that crossed my mind was that it sure must have been a lot of work being a princess. They'd dressed her in that ceremonial armor at the crack of dawn, so she was well within her right to tell us off for being greedy.

"In accordance with the Eight Grand Kingdoms' custom! Those pupils who fly from this spot before the sun hits its peak will be allowed entry into the floating cemetery!"

Sasha herself probably couldn't care less about the cemetery.

But as she carried out her duties as a princess, the wind fluttering through her silvery-white hair, which glistened in the divine morning rays, made the beautiful girl absolutely breathtaking to all who laid eyes upon her.

Then...

"Only those who will not lament if they are struck down as they make their way to the cemetery should take flight!!"

After we were taken aback for a moment by her encouragement, which sounded a whole lot more like scolding, everyone sprang into action.

"Eye of lightning, piercing the skies, the one who holds the name of a star—"

"Stone plumage, born of flame—"

"Behold Karoma's gusts. Echoing through the night—"

"Kizma Kazma, carry the rain clouds, the great glass of daybreak—"

Summoning incantations started up all over the roof.

Of course, the place descended to chaos immediately. And that was because the whole area filled with a bunch of spreading wings— of monstrous birds with wingspans of multiple mejals, of wyverns with front legs made of membranous wings, of giant centipedes with dragonfly wings at each joint, of a gigantic demon with a wolf's head, and much more.

But it wasn't like all hundred students were gonna just take off into the air at the same time. The chaos only started in the beginning, and eventually, something like a natural order started to form. Once one team went up, then the next would go.

"All right. Guess we should get goin' soon, too."

"Wait, Feil—N-no, Myfila. You can't fall asleep now. Wake up. You need to wake up. Please wake up!"

"Uh…well, it's not like we're in a competition to get there sooner," I said.

Since we couldn't wake Myfila up after she'd passed out again, we were the last team to take off…by a wide margin.

"All right. We're heading out, Feil Fonaf. Good luck."

"Yeah, you too. Don't go too hard and die out there."

"I hope that Myfila wakes up for you."

I watched Lulua gently wave at us before leaving, all three of her teammates riding on the slender neck of a white dragon that had beautiful, long fur instead of scales.

And then…we waited.

For a sec, I was panicking about what we'd do, but finally, Myfila woke up with a "Shut up, Cyril, and don't tug on my cheek, Feil. I'm actually awake, okay?" Once she was up, she summoned the king of winged creatures: a dragon—or rather, its carcass.

It was the type of thing that the necrospecters could just *barely* manipulate. Only the strongest and largest necrospecters Myfila could summon were capable of entering its dead body.

Cyril looked up at the giant, jet-black body, which was big enough—if its wings were included—to cover most of the Academy roof, and muttered, "Actually, maybe it really was a blessing we had the last summoning. We're pretty used to the stench, but…I think this would have sent some people to the infirmary."

I picked Myfila up by her delicate waist with both my hands and lifted her high into the air.

"Even maggots wouldn't eat a dragon's necrotic flesh. I've heard the only things that'll get near 'em are a handful of microbes and necrospecters, so it's supposed to be cleaner than you think. Some studies suggest that it smells so bad because their remaining abilities to preserve magical reserves go off-kilter."

Then the dead black dragon extended its neck and lowered its long snout before me and Myfila. It was like it was telling us to get on.

My eyes met its hollow eye socket.

It was covered head to toe in black scales that wouldn't be damaged very easily by any normal magic. I knew it was a corpse, but it was still pretty intimidating. It could fit three entire horses in its mouth.

It had probably been a majestic ruler of the world's skies right until the very moment it breathed its last. It might've even been a tyrant without much respect for life, for all I knew. A lot of black dragons were known for having violent temperaments.

"Myfila, could you ascend in one go? If the town catches a whiff of this, the Academy'll get complaints," I said after climbing onto the dragon and finding a spot that was easy to sit atop its broad back. I grabbed its thick scales and used those to hold myself in place.

"You took your sweet time. Please put yourself in our shoes and think about how we need to catch up to everyone else now."

When someone said that to us, I turned to find Sasha on her pegasus overhead.

"Sorry it took so long," I told her. "Are ya gonna catch up to the first group right now?"

"I do need to help those who drop out, of course."

"You're somethin' else, ya know that? First, you see everybody off as a royal family member, *then* you've gotta go around as the

Academy's number one and clean up after everyone who gets eliminated. Sounds like a weekend down the drain."

"I have little choice in the matter. This is my lot in life."

"I've got no clue when they started havin' the top-ranking team
do the dropout recovery, but it sure seems like you got the raw end of
the deal."

"It's a better deal than losing a precious summoner. It is merciless
over there, after all."

"We'll do our best to not add to your burden."

"Yes, I would certainly appreciate it. Cecelia and I would have
some qualms carrying the three of you in our arms now that this
stench has permeated through you."

She smiled, looking a little worried. We waited until her pegasus
was safely out of the way before letting the dragon corpse flap its wings.

It shot straight into the air, all three of us on it. I waved at Sasha
below from the dragon's back. Then Sasha waved to me like a princess—go figure.

"See ya, Sasha!"

"We're sorry for causing a delay!"

"Buh-bye!"

After just five flaps of its wings, we were above the clouds. The
morning air was ridiculously clear, and I felt I could almost make out
the deep purple of the starry night, which lingered at the edge of
the sky.

Suddenly, the dragon carcass's neck writhed as it let loose a ferocious roar.

It had probably been the necrospecters that'd crawled into the
dragon doing that, but the low growl still vividly made me imagine
the dragon as it must have been while alive. Then its giant black wings
changed course to head west.

"Hey, Cyril, how long do ya think it takes to get to the
graveyard?"

"Well...the wind's pretty strong today, so I think an hour and a
half would be a sensible estimate."

"Urk. But I'm already feelin' pretty chilly. Also, there's no bathroom on this dragon."

"Well, of course not... This isn't some royal's wyvern boat."

"You can pee over there somewhere, if you wanna," Myfila offered.

"Aw, well... Suppose nobody's goin' to be around in the middle of the woods or on the top of a mountain."

It wasn't even a long trip or a harrowing journey. But thinking of the "trial" that awaited me an hour and a half from now was enough to give me a case of nervous bladder. The one saving grace was the beautiful sky spread out before me.

The Summoner Is Treated Kindly by an Old Death

"I can't believe the stunts these ancient summoners used to pull," I said.

"Back when I was a kid, I saw the floating cemetery from directly below once... So this is how it looks when you come in from the side. Almost makes me dread it."

The actual floating cemetery, which we were seeing for the first time, was way wilder than we ever imagined. It wasn't idyllic like the one you'd expect. At that very moment, the thing floating three thousand mejals above ground in front of us was a monolithic fortress equipped with an uncountable number of magical gun turrets.

First, in the center was a hemisphere, flat side up. Then around the hemisphere were eight hexahedrons extending vertically, which made me think of some fancy chandelier. The entire area of the cemetery was probably as large as a town and was covered in greenery resembling a thick lawn. I could also make out some squarish buildings. Now, the issue with all this was the eight hexahedrons that surrounded the hemisphere.

All six sides of each hexahedron were open, and each one contained a large number of protruding gun turrets. Each side probably had about thirty openings. Since there were eight six-sided hexahedrons, there were likely more than 1,440 gun-turret openings each, at least.

There was something vindictive about it, like there wasn't an end.

I didn't know if this was just the wrath they had for the grave robbers attempting to steal the cemetery's artifacts or if it was the summoner's collective's fear of the infernal wyverns coming back, but at the very least, I knew that if we approached, the cemetery would recognize us as enemies.

Not to mention the fact that the Academy summoners were swarming the cemetery without any luck. No one was getting through the barrage. The mass of gun turrets, which fired destructive beams of light without pause in all three hundred sixty degrees, were shooting down one summoner on their winged mount at a time.

"Uh, so Lulua's group is—there," Cyril said. "They're still in flight. I see… So even Lulua's Holy Shield is as flimsy as paper when faced with the cemetery. Doesn't look like relying on resilience will be a good way to progress."

"Look, Feil. Sasha's summon, Cecelia, is there."

"'Course she is. Even Sasha couldn't collect all the dropouts without her archangel."

"Oh, I was just saying that she made it in time."

"W-well, yeah. She probably had to bolt to catch up with the first group."

"She's so fast… She's zooming past all the cemetery's turrets."

"Sasha's archangel is fast, sturdy, and powerful—the trifecta. But she doesn't have Zylgar beat in speed. It's actually no contest," I said.

"Ha-ha. That's enough flattery."

"It's not flattery," I said. "Zylgar's an integral part of our rush strategy."

"That's just absurd. This all hinges on *your* effort, Feil. That's what Myfila and I believe."

"You've gotta keep going until you're bleeding out your nose, Feil."

With Cyril and Myfila saying that, I whistled instead of giving them a strained smile. Just thinking of the turrets turning their sights toward us made me choke on my own breath, but we couldn't give up without making an attempt after getting all the way here.

"Ah, well. Guess it's time to get this goin', Cyril, Myfila."

Half the summoners making an attempt on the cemetery had been eliminated.

Some headed home in dejection, others lost their summons and were rescued by Sasha's archangel, and as the number of dropouts increased, so did the intensity of the turrets' attacks on the remaining challengers. There was no time for deliberation.

"We're goin' at this accordin' to the strategy we decided beforehand! There's no callin' it quits now, even if you're scared!"

My words served as the start of it all—the dragon corpse sped up in an instant. We circled the cemetery below a single time, only receiving three or four warning shots, likely because we were still so far away.

But even that was enough.

"Whoa! *This* is what Lulua's been dealing with?! Good god!"

I didn't know whether I wanted to laugh or cry at the destructive force aimed at us.

I gritted my teeth, my jaw audibly grating as I tried to force down my cowardice. Just as several of the turrets shifted targets, I cried out, "You're up, Myfila!!"

Immediately, the giant dragon arched and lowered its head.

It whipped its wings, beating at the air to gather speed, then after that, it stopped fighting against the wind or gravity. Before I knew it, we were going so fast, I couldn't even catch my breath. We'd rushed through the storm of destructive beams, which had been launched a moment too late.

In all, it took just five seconds—the gigantic dragon corpse, the champion of the skies, disintegrated in just five seconds.

The black scales were sent flying by the blast of the beams. As the light pierced through, opening gigantic holes in the corpse, the wounds spread and tore the flesh asunder. The dragon's head, no longer able to maintain its shape as it was obliterated, tumbled onto us in pieces where we were on the dragon's back. Its folded wings were pierced through the base, sending them flying through the air while the concentrated fire atomized the remaining bits.

All I could do was pray we wouldn't die.

The dragon's decrepit flesh scattered into the sky around us and fell to the cemetery like snow.

As the time approached when even the chunk of flesh we were clinging to would be obliterated, I heard the terrifying roar of a great beast. Something tugged at the back of my cloak with unimaginable force, and the scenery revolved around me.

It was the Tiger-Saber King, Zylgar.

When I got a chance to look, a four-legged beast was carrying both me and Myfila in his mouth, inexplicably sailing through the air. He held both our cloaks like we were kittens in a mother cat's mouth. Only Cyril sat on top of Zylgar's back. He held on tight to Zylgar's long fur with both his hands, stooping his body as low as possible as he expertly rode the beast.

Then...

"Run, my spirit! Zylgar!"

...Zylgar sprinted across the firm ground. Several of the horns that extended from his body cut through the air.

Zylgar had no wings. The footholds he used on his path through the air were the fragments of dragon that had been scattered throughout the sky.

He wove to the right and left so fast that human eyes wouldn't have been able to track him.

"C-can't...breathe..."

"Just bear with it, Feil. Don't you dare pass out."

As we zigzagged down, we fully dodged dozens of beams shot at us. Even the floating cemetery couldn't keep up with a thunderbolt.

It would've been easier to blast away each of his footholds than to shoot Zylgar, and whatever was pulling the trigger on those turrets likely had the same thought. In the next moment, the beams were all targeting the dragon's pieces of flesh.

Cyril yelled, "Feil! You're up!"

I'd been whipped around so mercilessly, I almost *did* feel a nose-bleed coming on as I shouted, "Dammit! Get over here, swarm!" Then I focused my powers on the scenery directly in front of me.

This was a summon without an incantation. You could only use it for simple summons, and it took a heck of a lot of magic, but it was fast. I could summon instantly through thought.

A giant swarm of insects spontaneously gushed from out of nowhere and formed a mass of ten thousand tiny bodies that became Zylgar's new footholds.

"If I summon too rapidly, I'll die, all right?!"

After Zylgar took a step, I immediately recalled the swarm and summoned them in the next spot. They wouldn't have been able to keep up with Zylgar's speed, so this was what had to be done. Zylgar made up for my timing inaccuracies. I searched around dizzyingly, trying to predict and send the swarm to where Zylgar was headed as his stepping stones.

"Feil! Your summoning is slowing down!"

"I see that! Just shut up for a second, Cyril!"

The beams, which continued to fire incessantly, blasted away half the swarm Zylgar had just been on—but honestly, who cared about that? My summon was literally just a swarm of insects. Losing half their number wasn't really an inconvenience. And if I recalled and resummoned them, they'd be revived to their original number.

We'd already gained some distance in our descent using the dragon, so we just needed a little more until we were on the cemetery's lawn. I could even see the waves of billowing ankle-deep grass from here.

Just like we'd planned, Zylgar had been able to beat the cemetery's turrets with his speed to reach this place from above. So long as he had footholds, that is.

"Th-this is getting tough…!"

I'd been using so much of my magic that I could feel a headache coming on in the back of my head and temples. My nether regions were clenched up, and I felt weak in the knees. My vision wavered for a moment, and immediately, everything around me was blotted by darkness as my vision tunneled. My heart had already been hammering away for a while.

How much longer?! How many more extempores until we'd be out of range?!

Any mistake here was life-and-death. Even Sasha's archangel wouldn't offer a hand in salvation here.

Was our future to touch down on the cemetery, or would it be death? Those were our only two options.

I'd come all the way here with the sole purpose of mobilizing the Legendary Beast of the Last Realm, Pandora. But putting our lives on the line for the floating cemetery had been a dumb move. This was the thought that crossed my mind as my reserves of magical energy began to fade along with my consciousness.

I was filled with regret, even after discussing today's floating-cemetery attempt with Cyril and Myfila.

That's why I gripped the breast of my cloak and growled to myself, "Get it together, big guy. I said I was gonna get this done, and I am." I grasped the coin pouch around my neck, which never left my person, as tightly as I could. Even my ears, which had turned ashen white and grown deaf, could hear the faint sound of the coins jingle.

In that moment, I felt an unpleasant feeling growing within me— rage, irritation, a sense of loss. I used that as my fuel for the final stretch to unleash a summon.

"I'm never! Doing this! Again!!" I yelled from the bottom of my heart. Immediately, another swarm, a new foothold, appeared, and as Zylgar instantly used it as a platform, he dodged another beam.

"We're through, Feil! You're done!"

I don't know what would've happened to me if Cyril hadn't yelled and I'd cast another summon. Maybe the vessels in my brain would've busted or my heart would've exploded.

The rough landing was probably a sign we'd been going at our fastest speed right before it.

The moment his paws touched the soft turf, Zylgar shook his head and tossed Myfila and me aside. Apparently, Cyril's quick reflexes had allowed him to leap off ahead of time, so only his beast bore the brunt of the harsh impact, tumbling violently on landing but sparing the rest of us.

I curled up on the grass and started to pant hard. All I could do was gasp for breath. I didn't even have the wherewithal to feel the pain from skidding on the ground. It was like I'd just come off a race running as fast as I could.

"Good job! Amazing, Feil! I genuinely thought we were done for!"

"I'm pretty sure no one's done thirty-six successive summons in a row before."

My friends rubbed my back, but I would've appreciated more air than their gratitude.

Using magical energy was as physically strenuous as running a footrace. If you utilized more than a certain amount of it, your heart and lungs would crave oxygen, and your muscles, which store magic, would all tire.

"Haah, haah—*wheeze*, haah, hah—haah, ah..."

"Slow down! Slow breaths, Feil! Just focus on exhaling! You'll be fine! We're not being shot at anymore!"

I couldn't even move one of my shaking fingers. Still, I gathered everything I had to get myself faceup on the ground. Then I saw the clear blue sky spread out before my eyes. I saw the sun, the drifting white clouds, and even a corner of the hexahedron that had been shooting at us until now.

...Apparently, we'd landed in a relatively secluded part of the cemetery.

"Zylgar, you looked pretty cool, too. How about a pet?" I heard Myfila say.

"Stop that, Zylgar. Don't lick Feil's face right now."

After I focused on nothing but sucking in huge breaths of air for a while, I eventually recovered enough to notice the smell of grass filling my nose. While Zylgar, the Tiger-Saber King, affectionately licked my hair all over, I murmured from the ground, "We made it..."

"Indeed. You have arrived."

Just then, I heard an unfamiliar voice.

I couldn't get up, but both Cyril and Zylgar reacted in my stead. Zylgar stepped forward, and I heard his menacing growl fill the air.

I got up as slowly as a turtle—which was actually as fast as I could manage in my condition.

Cyril loaned me a shoulder, so I made it to my feet somehow and saw the clearing up ahead, as well as a girl standing there, legs cemented far apart, just ten paces from us. She wore a white dress that exposed her shoulders.

"Welcome to Zelame, the floating cemetery, you delightful daredevils."

She looked to be around twelve or thirteen, and she had long, black hair, but the air she gave off was all wrong. Her grin was equal parts joy and mischief, and there was something contrarian about her— some sort of quality only someone who had watched over the rise and fall of human society for many years could possess...

I immediately realized who she was. In a rasping voice, I asked her, "Are you the necrospecter Tory?"

"Indeed," she replied at once, a giggle in her voice. Instead of scolding us for entering the cemetery, she closed her eyes to the wind that blew by and scoffed. "I do believe it has been two decades since the living have stood before a grave. Now, send that overgrown kitten back from whence it came and let us join hands."

"You really think we're gonna let our guards down now?! We were almost murdered back there!"

"Murdered? Ah, yes, I suppose you were. Zelame, the architect of this place, was a rather overzealous fellow—enough to boast that those who did not know their place deserved to die without exception, yes."

"I see. Then we don't know our place, either. We were pretty close to bein' goners ourselves."

"It would be no surprise. Now, that archangel hanging about outside—that is the level of summoner we seek as a guest in the cemetery."

"So then, what? Does that mean you're here to haul off any unwelcome guests who do make it?"

"Not quite. I won't be doing anything at all."

"What?"

"I will not hinder you, nor will I help you. If you wish to rummage through the graves, then you are welcome to do so. However, the defenses that protect the dead cannot be compared with the outer net that you slipped through."

Cyril and I shared a puzzled look with each other at exactly the same time.

We had probably both concluded that it would be best not to get on the wrong side of the greater elemental. Cyril started to recall Zylgar, but I immediately stopped him and threw another question at her.

"Aren't you the gravekeeper of this cemetery?"

"No, I am not a venerable servant of the dead, but simply a pensioner here to rest. I sleep as I wish, lose myself in my thoughts, and travel as I please."

As she was talking, she suddenly yawned deeply. She didn't even try to hide it with a hand, instead opening her mouth wide to show us the back of her throat. Once she was done, she lightly slapped herself on the cheek. She acted kind of like an old man on his day off.

She didn't seem anxious in front of us three summoners or Zylgar.

"I simply came here to speak to some interesting people who made their way to this place. If the master of the archangel were to enter, I would have found the event so commonplace, I never would have bothered appearing."

The black-haired girl, the necrospecter Tory, seemed completely defenseless, and we lowered our guard.

The decisive blow was when Myfila piped up, "If Tory wanted us dead, she would have killed us already." This time, I didn't stop Cyril from recalling Zylgar. We whispered to each other.

"Seems like it was all rumors. She's not capricious at all. She's even *easy* to talk to."

"Nah, this whole thing was just a miracle. She only came out here 'cause we caught her eye."

"So you're saying she's capricious *because* she normally doesn't appear?"

"Maybe we should consider that the defense systems might be run by elementals."

I looked at Tory again and found that Myfila had gone over to her. Myfila was practically ogling the necrospecter's flesh, which was more or less a suit Tory was inhabiting.

"What a pretty body," Myfila said.

"Isn't it? I came upon it a thousand years ago. It previously belonged to a girl who took her own life because of failed love."

Cyril and I walked over with me still hanging off his shoulder. I nodded at Tory, her frame small and delicate.

"I'm glad we met you. It was worth riskin' our lives to get here."

"Oh? So you were looking for an old spirit like me? How commendable."

I didn't like the look on her face as she stared up at me. When she smiled, she bared her teeth on only one side of her mouth.

"Then tell me your name."

"I'm Feil Fonaf. This is Cyril, and the cute one is Myfila. We're students from Raddermark."

"If you are students, you ought to make use of your instructors, then. Or are you here to hear fables of yore?"

"We need to know the limitations of the necrospecters."

"What did you say?"

She seemed taken aback by my directness.

I might've damaged her pride as a great greater elemental, but I wasn't planning on going into a long preamble. I pulled out my leather-bound book from my inner pocket and opened a random page to thrust before Tory.

"My Counterpart is the corpse of the legendary beast Pandora, and I need to somehow get him to move."

Pandora—the name of the being who had once fought the gods in ages past seemed to have caught Tory's attention, though that was only natural. After showing a moment of shock, she read through the pages at inhuman speed, whispering to herself at her lowest volume.

"_____"

I'd never heard any of those words in my life. It seemed like Tory, greater elemental that she was, had the knowledge to read the text I couldn't. So what the hell was written in those pages? But that wasn't our goal right now.

"This does look like Pandora's description...but is it true? A human, able to summon Pandora?"

Even though I could hear the shock in Tory's quivering voice, that didn't make me any happier. A strained smile wormed its way onto my face in due course.

"It's Pandora immediately *after* being killed by the gods," I said.

"And he cannot move?"

"Not a finger."

It seemed that'd been enough for the sagacious necrospecter to more or less figure out what was happening. She let out a large sigh and composed herself. "So this is why you wish to know the limitations of necrospecters. I suppose I cannot be so discourteous as to become upset now that you have brought up Pandora." A dull smile crept onto her face.

She casually took my hand and started to walk off.

Once I was separated from Cyril's support, I had to do as Tory asked. I stumbled, but I managed to walk.

"I once admired Pandora while he was alive. This was when I first separated from the origin elemental and was led by the hand, just as you are now... Pandora was more heroic than any god. Why, he could mold the very mountains like soft clay. A taciturn fellow, he was. The

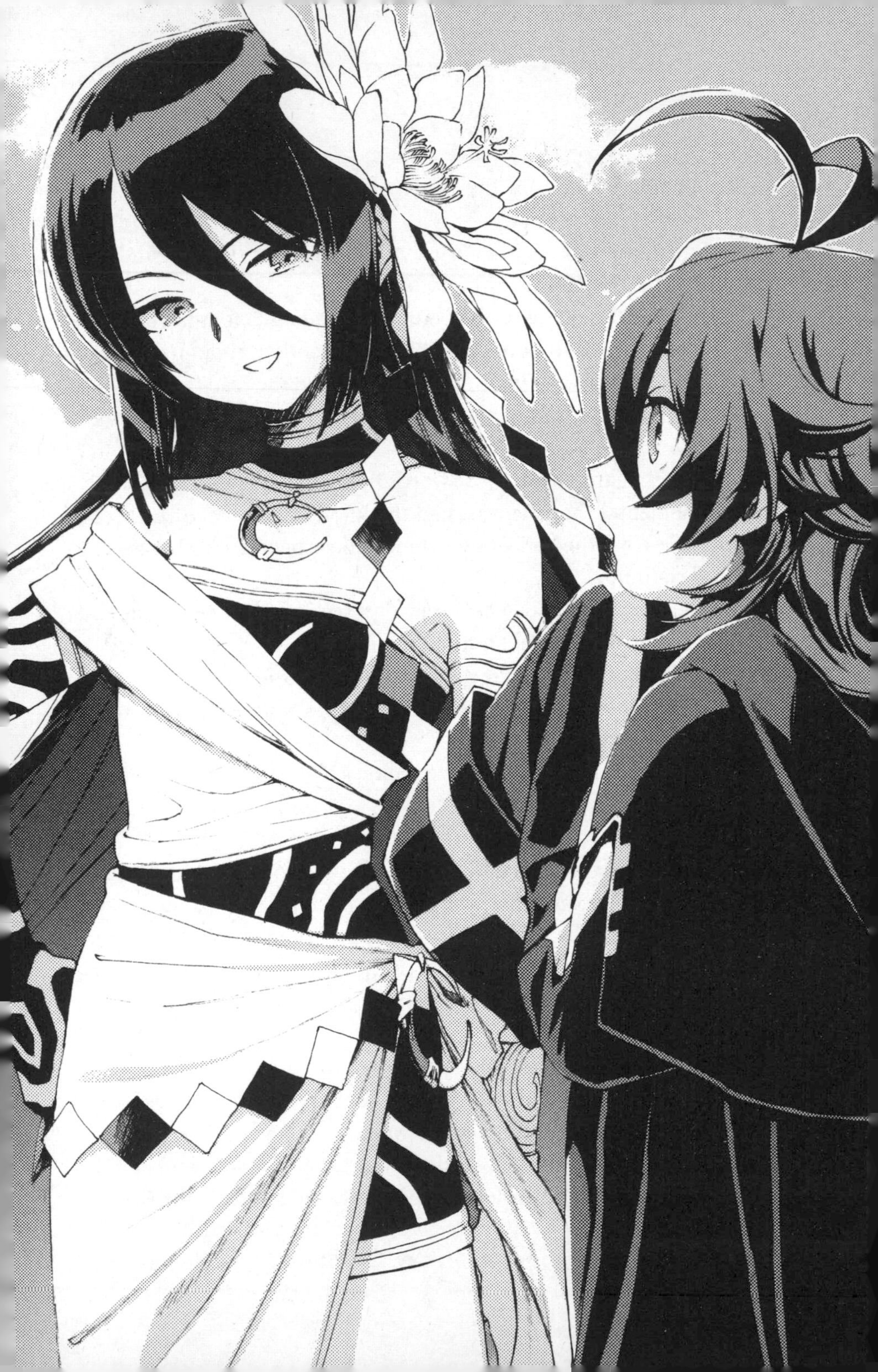

goddesses and sprites would ceaselessly pester him, and he often seemed annoyed."

A gentle smile came over Tory's face as she reminisced about the past. It probably hadn't been a bad time.

Cyril and Myfila followed after us. It was so quiet, even our footsteps sounded loud as we trampled the grass, likely because the turrets made no sound as they shot the destructive beams without recoil.

"According to legend, *Pandora* was the old name of the goddess Pearla, who became the wife of the beast. The beast appeared at some point or another before anyone realized, but it had no name, and Pearla gave him one—though considering her antics, it was more like she forced one on the beast instead."

"Then do you know about the end of the age of gods?"

"Perhaps? I was present at the time, I suppose."

"The temple describes the end as though it was sudden. According to them, Pandora wanted the throne of the head of the gods and started a war with them, then in the end, he was slain."

"That's all ancient history now. What use is it for a human to know the history of the gods?"

"...Is it so wrong to want to know how my partner died?"

Since I wasn't wary of her anymore, I opened up to Tory. I didn't know how many seconds the silence lasted after that.

Eventually, the ancient greater elemental told me in a serious tone, "He did not die a dishonorable death. He was not tempted by anyone else into his actions, nor did he seek glory out of greed. I can guarantee you this, on my name."

"Good enough for me. Now I just need to know a way to get him to move."

Just then, Tory stopped, still holding my hand.

Had something happened? I looked around, but I didn't see any graves or buildings nearby. Tory had turned around and was staring into my face.

"Though, Feil Fonaf, I can see it—you are a working scholar."

"—?!"

I hadn't expected that. I withdrew my hand instinctively.

I could tell right away that she'd peered into my past. For a powerful necrospecter like Tory, it would've been a piece of cake reading someone's entire past just by holding their hand like she'd done to me.

She could have done anything to me the moment I let her take my hand—I'd actually known that from the start.

I hadn't withdrawn because it was unpleasant, however. I was just so surprised by the experience of having my memories read for the first time that I was genuinely shocked.

"Apologies, apologies. I was just so curious to know what circumstances led to Pandora becoming your Counterpart."

She didn't seem upset by my reaction. She hid her hands behind her back and smiled.

"Did you see something we had in common, then? Me and the legendary beast?"

She didn't respond directly. "Heh-heh-heh," she cackled nastily. She brushed aside the black hair on her shoulder and said with eyes that looked like they could see through everything, "As an apology for peeking without permission, I will answer your question."

That was exactly what I'd wished for. If I could get any advice about Pandora from Tory, I'd let her look into my memories as much as she wanted. That was the whole reason we'd ventured out to the floating cemetery in the first place.

For a moment, I was almost so tense, I could've keeled over waiting to hear what Tory would say.

"I—nor even the origin elemental who birthed me—cannot control the Pandora you have summoned."

My knees almost bent when I heard those despair-inducing words.

"...However, that does not mean it is impossible."

My mind went blank when she smiled at me in a way that suggested there was still hope. "Did you hear that, Feil?!" Cyril clapped me on the back, and I couldn't help but pitch forward.

Tory stopped me before I could actually tumble.

"Oh, my, my, you pitiful child."

"Well…it's just, I've felt dead on my feet the last couple days."

Even though she was the corpse of a girl who had died a thousand years ago, she didn't smell. In fact, I caught traces of something floral from her. I needed to know the answer as soon as possible and grasped her by the shoulders. I looked straight into her eyes and asked, "So how do I do it?!"

"I will not go so far as to reveal *that* to you."

She grinned in reply. As for me, my face had frozen without a trace of a smile because of the anticipation.

"Are you not a scholar? Think of the answer for yourself."

Now that I knew there was actually a chance I could get Pandora to move, it was all the more disappointing she wouldn't tell me how to make it happen. Even though I was in front of people, I let out a dejected "But…"

Tory seemed to have developed an appetite for my despair, and she chuckled.

She prodded my forehead with her index finger, and suddenly, she had teleported. She'd disappeared from in front of me, appearing in the next second seated on my shoulders. I could feel her sitting on me, but not any weight. She was floating.

"Feil Fonaf, the answer is within yourself. You simply haven't thought of it yet."

The moment I shook my head, she teleported yet again. This time, she stood in the air above Cyril's head and looked down at me.

"In the past, magic used to be a part of we elementals and beasts."

Next, she was in front of Myfila. She reached a hand toward my teammate and kneaded Myfila's soft cheek.

"However, once humans obtained magic, they began to develop it, cultivating it into something much, much stronger. And among those methods, there are some that departed from the orthodox ways of thought."

Myfila didn't stop the elemental, so Tory kept messing with her cheek. I got the sense she was so occupied with that, she didn't even bother to turn around to face me.

"It's nothing special. In fact, you are viewing Pandora in *too* special of a light. He is dead, but only in the way that death exists for every creature. As long as you do not forget that he is a living creature, you'll soon come upon your answer."

"......I see."

I sat cross-legged on the grass and propped my chin up against my knee, hunching over to think about it for a while.

Pandora was a living creature, too... Why hadn't I ever thought of that these past few months? I'd been so preoccupied with his towering body, which seemed to pierce the sky, and the ancient legends that I'd ended up deifying him and hadn't considered him as my partner. I was an idiot.

"I studied magic for over ten years, and this is what I've come to..."

I recalled back when my mom, the village's conjurer, had still been alive.

What had I done when I'd learned magic? I remembered doing plenty of terrible things in the name of mischief, testing the limits of my crude spells through trial and error.

I'd zapped the nearby lake with an electricity spell to catch fish, then used another to power up a dead giant old frog into temporarily jumping out of the grass to scare the neighborhood bully who'd wailed on my friend.

"I was a li'l terror."

I started to feel grateful to the adults who'd set me right with a reproachful whack of their fists when I'd been up to too much magical mischief. We were a poor village without anything special to offer, but there are some things you can't gain from just living in sophistication.

"From the look on your face, it seems you've come upon a realization." Tory looked at me, one side of her mouth lifted way up.

"I almost feel like kneeling down and kissing your feet," I said.

I scratched the top of my head, smiling awkwardly. I wasn't just happy about the breakthrough—I was pretty embarrassed by how quickly I got to the right answer after just a little advice.

"Heh-heh-heh-heh. Now, I *would* ask you to try it out right this minute, but you'd better not summon Pandora here. The weight alone would be enough to send us plummeting."

Tory slowly cast her sights over the outside of the cemetery. We were also led by her gaze. We noticed for the first time then that the turrets of the hexahedrons had gone silent.

They hadn't run out of ammunition. The summoners whizzing around the cemetery had simply started to leave.

"Oh, how spineless the youth have been as of late."

"That's because those turret guns the cemetery uses are absurdly powerful. What are those things?! They blasted away a dragon carcass in a matter of seconds."

"Look, Feil. Lulua didn't fall," Cyril said.

"She must've boosted the power of her Holy Shield using her summon. But you'll need more than high endurance to win against those things."

Cyril paused before saying, "I can't believe we were able to accomplish what Lulua couldn't."

"Well, we did put our lives at risk. I reckon we'll be in for a scolding from either Sasha or the professors when we get back."

Just then, the absurdity of what we'd managed to accomplish really started to sink in...and we'd even met Tory in person! I felt like running myself ragged had totally been worth it... In fact, all things considered, everything had gone so smoothly that I was actually a bit terrified by our achievement.

"Well, then..."

Seeming to have had her fill of squishing Myfila's cheeks, Tory finally released our teammate. She turned her back to us and started walking alone toward the center of the cemetery. Her pace was slow, almost as though inviting us to follow after her.

"You'll travel past Raddermark in the evening as it is. Why not tour the flying cemetery in that time?" she said. "Would you care for a treasure hunt? I can tell you the way down into the tombs, at the very least."

Cyril and I shared a weary look, then I gave Tory's slender back a strained smile.

"You'll have to forgive us, but I've already used up all my magical reserves."

"And I'm sure you saw in his memories—he doesn't steal from others," Cyril added. "He even hates being treated to anything unless he can pay a person back."

Damn you, Cyril. He didn't need to say that. But Tory laughed and seemed to have accepted the explanation.

"Pfft! Ha-ha-ha!"

She laughed high and toward the sky, then pointedly stopped to look at us. I could clearly see she was pleased through her eyes, which had arched into the shape of crescent moons.

"Your austerity is not altruistic," she said. "You inexplicably exacerbate your own poverty, but it's endearing in a way."

Cyril elbowed me.

"I'm fine livin' this way," I said. "It's been like this ever since my dad died."

I set my mouth, then stuffed both my hands into my cloak's pockets.

"Since I don't have any money, if I start accepting handouts, people will start thinking I'm some sorta charity case. And stealing's even *worse*. I'd be a sorry excuse of a son after all my parents invested in me if I turn out like that."

I was more talking to myself than anyone else, but Tory still picked up on my low voice and replied, "You already are such a selfless child, Feil Fonaf. To keep paying back the dead in this world where no such thing as resurrection exists requires compassion."

I'd never known my grandparents, but I imagined that they would've been something like her. After today, I'd probably never have a reason to see her again, but I decided that I could come by for another graveside visit just for the sole purpose of seeing Tory. The thought flitted by for a moment.

"Lyle and Roselle have such a dedicated son," Tory continued.

It'd been a while since I'd heard my parents' names.

The greater elemental, who'd been alive since the age of gods, had said their names in the famous flying graveyard. That alone seemed like a special condolence, and it made me want to ask my mother and father directly how they felt about it.

A cold wind swept by, reminding me of the loneliness I'd buried.

The Summoner Starts with the Right Hand

"How's it going, Feil? Can you see?"

As I heard Cyril's voice come from above, I checked on the image of the scenery projected on the wall.

"Crystal clear! Keep it 'round that height, could ya? I want a view of the whole body!" I shouted back at where his voice had come from.

Looking up, I saw the sunlight streaming in from a large crack in the ceiling. The person moving up above was Cyril, who was projecting the state outside using magic after he'd summoned a large bird.

The previous day, once we'd returned from the floating cemetery, everything had been chaos. Since we were the first in decades to get through the barrage of destructive beams into the cemetery, we'd been greeted with celebration and applause from the dropouts. The students from our year who'd heard about our success started interrogating us during mealtimes, asking whether we'd brought home any artifacts or seen the necrospecter Tory.

And after Sasha saw our reckless charge, she called us into a classroom to scold us, just like I'd expected. *Do any of you value your lives even a little bit?! If anything happened, I wouldn't have been able to save you in that situation. There is a point where an endeavor becomes unreasonable.* I probably haven't been scolded like that since back when my mom would sit me down on the ground and chew me out for being up to no good.

After sleeping like a log, the next day—in other words, today—I'd been restless since morning.

We didn't have lectures, either, since it was a Sunday, so all three of us got together right after the morning meal and got to talking.

"Have you recovered your magical reserves?"

"Enough," I'd said. *"Finally got a decent night's sleep for once."* Then we flew off to the Agona mountain again to summon Pandora in the deserted, sprawling wasteland.

And here we were now...

"Feil, are you done yet? Go faster. I wanna see it."

"Don't rush me. This looks like a good spot. The membrane looks broken, so I'd be able to get my arm in."

Myfila and I were inside Pandora's head—and that was no metaphor. We'd actually slipped into a crack in his skull and were walking along his gray matter. Normally, it would've been chock-full of stuff, and we shouldn't have been able to get in there, but when Pandora was hit with the Supreme God Zen's thunderous hammer, it seemed a ton of his brain matter had evaporated. The space inside his head was about half the size of a classroom and ten mejals in height.

In addition to the light streaming in through the crack, Myfila had also conjured up two light orbs to make the projection, so it was pretty bright inside, all things considered.

"Still, just figures with Pandora. He's pretty different from any other creature I've seen. I think if a normal person cracked their skull, this whole space would've been flooded with blood by now."

"It feels like soft cement. It's not very brainy," Myfila commented.

The first issue at hand when it came to manipulating Pandora was visualization.

If I was inside Pandora's head, I couldn't see outside, and that'd pose an issue when trying to control him. But we figured that out quick.

We just needed to project the eyesight of a bird that Cyril summoned. We were using the same method as the Academy's match broadcasts. All of us could use projection magic, and Pandora's skull made for the perfect wide screen.

"Feil! Are you already moving him?! I just saw a finger twitch!"

"Not yet! I think you're so worked up that you're seein' things!"

We were projecting Pandora as viewed from above on the matte white wall—the same image of an immobile Pandora that I'd gotten fed up with the last few months.

"I'll count down to three! I'm goin' to really focus, so give me some time!"

"Got it! Once we're done, we're celebrating with tea! And you have to drink it!"

"Only if it works!"

Then as Myfila watched over me, I got on both knees on top of Pandora's brain.

"Sorry, partner. This might tickle a little," I murmured as I thrust my arms straight into the gray matter through a tear in the thick membrane.

Sure is chilly...

I only went down elbow deep. I exhaled a long breath, clearing all the air out of my lungs. Then I breathed in the smell of Pandora through my nose. He had a slight iron scent to him.

Electromagic was probably the one and only way to get Pandora to move in his state right now.

Doctors and scholars had known for a long while that living crea tures moved using electrical impulses. I'm not sure if I read it in an electromagic enchantment tome or what, but I knew I'd learned that from some book somewhere as a kid.

Then again, there were still many mysteries about the brain, and nobody had established through research where or how the electric ity traveled from the brain to move the body, so that was a blind spot.

"You can do it, Feil," Myfila said.

"Yeah, yeah. I know I'm the only one who can do this."

There was no way Pandora would react to either Cyril's or Myfi la's electromagic. But as for me—the one deeply connected to Pando ra's corpse as his Counterpart—I might be able to intuitively figure out how to zap Pandora so he'd come to life.

....
"Three!"

If Pandora had no soul, then *I* could take up the job.

"Two!"

Even if I couldn't make him move like he had when he'd been alive, just getting him to do anything with his mountain of a body would make him plenty strong enough.

"One!"

In the next moment, I concentrated everything I had into a Thunderbolt. I could tell that the electricity was charging in through his cranial nerves, traveling through his neurons one after another.

This just proved how deeply we were connected. It felt like a tiny centipede was crawling around inside my own brain—and I was the one controlling it. I was also the one who felt just how *nasty* the sensation was.

But that also meant I could direct the centipede into the muscles of my arm. And somehow, I even knew how to direct it through the labyrinthine maze of nerves to get there.

"Okay, that's it—how's *that*?!" I shouted, before I even realized I was talking out loud. I stared at the projection illuminating the brain wall.

Pandora's right hand had moved.

First, I made him form all five fingers into a firm fist, then I gingerly raised his clenched hand into the air.

"Feil! His arm! Pandora's arm is moving!" I heard Cyril's worked up voice.

Myfila was also staring at the wall in a daze. And as for me—well, I'd just realized that continually discharging electromagic was *freaking* exhausting.

The Summoner Learns of the Electro-Arachnid Tome

"I can't anymore! This ain't workin'!"

Too spent to continue, I collapsed onto my butt. I panted like a dog as I turned my head upward and closed my eyes, sweat streaming down into them like a waterfall. I couldn't even keep them open.

"I ain't a dragon or an elemental. I can't use Thunderbolt for thirty minutes straight."

I'd made the right decision taking off my robes before I tried to cast a prolonged Thunderbolt. The whole thing felt like doing push-ups and squats simultaneously without a second of rest. After a certain point, things suddenly got super hard—I started panting, and it felt like every single pore in my body was gushing out sweat.

My black tank top and cotton pants were sopping wet. I realized I shouldn't have tried to test out my limits on a whim like that. Or at the very least, I should've prepped a change of clothes.

It was afternoon, after all the morning lectures, and we were in a practice room on the first floor of the Academy. The place was big enough to fit three dragons lying down and featured a super-tall domed ceiling, all built from heat-resistant bricks that could withstand temperatures of more than thirty-six hundred degrees. The floor was made of solid white clay.

Only the three of us were using it at the moment.

After watching me discharge powerful waves of electricity from afar, Cyril and Myfila came over to talk—and it sure sounded like they were trying to console me.

"I think five minutes and twenty seconds is impressive for anyone, really."

"I know you're throttling the output, but you know Thunderbolt is a hefty spell. An average conjurer's spell would dissipate after a minute. Isn't five minutes of manipulating Pandora plenty?"

I practically spat my words back at them. "You idiots. What good will it be if I can only move his *finger* for five minutes?!"

I staggered to my feet and slung the robes that I'd abandoned over my right shoulder.

"I'm not gonna stop till I can get 'im to stand, run, and punch. If I'm goin' to make his whole body move, I'll need to be able to cast *multiple* Thunderbolt spells. I'd barely manage ten seconds based on my attempt a moment ago. It'd take everything I have just to make Pandora stand!"

"Is that why you keep going on and on about getting to thirty minutes?"

"I'd be able to deliver a punch to Sasha's archangel if I could manage a minute."

"Are you sure? Cecelia's really fast."

"Then you can just give me pointers on hand-to-hand combat, Cyril."

"Are you planning to do some light boxing with Pandora? Now that'd be a show."

Then the next moment, the double doors of the practice room opened, and a whole bunch of people sauntered in.

"Looks like you're working hard, deadbeat. Tell me, is spellcasting really this hard for *all* poors?"

Another day, another visit from the head dumbass, Bernhart Hadcheck and his goons. He had no idea what I'd just been putting myself through, but he sure loved to run his mouth.

"Looks like you made it into the cemetery. Couldn't you make a fortune selling off those artifacts, then? Oh, sorry. Just remembered you didn't manage to bring any home. Ha-ha! Sucks for you! I would've paid you so much for one of those things!"

The moment he spread both his arms, his cronies also burst into laughter.

He'd been quiet since making Cyril upset the other day, but it seemed our success at the cemetery had rekindled his jealousy to its full vigor again. The last few days, he'd been nothing but persistent at mocking us. He was getting on my nerves like never before.

Then again...

"Warmin' up for your first match of the afternoon? Break a leg out there."

Instead of giving him the satisfaction of riling me up, I headed to the wide-open doors. "Want to teach them a lesson?" Cyril asked me.

"Let 'em talk." I snorted. "Who's got time to deal with some rich kid? I've gotta focus on drawin' out the time I can use electromagic. Gotta think of somethin' that'll work. No human has got the ability to cast Thunderbolt for thirty whole minutes."

"You don't need to feed it more power?" Myfila asked. "You were casting a really weak version of the spell."

"As long as I choose the shortest route through the nerves, a hundredth of a normal Thunderbolt's power is enough."

"You're ridiculous, Feil. That wouldn't be a Thunderbolt anymore. If you restrict your magical output to that extent, the spell won't even invoke."

"I know. That's the conundrum, ain't it? But Thunderbolt's the easiest spell to regulate. Electromagic eats up a ton of magical reserves."

We talked as we headed out. We'd probably hurt Bernhart's pride in the process, but who cares? He'd probably vent his bad mood by punching one of his cronies anyway.

None of us looked back to see what kind of face Bernhart was making as we left him and the practice room behind.

The late-autumn sunlight filtered through the hallways.

"What are you two up to after this? Want to go watch the ranking matches?"

"Today's lineup doesn't look all that interesting," I said. "Plus, I've gotta finish up my bindin' enchantment assignment first."

"Oh, right, there was that. Undoing the seals seems like it'll take a while."

"Which kind did you two get?" I asked. "I got the lousiest one—the one that's on the Azoton ruin entrance."

"Wow, Feil…my condolences."

"Doesn't that one have the most seals, too? Do you think you'll be able to break it today?"

We were trudging along just talking when suddenly…

"Feil, Feil…"

…I heard someone calling out to me in a haggard, weak tone, and all three of us turned around.

A thin middle-aged man, his long white hair tied behind his head, was jogging along between the thick pillars of the open corridor. I could immediately tell he was a professor without looking at his face from his black-and-red conjurer's robes he wore.

"Perfect timing. I was looking for you three."

It was our high-order magic professor. He was also head professor of the first-year classes, the liaison for ranking matches, a guidance counselor for all sorts of things, and generally the point of contact for a lot of people.

We stopped and waited for him.

"We've decided the next schedule for ranking matches," he said, "so I wanted to inform you three. It'll be in three days, against Lulua's team."

We all shared a look at this sudden news. We weren't exactly unfazed hearing that we were up against number two in our year.

"Well, regardless, take care not to injure yourself too wildly. Especially you, Feil. You have an appetite for the wild."

At a glance, I could tell he'd run all this way even though he wasn't in shape. He let out a tired sigh and then gave me a weak smile.

"I think your extempores and those bugs of yours will probably serve you well."

Then he about-faced as if his work here was done.

Something occurred to me right then, though. "Sir, I wanted to ask you somethin'."

When he turned around, I noticed a hint of delight that I'd called him back.

"A question? Very good. Oh, what diligent students you are. Your and Lulua's teams are the only ones who actually seek me out with questions every now and then."

"Um, it's not about the lecture, though."

"Gosh, then I suppose my hands are tied... I met my wife through a blind date, you see."

"It's not about romantic advice, either, sir," I clarified. "Actually, I'm lookin' for electromagic that isn't physically draining to use."

The professor looked like he'd been put on the spot for a second, but then he appeared relieved I was asking him a question about magic. He crossed his arms and seemed to be thinking about my question, then finally proposed, "You could throttle the output of a Thunderbolt spell?"

"I need it to use even less magic than that," I explained. "It needs to consume very little *and* be precise to manipulate. Ideally, it'd also be able to take on multiple targets, if that's possible."

"Up to one of your schemes again? You're essentially asking about the limitations of electromagic."

I didn't know how to reply. I could only give him an awkward smile now that he was wary of what I was planning.

"Please abandon the thought. Every time you come up with another wild scheme, you put the entire faculty council into chaos. Last time, when you tried to disrobe poor Sasha, the headmaster classified it as inventive so you skated by. Though, I can understand why you resorted to such methods. Sasha *is* very powerful, after all."

Even though he was grumbling under his breath, we knew that he was supportive of us and had our best interests at heart. "So? What was it again? Electromagic that needs to be lightweight, easy to manipulate, and capable of multitargeted attacks?"

"Yes, sir. It only needs to be one hundredth as powerful as a normal Thunderbolt."

"You're looking for an awfully peculiar spell. I'm afraid I don't have one in my repertoire that's capable of that."

"I see…"

"At times like these, an air elemental should do the trick. Electricity is within their jurisdiction. Even a young, weak air elemental can transmute electricity for you."

"That's the thing. It won't work unless I'm the one castin' it. It really wouldn't work out with a third party in the mix—"

"Quite demanding, aren't you? Just a moment."

His arms still crossed, he turned up to look at the ceiling and started rocking lightly from front to back. Sometimes, he'd do this during lecture, too, and I'd come to recognize it as his thinking stance. Eventually, he stopped rocking, and our eyes met—his with deep creases at their corners as his slender, pale face took on a strangely persuasive power.

"Feil, do you know of Torrenos, the great arachnids?"

"I don't believe so, sir."

"They're curious creatures that weave their webs from electricity. Now, when one of those buggers sets up, their web will last a whole summer."

"It's not that they're weaving electrified spiderwebs?"

"Torrenos live within a ravine that's used as a flight passage by dragons. It seems only dragons are able to pass through the nests—using their electrical resistance, you see—so the spiders weave using intangible electricity."

I didn't get what he was telling me—or rather, I did, but just the words and not the intent behind them, so I just answered with an "Uh-huh, I see."

I was anxious for a moment before he continued. "Now, I just so happen to remember a tome named the *Torrenoxion*—after those great arachnids. There was a spell to conjure a large number of electrified threads, I do believe. However, the threads on their own were rather weak, so I thought it qualified as little more than a magic trick…and I don't believe the tome itself is even in the Academy's possession."

And *that* was exactly the info I was looking for. In my excitement and reverence for the professor, the corners of my mouth lifted naturally, and I ended up rudely goggling his face as I grinned.

"Ha-ha-ha. Based on your expression, I'd say I've fulfilled my duty as an educator."

The Summoner Is Bewildered by the Drunk of the "End"

"One fried chicken! It's hot, so be careful!"

After I set the giant plate piled high with fried food on the table, the men with their wooden tankards were whipped into a frenzy. "Food's here!" They stabbed at the chicken one after another and eventually drained their tankards of beer dry. "Whew. This place serves fine chicken. Pairs with the beer a little too well, if you ask me."

"You there, another round. Chop-chop."

"Thanks, sir! I'll get your order in!"

After gathering up the empty tankards and plate, I passed through the turmoil of customers in the dining room and headed into the kitchen.

"Table eight ordered another six beers! I'll bring out table one's whiskey!"

"Feil! Take this, too—table eleven!"

"Ya got it!"

"Would you believe those buggers put in such a picky order?! I'm tacking on a service charge! Also, Feil, call in Ilecia, will ya?! If those geezers so much as grumble, you stick a knife right into their table, ya hear?!"

"Ya got it!"

We were so busy, I barely had time to catch my breath.

Once I finished serving up the drinks and food, I went to grab the arm of a busty brunette who'd been sat down by five regulars—

the old "geezers"—and started hauling her back with me. It was Ilecia.

"Sorry. Time's up, so I'm 'fraid I'll have to take the young lady back," I told them. I gave the red-faced old men a service smile. I saw them practically every day.

"Feil! Who gave ya permission to take Ilecia away from us, huh?!"

"It's the young'un! Don't do this to us!"

Just as anticipated, the perverts started their caterwauling. I didn't hesitate to smack a fist down on the table.

"Keep it down! Quit groping the lady's behind and just drink your beer!"

That shut all five of them up fast. They stared at one another over the table like kids who'd gotten caught red-handed.

"Frightenin'. Just downright *terrifyin'*. Feil's basically turned into a mini-me of the cook!"

"Ever since the ball and chain gave him permission to tell us off, the kid's changed on us."

"When he just started back in the spring, he used to be so kind to his elders."

I collected the empty plates on their table. "Aren't your wives comin' to collect you soon, sirs?" I reminded them. Then, with a sigh, I said, "You'll be caught droolin' over Ilecia again. Remember all the trouble you got in last time?"

As I left them, Ilecia happily called out to me. "Feil, take a look at this!" Then she showed off her open apron dress—or rather her exposed cleavage.

"I got a tip!" She showed off two copper coins buried between her breasts.

I just scowled at her.

"Please go back to work," I said. "The boss is already 'bout to blow his top."

"You got it!"

The Horse's Drool Pavilion, where I worked, was packed yet another night. It was getting pretty late, but the guests were showing

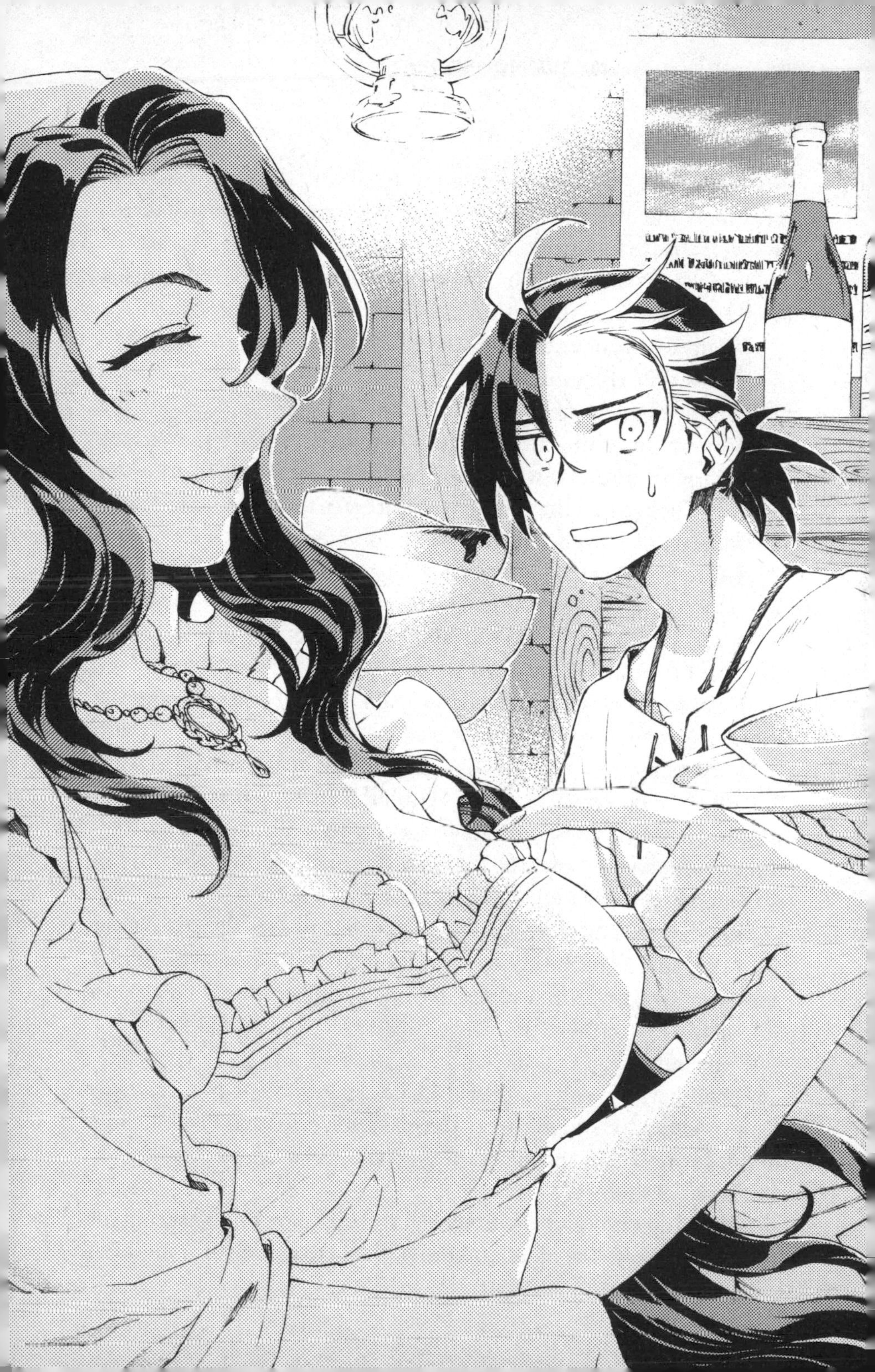

no signs of easing up, and the place was filled with their bellowed conversations and the smell of booze, fried foods, and middle-aged fogies just back from work.

Ilecia went back to serving the dining room, and I started quickly heading back to help the boss in the kitchen.

"Waiter, you got a sec?" Somebody whispered at me to stop.

"Yes, sir! Be right there!"

I whipped my head around.

A thirty-something man, haggard and wearing a dark-green cloak crowded with pockets, was inconspicuously drinking in a corner alone. He looked like the traveler type. It wasn't unusual to see them in Raddermark, considering this was a commerce town.

"Were you born and raised here?" he asked me.

"Uh? No, sir. I came here as a student."

"I see… Good, then. Sounds like you'll have no worries, even if you've got to abandon the town someday."

He propped his chin in his hand against the table as he drank the stiffest booze we served. Then he eyed me blearily.

I had no idea what the guy was going on about, but I couldn't wave him off since he was a customer. "Uh-huh," I said as a response and tried to manage my best, tiniest service-worker smile. I didn't say anything significant to him. The best way this could end was for him to get bored of me and for me to get out as fast as I could.

But the guy didn't care what I thought and just kept jabbering away.

"Did you know? This town's doomed soon. The will of the god—her wrath—will swallow it whole. And no one'll be able to stop her."

"Uh-huh."

"But that's a secret, you hear? I hold the key to doom. As soon as I got it, I heard what I'm sure is the god's voice. So that's why I came to this town. I'm an apostle of the god who seeks the end."

"I see," I said.

"And right now, I'm picking out a sacrifice. Something sacred for that thing to eat. The older and purer, the better. I've got something in my sights, but I need to escape the eyes of the people who want to get in the way of my mission, you see."

"Sounds very tough. In that case, are you sure you should be drinking here, sir?"

Something felt off about this. I felt like I'd heard all this before, about someone looking for something... I tried to search my memories, but nothing came to mind right away. If I really thought about it, I'd probably come up with an answer, but I couldn't find a reason to spend so much effort thinking about the ramblings of a drunk man.

Then again...

"I'll tell you something. A treat for you. When you see silver in the sky, you scram. The end will begin with something beautiful. Don't know if you'd make it if you take off right then, though."

At the same time, everything he was going on about seemed strangely specific, and I couldn't help but start to get drawn in.

"Feil!! Quit chattin' up the customers and get your ass over here to cook!!"

If the boss hadn't stuck his head out from the kitchen and bellowed at me, I might have asked the guy an actual question myself. But I was so shocked by the stiff scolding, I remembered I was at work. It was time to do my job.

"Yes, sir! Sorry, boss!"

I put on my best customer-service smile, bobbed my head, and moved to leave the drunk, who'd shown no signs of ordering anything.

"I'm sorry, sir," I told him. "I'm 'fraid my boss has called me over."

When it came down to it, my work for that day was more important than the hypothetical end of the world—the hunger I'd be in the next day was more tangible, after all.

The Summoner Accompanies the Princess in the Early Afternoon

When I needed to search for practically unknown spellbooks, I'd head off to large secondhand bookstores open to the public. It was something of a secret.

Spellbooks made use of a particular ancient script called Catagmark. In this day and age, the only ones who could read it were conjurers and summoners, so there were a lot of cases where the family members of recently deceased mages would sell entire collections of books to public secondhand stores like this.

Since spellbooks tended to go for a high price, the shops rarely sent them off to specialty shops, instead setting up their own sections for grimoires. But that also meant they wouldn't particularly push to sell the minor tomes, which would end up collecting dust.

At the end of a three-year search, I'd been shocked once to find a book being sold in a secondhand place like this as though it were any other merchandise.

And then there was the *Torrenoxion*.

As soon as the high-order magic professor had told me about the tome, I'd rushed off to the specialty spellbook shop right away but hadn't been able to find it. Even the owner I was pals with told me he'd never seen a book like that before, so I was going around the larger used bookstores in Raddermark just to test something. If that turned up nothing, I'd try privately owned shops next.

"Can't find it...," I murmured to myself absentmindedly as I searched the spellbook corner from one side to the other with no luck.

According to the professor's memory, it had a black cover, but that was a pretty popular one for tomes. In the end, I'd had to read every spine. I started again, scouring the giant bookshelf that towered over me all the way up to the ceiling.

As I read each title, I scratched my head.

"Um—may I ask you something?" someone suddenly asked me in a quiet voice.

I took a look and saw a girl in a white hooded cloak. I couldn't see her face since her hood was pulled low over her eyes, and she seemed to be shrinking in on herself.

"Sure, what is it?" I asked, trying to cover up my drawl.

Why had she talked to me? As I thought that, I scanned the shop and couldn't find any employees around—not even at the counter I could just catch a glimpse of from here.

Since I'd already said yes, I looked down at the reserved girl's head and waited for her question.

Then she said, as though she'd resolved herself, "Do you happen to know where the manga artist Rifris's autograph event is? I heard it's today at Tabitha Books." When she asked that, I genuinely was confused.

"You're lookin' for a *what* now?"

Shoot. I'd been so caught off guard that I'd reverted to my normal way of talking, which was guaranteed to spook a timid girl like her.

I covered my mouth with my hand as I set my mind on figuring out how to fix this.

I felt sorry for the girl since her shoulders were quivering from the shock. She'd probably screwed up her courage to ask me, considering she genuinely needed the help. Then I thought of what to do right away.

"That would probably be in the shop that handles new releases. Tabitha Books has a secondhand location and a new books location, but they're separate buildings."

The hood covering the girl's head shifted slightly. I realized it wasn't because she'd nodded or anything like that. Seemed she'd recognized my voice.

"Feil Fonaf?"

"Oh, it's you, Sasha."

I was the one taken by surprise when her pretty face appeared in front of me.

I couldn't mistake that for anybody else's. Nobody had a face like hers—with her platinum hair and amethyst eyes that even bards from other lands called the second coming of the goddess Pearla.

She'd hidden her long, full hair under her hood. When she looked up at me with wide doe eyes, instead of her usual majestic and dignified self, she seemed more like the young girl she truly was.

"What are you doing here…?" she said.

"I'm searchin' for a book like anybody else. Actually, shouldn't I be askin' you that? Had no idea it was you."

"I—I couldn't see in front of me very well because of the hood—"

"Uh-huh. Well, anyway, glad it worked out this way. If you'd asked anyone other than an Academy student, they would've swooned soon as they realized they were talkin' to *the* Sasha."

"How silly. I can't avoid excursions to town simply because I'm royalty."

"…You're incognito, then?"

"…Yes," she whispered and seemed to scan her surroundings. I naturally dropped down to a whisper, too.

"You sure were askin' weird things. What's this about a manga artist and autographin'?"

"That's—"

I wasn't trying to be malicious in the slightest, but Sasha's face clouded over when I asked out of curiosity. "Sorry. Shouldn't be pokin' round your hobbies," I apologized immediately. Then I asked, "Did ya look up the location where the new books are sold before comin' here?"

She shook her head weakly. When she did, her sweet fragrance wafted from the hair under her hood.

She was acting so meek today, it was almost giving me the creeps. Where had the third princess of the land of Shidoh, the strongest summoner in our school who dealt with us effortlessly and had a hand in managing the Academy, gone?

As a way of apologizing for earlier, I said, "Would it be okay if I took you? Better than gettin' lost somewhere."

She seemed to perk up after that.

"Are you sure? What about your spellbook? You used one of your valuable Sunday breaks to come all the way out here."

So she said, but she'd already pulled the hood low over her face and looked ready to bolt out the door.

Once I started walking, she glued herself right to my side as if she were my little sister or girlfriend or something. *She seriously has no sense of personal space*—I thought but didn't say out loud. As usual, I was self-conscious of it, but I simply cracked an awkward smile.

"I was just goin' round to bookshops before work. I left the dorms real early today."

"How fortuitous that I ran into you of all people, Feil Fonaf."

"Sheesh. You could've brought a friend or somethin'. Anybody would've gone with ya... Considerin' the complicated roads, I dunno if they'd know the way in this part of town, though."

Once we were out of the bookshop, we passed through small roads lined with independent shops and houses, heading over on the quickest route to Tabitha Books. Sasha was looking around curiously all over the place, but she probably wouldn't come by here again.

We headed down a tidy lane where there wasn't even a single beggar.

The land of Shidoh had been known since ancient times for being a place that treated its people well, with workhouses, free hospitals, and places for occupational training. Though there was a class difference to a certain extent, Shidoh was top in the eight grand kingdoms for having the lowest crime rate. Even this comparatively safe alleyway was just one blessing provided by Sasha's father and the other ancestors of the genial and sensible royal family.

"Urgh… Looks a tad snug over there…"

"Wh-what should we do? Do you think we'll make it if we line up now?"

As soon as we caught sight of the three-story Tabitha Books building, it was plain to see the store wasn't in its usual state. The line was already out the door and stretching three buildings past its neighboring shops.

I couldn't stand seeing Sasha so anxious, so I talked to an employee who was managing the end of the line. "Um, scuse me. Are there still autographs for who's-it-called available today?"

"You should barely manage to make it. There's also a spot to buy books right before the autograph area, so please purchase the new release there."

"Really?! Thank you!"

She broke out into a cheery smile and was looking up at me just like a normal girl from town. I almost felt my heart flutter until I reminded myself this was also the girl who'd mercilessly crushed my team—then I managed to regain my composure.

Once I got Sasha queued, she was at the end of the line, and so was I—with my duties.

"Well, see ya. Make sure you get that autograph."

But when I turned around, seeing Sasha standing all on her lonesome at the edge of the crowd was so heart-wrenching that I couldn't bear seeing her like that. I sucked in a breath through my teeth.

"Ugh, fine. Nothin' else to do about it."

I scratched my head in defeat and headed back to the line.

"I'll keep ya company while you wait. I'd never be able to forgive myself leavin' you alone when you don't know what the real world's like."

She immediately replied, "I know plenty about the real world," which earned a snort from me.

"Says the girl who went to the wrong store for an autograph."

"What about your work?"

"Got an evening shift today. I'll head out when it's time, so don't worry 'bout it."

Then we didn't talk for a while.

It wasn't like we were particularly close. This wasn't like my relationship with Cyril and Myfila, where sudden silences didn't bother me, or like at work with Ilecia, who I could laugh and gossip with.

After half a minute of agonizing in silence, I started to search for a conversation starter.

"So...ya read manga."

"Am I not allowed to?"

Her reply was cold and curt. *Why you little*—that irritated me a bit. It wasn't like we were some bickering couple, so I wished she'd just be a little more amicable.

"I'm not askin' for bad reasons. I don't read 'em, so I don't know what they're like. You said the author's name is Rifris? What kinda manga is it?"

I won the battle holding back my annoyance and managed to sound reasonable. With her face still hidden in that big hood of hers, Sasha answered, still a little cautious but willing to engage, "...It's a romance. A girl who works as an apothecary meets a prince in battle, and then they're drawn together."

I started teasing her, ready for the possibility she'd snub me after. "Well, sounds more like a *fantasy*, then. Not like princes grow on trees."

"That's not true. Mother—ahem—the current Shidoh queen was originally from the minor aristocracy. Sometimes, fate has a way of playing tricks."

"Well, I think it's great the main character works as an apothecarist. People need ta make a decent livin'."

"Well, Akasha isn't anywhere *near* as foulmouthed as you, Feil Fonaf."

Then both of us laughed lightly at the same time. After that, Sasha let out a small sigh as though the tension had left her.

"She perseveres despite so many difficult circumstances that I almost can't help but worry seeing it. I've never been drawn into a manga before, not like this... There's a part where she braves a snowstorm to deliver medicine, and I actually wanted to take her place—it was so bad."

"Ha-ha-ha! Well, *you'd* manage in negative hundred degree weather— Ouch."

When I'd been too candid with my thoughts, she elbowed me in the side. Actually, I fully deserved that. She'd saved the situation so we didn't end up getting awkward again.

"I'll let you borrow it, so why don't you read it? You might empathize with Akasha."

"After the summons festival, sure. I'm a tad busy now."

"Are you up to another one of your schemes again?"

"Possibly. Might depend on the person whether they think it's one. Some might get mad an' call it underhanded. Others might laugh an' say it's an impressive accomplishment."

"I don't understand what you mean to say. Are you *sure* you're okay?"

"Dunno. It doesn't violate a single Academy regulation, but the temple might have somethin' to say about it," I murmured and stopped myself there, which seemed to have more or less given Sasha an idea of what I meant.

"I see...so that's your Counterpart, then..." She nodded slightly as though she'd come to an understanding. "It seems very like you— but why would you need to worry? The Academy wouldn't forbid any summons."

"I'll make sure it kicks up a fuss. Only thing I got talent for anyway."

I didn't know what kind of appalling monster she'd imagined, but Sasha more than likely had assumed I was talking about a devil-type summon from the moment I mentioned the temple. She'd never realized that my Counterpart was the Legendary Beast of the Last Realm, Pandora, who'd killed gods and fought against Zen.

"So it sounds like you're finally making progress with your Counterpart, then?"

When she sounded happy for me as she said that and I realized I was duping her in a way, I felt a little guilty. All I could do was cross my arms and murmur, "Well, yeah."

"You had a great match with Lulua, Counterpart or not, so am I to assume you'll show it off at the summons festival?"

I could only smile awkwardly when she brought up the loss from only four days ago. We'd put up a good fight against Lulua Folicker, but it'd still been a defeat I didn't want to acknowledge. But wait, she'd been watching?

"Cyril just put up a good performance last time," I said.

"But you and Myfila managed Lulua's white dragon."

"We lost 'cause we *didn't* manage it. Shoulda hightailed it outta there the moment it turned into a battle of spells."

I still felt annoyed even recalling it now. To be frank, we could've won the match. Until the endgame, almost all the developments had been advantageous to us—and then everything turned on its head right at the very end.

"It was also a close match for Lulua's team," Sasha said. "I think you would have had it if Cyril's breakthrough had been a slight bit quicker."

"It's a bad habit of ours, relying on Cyril's offensive abilities. We've got an obvious and giant weakness in our team, and when things go wrong, that's where it always starts snowballing."

Sasha giggled quietly when she heard me say "weakness."

"By that, do you mean your own inadequate summons, Feil Fonaf?"

That wasn't even anything to hide. The corner of my mouth lifted as I said, somewhat self-derisively, "Everyone already knows. The first-years and the whole Academy."

"But you're not one to stay down, are you? You *are* participating in the revered summons festival, after all."

"Yeah...we had our wins and losses, but we qualified to enter."

The summons festival was held every year in December and included the top five teams of every student year, making it a knock-out competition between fifteen teams in total. The merciless single-day tournament allowed no second chances for losers.

Apparently, it'd started off as some fight between strangers when a first-year had challenged an upperclassman to a match, but since then, it'd turned into a thousand years of Academy tradition and was now hailed as a festival. If you won, you'd be established as number one in practical skills, and there was tons of prize money, including auxiliary prizes, too.

"Now you just gotta look forward to it on the day of."

"I am. I wonder how you'll fulfill your promise."

Promise? What promise?

I really didn't remember for a second, but when I dug deep, I unearthed that memory of when Sasha Shidoh Zultania had practically been undressed in a single thin and clinging robe in the bath, and the alluring curves of her chest, and the slight fullness of her hips and thighs...

When I remembered our chance encounter in the bath, I keenly realized that this was the same person next to me. I stared at her as she stayed hidden under her hood.

Come to think of it...I vaguely remembered getting riled up and telling her to wait until the summons festival in the heat of the moment.

"Well, just you watch. I think even you'll be in for a shock."

The line at Tabitha Books progressed slowly. There were several people who came in after us for an autograph, but the employee politely turned them away, and they ended up trudging back home.

"So change of topic—how do ya accurately manipulate electro-magic? Do ya set up conduit lines prior to invocation like the theory calls for?"

As Academy students, talking about spells seemed like the safest bet to kill some time. She wouldn't think twice about it, and there was a chance I'd get some secret pointers from the strongest summoner in the Academy.

"I prefer manipulating it by the root after invocation. Setting a line will increase precision, but it also consumes a lot of magic and creates some invocation lag."

"There it is. So ya manipulate it at the root. Myfila says she does the same thing, but only geniuses do that."

"It's easy once you learn the trick behind it. I won't say anyone can do it, but I believe you could."

The next ten minutes were nothing but beneficial.

In the past, Myfila had tried to teach me magic manipulation, too, but she'd mostly made sound effects to explain it, and none of it had made sense. Sasha put what Myfila had failed to convey into proper words and started demonstrating in front of me.

So she's even a genius at teaching...

I'd been asking her that casually, but now I felt like I kind of needed to pay for the lesson.

If Sasha had actually worked as a teacher for her job, I probably would've been really grumpy and telling her I didn't want handouts.

Eventually, the line kept moving, and we got into the store.

That was where the real problems started.

The moment we set foot into the retro-chic atmosphere of the bookstore, Sasha's entire demeanor changed. She seemed to lose all ability to speak, her shoulders froze, and when I took a look under her hood (without asking), she avoided my eyes.

"You okay?" I whispered to her, and she bobbed her head up and down to say yes.

That was when I realized she was a lost cause.

I couldn't understand why she was so nervous about meeting somebody. This was just an autograph event. She'd buy a book, meet the author, and have them write their name inside—that was all. Wasn't like somebody was going to eat her or anything.

"You can hold on to my clothes till we get there. I'll walk for you," I said, offering her help.

Even if I didn't understand why she was so nervous, this whole thing was apparently just that important to her, so I at least owed it to her to be considerate.

If I ever had time, I guess I'd borrow that manga from her. I was starting to get more and more curious about what kind of book had spellbound a princess to this degree.

We got to the second floor, at which point, one of the employees called to us, "Here! Please buy the newest release over here." The girl under the white hood seemed like she'd lost her bearings entirely as she thrust out her money with a quivering hand.

"I'm beggin' ya, please don't faint on me."

"I—I wouldn't…! I'm not a child…!"

I caught sight of the manga artist—Rifris, or whatever it was. She was a thirty-something slender woman who wore her hair in a large braid and was dressed in a plain white sweater and a brown cardigan. Her back faced the store's wall as she sat at a long table. She didn't seem to look too famous like that.

"Next, please. You may come forward."

Once the employee next to Rifris nodded at us to go, it was finally Sasha's turn.

It was my first time at an autographing event, but I gathered that she was drawing a character on the endpaper of the books and also writing a direct note.

I was convinced Sasha would go up by herself—"Wait, me too?"—but she kept a death grip on my sleeve as she headed forward to face Rifris.

In the end…

"Hello. Nice to meet you." I was the one to greet Rifris when I met her gentle eyes. Sasha still had her hood low over her head, and she'd frozen up stiff as a statue. She didn't seem like she'd make herself useful at all.

"My *little sister* is a huge fan of yours," I said. "Sorry, looks like she's so nervous, she's frozen up."

What kind of sick joke was this? Here I was, the destitute son of a farmer, pretending *the* Princess Sasha was my little sister.

Then again, if anyone figured out it was Sasha Shidoh Zultania hidden under there, it'd be chaos for sure. That'd create trouble for the author, too—and it was probably why Sasha had put on such a big hood to keep her face and hair hidden in the first place.

"Th-thank you. I'm glad you enjoyed it." Rifris forced a smile. Well, figures. Here was her last fan at an autograph session, and it was a hooded girl with a random guy.

"C'mon, give her the book you bought. Don't you want her to sign it for you?"

Once I gave her some encouragement, Sasha gingerly offered the book she cradled to Rifris.

The author took it in both hands. Then she asked—not me, the tagalong—but Sasha, "Do you have a favorite character?"

Which character someone got drawn on the endpaper was an important choice. But how low was Sasha gonna stoop her head instead of answering? All she did was deflate even more, like the embarrassment was weighing down on her.

Internally, I was screaming at her to stop messing around, but I didn't let that break my polite smile. I remembered my talk with Sasha and the main character's name.

"What was it again—Akasha? Akasha would work, right?"

That seemed to be the right answer. The hood nodded—a whole two times.

"All right. Then I'll draw you something nice."

Rifris drew with her brush for just barely a minute. The character started to appear like magic. She looked like a determined girl with short hair. There was a speech bubble that said, "Thank you for your support!"

"And, um, who should I address it to?"

"Sasha, please."

"Sasha—just like the princess."

"Yes, that's right. I wish she could be *nearly* as composed as Her Highness."

"Ah-ha-ha-ha. All done. Here you go, Sasha."

Finally, Rifris closed off with a fluid signature and the words *To Sasha*, and the only signed book in the world made specifically for Sasha was done.

"C'mon, Sasha. Aren't ya gonna thank her?"

I felt bad that she'd been silent the whole entire time in front of Rifris.

With that little bit of encouragement, Sasha managed to squeeze out a whisper. "Th-thank you so much..." Quick as a little creature, she bowed real low and deep.

I led Sasha along out of the shop while she continued to cradle her autographed book in her arms.

Outside was overflowing with the normal crowds. *I'm finally back.* I sighed as though I'd just finished a job. It seemed like Sasha had finally come back to her senses, too, and she sheepishly looked up at me.

"Th-thank you, Feil Fonaf."

I didn't say anything—just roughly set a hand on her hooded head and tousled it. Normally, that'd be the equivalent of blasphemy and would've gotten me sent to prison, but until that point, this princess had been my little sister.

The Summoner Is Teased by a Nocturnal Intruder

"Urgh?"

When I turned over where I lay, still partially asleep, I felt the corner of a spellbook poke me in the shoulder.

Odd. I was pretty sure I'd just been reading the spellbook *Practical Combat Magic for Devil Dialogues*…but apparently, I'd dozed off at some point.

I'd been fighting a Sasha-and-Lulua combo team in my dream.

In it, Cyril, Myfila, and I were pushed to the verge of losing, but then I'd remembered a new kind of spell I learned in *Torrenoxion* a long time ago and decided to revive my Pandora summon from the dead.

When I cracked open my eyes, I saw my familiar room tinted in an orange hue. A candle lantern hanging off the ceiling on a string provided the light. The worn lantern was lit with a heatless flame I'd cast. It would've lasted two hours at most, based on the amount of magic I'd imbued in it.

It was the little free time I had after working into the night and taking a bath.

If the flame was still lit, I couldn't have been asleep for very long. Maybe a couple dozen minutes at most. Since I hadn't gotten a proper rest, I felt real tired.

"Dammit…wasted my precious time…"

I was in my own room, which didn't have any bookshelves. Not even a bed or desk or chairs.

The most I had that amounted to furniture and bedding was a straw-filled mattress and a blanket. I also had a few dozen thick magical tomes piled directly on the ground.

And then there were the huge number of notes that blanketed both the ground and the mattress.

Whenever I read from a tome, I'd write down any ideas or sentences that piqued my interest at random. I had some scraps where I'd written the same sentence over and over again to memorize it, and others where I'd just written out a patchwork of ideas—like about the potential of magic that could absorb the water element, practical applications for defense spells, or slapdash summoning circles.

I didn't have the time to clean up my notes, so they stayed as they were written at the time I made them.

And then there was something that caught my eye...

"That's why I always tell ya to watch where you step in my room."

A girl had fallen flat to the floor after getting tripped up by my notes. She was splayed on the ground, her small arms and bare feet outstretched. She was wearing a men's collarless short-sleeve shirt, which had turned up, exposing her white thighs. Luckily, she just barely escaped showing off her underwear.

The sound of her biting it had probably woken me up.

I sighed as I sat up and talked to the girl's conspicuous cowlick on the top of her head.

"You never come by. Why're ya here in the middle of the night, Myfila?"

Right then, she slapped her arm against the floor. Her entire body was giving off an unsettling vibe as she slowly, gingerly got to her feet.

Her long bangs were haphazardly pinned up by a large barrette, showing off the glint in her gold eyes, which were normally hidden.

When Myfila abruptly started to walk, each time she thrust out a leg, the edge of the shirt would flutter and show glimpses of her thighs. They were curvy in a way one wouldn't have guessed from her small form.

Eventually, she stepped onto the mattress.

"...Let's hug, without clothes."

She thrust her chubby thighs in front of my eyes. Shadows from the flame of the lantern faintly wavered over her baby-smooth skin.

I looked up at her while still sitting down. "..."

Her gorgeous golden eyes stared down at me. Her charming face had a way of arousing the protective instinct in men and women of all ages, kind of like a kitten.

"You...look stunning as ever."

Her large golden eyes sparkled. The bridge of her nose was beautifully sloped. Her lips were moist and plump. She even blushed an amorous pink.

And that wasn't just me being biased as one of her friends. Myfila was talented enough for bards to sing about her being a goddess, much in the same way as Sasha Shidoh Zultania—when Myfila's bangs were pulled up.

"C'mon, Feil, let's hug without clothes."

When she said that, she licked her lips and smiled suggestively. She placed her hands on the shoulders of the Academy robes I was wearing as my pajamas in fall and winter, then moved her hands to my neck, then to my chin, then worked her fingertips up to my face.

It was almost like she was *actually* trying to seduce me.

"I didn't know you went into heat, Myfila. I've gotta warn Cyril about this."

I tried to brush aside her ticklish hands, but she ended grabbing mine instead. She tangled her fingers into mine like a couple having a tryst for the first time in weeks.

"That's not allowed. What happens secretly at night is supposed to be left in the dark."

She smiled with just her mouth as she knelt and placed her face against my hand. Then she said, "And it's against the rules to remember anything that happened once the sun rises," then she chomped down on my thumb.

Somehow, she bit just light enough that it was tolerable until she spat it out. She was surprisingly gentle as she carefully licked the impressions her teeth had made.

"...You're okay with that, right, Feil?"

After she slobbered all over my thumb, she started to act openly demanding. She pushed me down onto the mattress and tried to stick her hand into an opening in my clothes.

But Myfila was going too far. I grabbed her wispy wrist to stop her.

"No way is that okay. I'm actually going to bed now. For real."

I grabbed the hem of Myfila's shirt, where her thighs had been peeking in and out of view, and tugged down hard enough that I'd probably stretched the fabric out of shape.

"If you want a hug, it'll be with clothes on. Otherwise, get back to your own room and sleep."

"Aww."

"Why're you playin' at sneaking into my room at night? What am I supposed to think?"

I tsked quietly and wrapped my arms around her back, giving her a firm hug.

"Well...I guess this works, too..." She wrapped her arms around me and hugged me back.

We stayed like that for nearly two minutes. I could smell her hair as she sniffed my chest.

It got hot enough that I felt like I was starting to sweat.

"Myfila...are you feelin' feverish?"

"No, I'm fine," Myfila said and shook her head.

"Sheesh...you've been wearing nothin' but that this entire time? Cyril's gonna be upset with you." I focused on the hand I'd placed on her forehead. "You might actually have a slight fever."

After concluding that, I got up from the mattress, picked up a pitcher off the floor, and filled a pretty wooden cup I had for guests to the brim before handing it to Myfila. She took it in both her hands and didn't even hesitate to bring it to her lips. Then she drank from it, her neck bobbing cutely.

"Fwah!" she exclaimed when she was done.

"So? Why'd ya come all the way here when you have a fever?"

"I was tired, so I came here to get human contact. Today, I felt like visiting you," she said.

"Uh-huh. But don't strip just 'cause it's more efficient."

I picked up the book I'd been reading earlier and sat down cross-legged on my mattress. When she sat on my lap, I didn't try to stop her this time.

In the end, I hugged her soft body from behind.

I put my chin on her cowlick and opened up the spellbook, almost like I was going to read a picture book to a kid.

"Aren't you going to praise me for working so hard at my invention, Feil?"

"It's great a genius like you is making somethin', but if you're going to work yourself sick, that's not gonna make me or Cyril happy."

"Hmph!"

"Don't get upset, c'mon. You finished the Temporal Lizard Incubator last month, right? I was surprised when you managed to control a temporal lizard's space-time teleportation..."

"I think this next one will be really impressive."

"Will it? Now that's got me curious. What kind of thing are you makin' this time?"

"It's a secret. I'll tell you tomorrow."

"Don't leave me hangin'. Actually, it must've been a tough fight choosin' between coming to me or Cyril."

I turned a page of the spellbook as I smiled, and Myfila pushed me as though getting back at me.

She wriggled around—not too heavy or bony, and slightly warm—until she found a good position. She buried her face into the upper arm of my robe and didn't move for a while. I just let her do what she wanted and kept reading silently even as she tickled me by sniffing my clothes.

"...Feil, you're reading a book about devils?"

"Was thinkin' it might be nice to have one devil summon."

"Their verses are pretty long, you know."

"That's generally the issue. A famous grand devil's out of the question, and if they haven't been alive for at least a millennium, a dragon'll beat 'em out with their fire. So the issue is whether it's worthwhile to fill up the pages I've got left for verses."

"I think adaptable bugs and slimes are a lot more to your taste, Feil."

"Well, I've seen a couple devils in the ranking matches, so can't hurt to have some countermeasures against 'em."

"If only you could use Pandora…"

"Yeah, if I could, we'd stand a chance against Sasha's team."

After that, I concentrated on reading the book in my hands, and Myfila clung to my robes until twenty minutes had passed before we knew it. Apparently, Myfila had gotten enough scent immersion and physical contact with a friend and suddenly murmured, "I feel better now. That was great." Then she stood up from my lap.

"Want me to walk you to your room?" I looked up at Myfila.

"That's okay. My fever's gone down." She shook her head.

"Make sure ya keep yourself warm when you sleep once you get back to your room."

"Hmph. You sound like Cyril."

"That's 'cause I don't want you to get sick."

Right as soon as I said that, she slid her hands over both sides of my face, then gave me a good-bye kiss on the forehead.

"Thanks."

She tottered out of the room, this time without slipping on the notes all over the ground. She opened the unlocked door and quickly slipped out.

"…"

After being left alone in the room, I lightly touched the spot on my forehead where Myfila had placed her lips.

"Guess it's time to hit the hay…"

I snapped my fingers.

In that moment, the light in the lantern flickered out.

The Summoner Obtains the Source of Vitality

"It's finally! Done...! Hee-hee!"

Myfila puffed with pride as she thrust out a vial full of some sort of dubious bright-red liquid. The glass test tube seemed to be capped by some sort of mystery meat. Several short hypodermic needles stuck out from the bit of flesh, and apparently, the liquid inside could be poured out by stabbing the flesh topper.

Cyril and I had been waiting for Myfila in one of the five parallel open-air hallways that ran midway between two of the large Academy buildings.

"You're already showin' us some ungodly thing at this early hour... Wait, is that what you talked about yesterday...?"

"Stop that, Myfila. That looks filthy. Throw it away."

After the genius girl had overslept her first morning lecture by a long shot, she seemed in a much better mood than usual when she'd come to the open hallway. She was rarely one to show emotions on her face. I leaned my back against the corridor wall, which came up to my chest, as I took one of the vials with the liquid and black-and-red flesh. "What's it made of?" I asked with a chagrined smile.

The moment I held the vial up, I sensed magic in the red liquid.

"This isn't dragon's lifeblood, is it?"

I looked over at Myfila, and she grinned proudly at me as she stuck her chest out and put her hands on her hips. "It's a tonic. You'll need magic in reserve to mobilize Pandora for a long time."

I didn't even hesitate to blurt out, "Are you an idiot?"

Then I kept going, "Dragon's blood is toxic. Even if I could replenish my magic with this, I'd still croak."

Then again, if that was common sense to me, it'd be a problem that a genius like Myfila would have already anticipated. "Don't worry. You won't die," she insisted, with a huge, very smug grin on her face.

"Dragon's blood normally kills people because their white blood cells keep proliferating and consume a person from inside. But if you stop the cells from multiplying, you won't die. You'll just feel sick."

"Still sounds unreasonable. Even if you decreased their ability to proliferate by two hundred whatever units, they still wouldn't be completely inactive."

"I extracted the peptic juices of the dracogestion tree and mixed it in."

"The what? Isn't that the rare tree from Great Schulnov Forest?" I said, and Myfila gave a big nod in the affirmative. She knocked together her two fists in front of her chest.

"Its peptic juices don't break apart the white blood cells, but it *does* prevent hematopoietic stem cells from forming into them."

"And that's really benign to humans? What happens to human blood cells, then?"

"It actually used to be prized as a salve for venomous snake bites in the past. Also, I already tried the tonic after I finished it, and I just felt a little feverish."

Cyril and I both spat out at the same time. Neither of us had been expecting Myfila to use her own body as a test subject. "What do you think you're doing, ya nitwit?!" Obviously, both of us were panicked by that.

Cyril picked Myfila up in his arms almost as fast as a beast.

"This is an actual nightmare, Myfila. Did you really inject dragon's blood into yourself...?" Cyril said.

He found the needle marks on her slender neck, which stuck out of her baggy robes. After that, he checked every inch of her to make sure there wasn't anything wrong. Finally, feeling that her face was just as soft and springy as usual was what seemed to have decided it for him that she was fine.

She didn't seem to enjoy the attention, but she also didn't stop him.

"If you want to test it out again, at least ask Feil to do it instead," Cyril said.

"Ya couldn't convince me to do that for a million gants," I said, but internally, I remembered the night before.

Why hadn't I noticed the injection marks on her neck when she'd come into my room? And why hadn't I asked her more about why she had a fever? And why had our normally mascot-like Myfila come on to me like that? I shouldn't have just been reading a spellbook without a care in the world back then.

"Hey, Myfila, next time you try somethin' dangerous, at least do it when other people are around. Ya could've even beaten me or Cyril awake if you wanted to."

"Uh-huh. Okay."

"Haah... You don't seem like you're takin' this too seriously... Please, Myfila. Cyril and I care about ya way more than you think."

"Uh-huh. I know that," she said again.

Cyril and I could only share a look and let out long sighs, then we somehow composed ourselves again.

"Sorry. She came all the way to my room yesterday, and I didn't even notice."

"How could you have? Nobody would have guessed that she injected herself with dragon's blood."

Then the two of us stared at Myfila as she just stood in the corridor, and we both sighed deeply again.

"Still, dragon's blood, huh? That's pretty ridiculous."

"Yeah, I don't want to admit it...but honestly, this is revolutionary."

"Heh-heh! I know!"

Magic tonics already existed, but they put a large burden on the consumer and also had little effect for the costs. But considering dragon's blood was basically almost pure magic, being able to inject it straight into your veins meant that it'd probably be incomparable to the current products on the market.

I held up the eerie test tube again. The summons festival had lax rules compared with the ranking matches at the Academy. I was pretty sure there were idiots who brought in artifacts that were practically national treasures in past festivals, so a homemade tonic was nothing. But that line of thought also frightened me a little. That was just how far people were willing to go to win in this world.

"...Must've cost a lot," I said.

"Don't worry. I knew you'd never try it out if it did, so I only used odds and ends I had around to make it."

"But why else would you use dracogestion-tree peptic juices?"

"For the temporal lizard rearing. It's perfect for melting off their old skin when they're molting."

"...An' what's the maximum dose?"

"In theory, four per day. But you should limit it to two. If you get a nosebleed, that's a warning sign."

"I see. Seems good, then."

Then I flipped around. I set both my arms and my chin on the edge of the hallway wall and looked over at the students walking down the next corridor as I murmured quietly to myself, "Can't even find *Torrenoxion*, and the festival just keeps gettin' closer."

"Didn't you inquire at the royal library for it? How did that go?" Cyril asked me as he gave Myfila a piggyback ride on his shoulders.

I gave him a wry grin and poked at the enigmatic piece of flesh stoppering the test tube. "They sent me a polite reply sayin' they haven't got it." When I saw a procession of girls appear at the end of the corridor as I absentmindedly watched it, my eyebrows went up.

"Far as I know, there might only be ten copies in the world—and they might be owned privately. Might need to go out on a long journey to find the legendary rare spellbook."

The girls were Sasha Shidoh Zultania's first-year devotees.

Then again, she sure didn't look like some rigid royal accompanied by her respectful retinue... She and the girls around her were all smiling. It seemed like they were chatting up a storm while heading to their next lecture.

Suddenly, Sasha, who'd almost been heading up the group, noticed me in the corridor next to theirs.

Uh.

She gave me a quick wink.

The girls talking with her hadn't seen it, so the only ones who'd witnessed the princess's little bit of mischief were me, Cyril, and Myfila.

Cyril, who was quick to pick up on things, asked me, "Did anything happen between you and Sasha?"

All I said was "I dunno." Then I changed the subject. "We've got two weeks till the summons festival. I gotta finally consider what'll happen if I need to give up on findin' the *Torrenoxion*..." I let out a heavy sigh.

"What do you mean you expect Sasha to win?! Huh?!"

We looked around when we heard the sudden shout and found a fight developing in the corridor right below us.

"I got the key! The key to doom that'll make sure nobody can stand against me!"

It was Bernhart Hadcheck, yelling at the top of his lungs to the point where his voice was on the verge of cracking. The guy had grabbed onto the lapels of one of his cronies. The other henchmen were standing around like they had no idea what to do about Bernhart's outburst.

"I'm gonna win at the summons festival! I'm the only name you pip-squeaks should mention when it comes to that!"

I raised my face and gave Cyril and Myfila a bold grin.

"Seems like everybody's desperate to win the li'l festival."

Then I handed the magical tonic Myfila had made back to her.

I planned to head back out that that day before work to run around Raddermark, continuing my search for the *Torrenoxion*.

14.

The Summoner Is Cursed

I was at the eastern end of the third floor of the dorms—right in front of the wooden door leading to Cyril's room, but I'd never remembered the threshold seeming this bleak.

I could give it a casual knock when I was asking him for advice on assignments or having a strategy session on the Academy ranking matches. I even normally thought the glossy varnish on the door, which had been well taken care of despite being old and worn, was beautiful.

"Haah…" But that night, I just sighed when I got to his room.

It was almost the next day—even though I'd actually come back from work early.

Well, it wasn't that I'd finished work so much as the boss ordered me to leave for the day, saying he didn't know what'd happened but that he could see the gloom and doom all over my face. He told me to head home and hurry and get to bed. It hadn't been a suggestion.

Once I'd gotten back to the dorms, I'd tried knocking on Cyril's door several times but kept losing my nerve. I'd ended up just standing there in front of it for ten minutes, unable to come to a decision.

Ka-chak.

I hadn't tried opening the door. It'd opened on its own. Cyril's face came out from behind the door, along with the soft light of the candle lantern.

"What are you doing here so late at night, Feil? If you need something from me, just ask me to come out already."

He gave me a dubious look, scowling, which somehow didn't detract from the handsomeness of his features. I couldn't look directly at him, though, and dropped my eyes as I gave him an awkward smile.

"Didn't think you'd be awake…"

"I was *woken* up. You were hanging around outside my room, so I was wondering what was going on."

"No wonder your family's full of heroes. Ya must've trained hard to get that skill."

"Cut it out, Feil. I know you didn't come out to my room just to tease me."

"…Well, I dunno how to put it… Had somethin' I wanted to talk about…"

When I said that and got stuck on my words, Cyril opened his door further without a word. I thought he'd tell me to save it for the following day so he could sleep, so I felt a little relieved, but I also still felt half down in the dumps.

"Sorry," he said. "I haven't cleaned at all lately."

"What have ya got to clean? If this is messy, my room's a dump."

"That's because you sleep on top of your notes. At least buy yourself a desk."

The inside of Cyril's room was small, like any other dorm, but it was full of expensive stuff that had me feeling self-conscious. The bed, his desk, the gigantic bookshelf, the curtains, the carpet—his entire room was decked out in expensive objects that would be out of a commoner's reach for their entire lifetime.

And it wasn't that anything looked particularly extravagant, either. But they'd still been constructed by craftsmen sure in their technique and well taken care of by the many previous owners. Only the noble aristocrats could get their hands on antiques this high-quality.

"Take the chair," he said, setting the lantern on his desk. He sat on his bed. "What is it? You look like you've gotten in trouble with someone."

He silently watched me as I refused to budge from the room's entrance since entering. It seemed like the late-November cold had bothered him, as he grabbed the thick cardigan folded at his bedside and put it on.

"Take the chair," he said again.

"Uh-huh...," I murmured as I walked over. I approached the beautiful desk made of black-brown macmiel wood but didn't sit down.

I tried to start talking to Cyril several times, but no matter how much time passed, the words just wouldn't come out. "Dammit..." I bit my lip.

...

It was just shy of midnight. The only things in Cyril's room were the faint light of the candle and the silence of night.

Cyril didn't try to get me to speak.

He just sat on the unmade bed as he stared at me with his gentle eyes and patiently waited with me.

Then after wasting who knows how much time, I finally managed to squeeze out a groan like I was a man on the verge of death. ".......Would ya...lend me some money...?"

Cyril said nothing. Didn't say yes or no—just stared at me with the same look as earlier.

He might have already guessed what was coming just from how I'd been acting—that I was going to talk about money—and also probably why, after avoiding discussions about finances all this while, I was asking for a loan.

Finally...

"Is this about the *Torrenoxion*?"

His calm voice slowly seemed to spread throughout the room, sinking into all the objects and almost seeming—in my eyes—to make the candle waver.

I nodded slightly and said, "I found it...in an old bookshop on Tile Street. But it's...a lot more expensive than I ever expected..."

I hated this. My heart was going wild. I felt like I was making up a terrible excuse for my actions.

"It's nine hundred thousand gants. Nine hundred thousand. Considerin' the summons festival, I've gotta buy it now to learn the spell, but that's not an amount I can get together right away. I couldn't afford it even if I sold off all the spellbooks an' textbooks I own."

I explained why I wanted to borrow the money to the teammate— or rather the best friend—I trusted from the bottom of my heart, Cyril Ojlock.

"I asked the guy at the shop if I could rent it an' he said it was too expensive an' to stop with the jokes. So, Cyril, that's why I want to ask you to let me borrow the money."

It was like a nightmare come true… I wish I could have just rewound time to before I even got to Cyril's room. If I knew it was going to put me through this, I wish I'd never found out about the *Torrenoxion*. I shouldn't have learned about it. And I—

I was the worst.

And I wasn't just doing this to Cyril, who I was treating as a source of money. I'd also betrayed myself up to this point—the person who'd been adamant until the previous day about never going into debt.

I grabbed the front of my own robes and dramatically inhaled and then exhaled. I really believed I wouldn't have been able to breathe if I hadn't.

Cyril continued to stare at me as I was basically self-destructing all on my own. He didn't talk until I'd exhausted myself to the point where I knew I wouldn't be able to manage any other words out of my throat.

"Is that what you want, Feil? Really?" he said, his eyes and tone indicating as though he'd seen through everything.

He was probably trying to be kind. He pointedly turned his eyes down and away from my face, looking at the boring carpet on the floor as he said matter-of-factly:

"I wouldn't mind. If you need it, I'd be willing to let you borrow all the Ojlock family assets I'd inherit—all three hundred billion gants."

Three hundred billion.

"Because I believe you'd never betray me," he said. "We haven't even known each other a whole year, but…you've done enough for me that I really feel that way about you."

What the hell? What was this baloney coming out of his mouth?

I'd forced Cyril and Myfila to humor all my whims. I'd made them go along with my ridiculous schemes during ranking matches and even monopolized every single free weekend and day off they had to work on Pandora. And if I hadn't been in a group with them studying together, I never would've gotten passing grades on assignments received after daily lectures.

"I'll do anything I can for you, too," Cyril was saying. "You can have the nine hundred thousand. And if you're really insistent on it, you can even pay interest on it… Everyone takes on debt anyway. Even the temple will take on debt to reconstruct their sanctuaries."

Our ragtag team had formed all because Myfila had talked to us at the welcome party right after the entrance ceremony. And the reason why we'd been able to successfully stick together was probably because of Cyril's perseverance.

"When it comes down to it…I think it's all about whether you can allow yourself to do it, Feil."

Then Cyril looked at me with eyes that didn't seem like they could have possibly belonged to a sixteen-year-old.

"It's not as though I could actually undo your absurd way of doing things."

I forced myself to stay and not run from the place as I faced not Cyril in front of me—but myself.

…My dad……

After my mom, the conjurer and main breadwinner of the household, had passed away, and we ended up poor from all the spell-books we'd bought for my education, he kept minding the fields, getting mud on himself without a single complaint.

And I loved the way he was oddly overzealous.

In the middle of the night, I loved watching him from behind as he balanced the household account book all on his own at the table.

"*Today, someone from the temple had some kind words to say about ya, Feil. Said yer the biggest genius this village's ever seen. Also reminded yer old man not ta slow ya down.*"

"*We'll take charity in this house over my dead body. That happens, an' it'll spread all over the village right quick. Ya know what's also important if ya wanta get into a summoner's school? Household environment, that's what. We may be poor, but we sure as hell don't have any debt to our name.*"

"*You wanna work? Ya nitwit. Ya pa'll get the money together, so you focus on your schoolin'. You remember what yer ma used to say. The fact ya got talent to become a summoner is amazin'.*"

"*Don't worry about school tuition. It'll be fine. Your pa's been gatherin' up the capital. It'll be the next crop, that'll be it for sure—*"

Whenever I resented not having money or thought about finances, I always remembered him.

".........I don't think I can change at this point..."

Cyril let out a deep, exasperated sigh. "Then I can't lend the money to you. I don't want you to hate me over something like this."

His tone was even, but his normally composed and beautiful forehead was not.

And of course it wasn't. I'd barged in here while he'd been asleep, and right when he thought something terrible had happened, I'd forced him to humor me about some half-baked decision I wasn't even sure about. Even I was fed up with myself.

"If you need the *Torrenoxion* for the summons festival, then you should just buy it as fast as you can. You keep complaining about being poor, but it's not as though you don't have any money at all."

Cyril pointed at my chest.

"You told me at some point that your dad left you the money to pay for school, but you couldn't bring yourself to use it and worked until you saved up three million. And that was why you didn't start at the Academy when you were sixteen."

"It wasn't just money I saved up..."

"I know. You said you sold off all the furniture in your home, right? Even your mom's favorite desk and bookshelf, and you and your dad's beds. All of it."

"..."

"So, Feil, I know it may be none of my business, but that pouch you keep around your neck—is that the money your dad left you?"

He'd hit the mark. The pouch around my neck contained the two gold coins and ten silvers that made up my inheritance.

I knew that Cyril wouldn't steal it, but I automatically put up my guard. As though I was protecting it, I drew my left leg back like I was getting in a stance to fight. I felt for the pouch over my robes to make sure it was still there.

"This is— This money isn't for spending..."

"Then our only option is to do the summons festival without Pandora. Well, I'm sure we can manage without him."

"We'd never win against Sasha's archangel without him. Just think of how she brushed aside every tactic we threw at her last time and the state she left us in."

"Then would you *actually* borrow money from me?"

"Well...I..."

"There's also Myfila's tonic. If you use five or six of them, you might be able to use Thunderbolt to move Pandora for tens of seconds, at least."

"Don't mess around. I'd die like anybody else doing that. I'm not just screwin' around here—"

I wasn't allowed to say anything more.

Cyril grabbed my face fast as a beast and pushed me straight back into a bookshelf. "Gah?!" I cried out.

"Screwing around?! You think this is screwing around?!"

He started yelling like he'd forgotten it was the middle of the night.

The impact was enough to send spellbooks and novels scattering down to the ground.

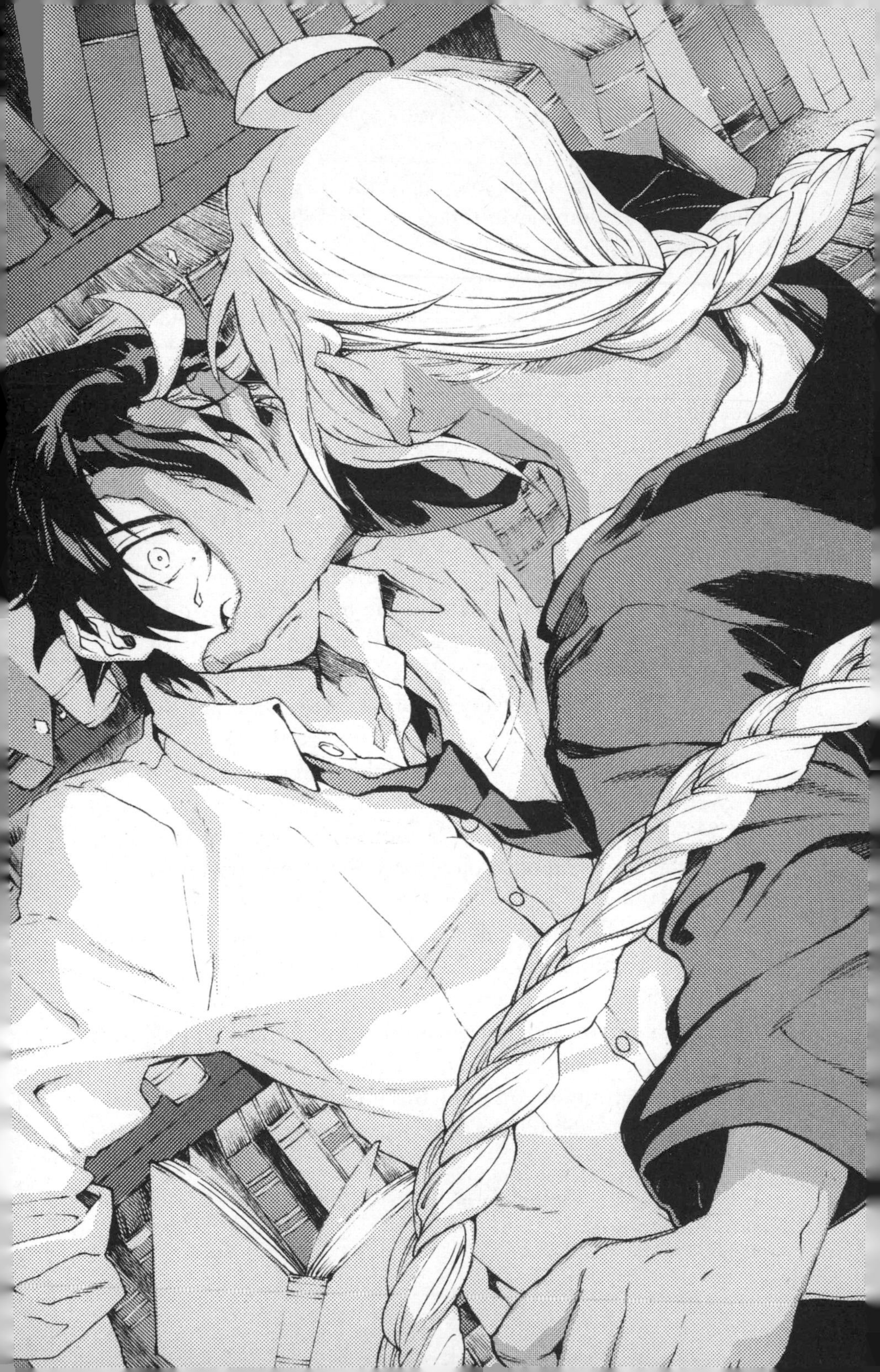

"Feil!! What in the world do you want?! What do you want me to do?!"

There was too much of a difference between our physical abilities. I didn't have the strength to immediately pry his right hand off my face.

"You refuse to borrow money! Or to spend what your parents left you! And you won't allow me to give it to you, either! So what do you want from me?!"

I could see his face through the cracks between his fingers. His eyes were wide-open, his nose was scrunched from his scowl, and his lips were raised in a snarl, even showing off his canines. He was genuinely angry.

"Feil! You're too intimidated by money! Money is just money! That's it!"

But I couldn't stand back and take it with him yelling at me like that. "It ain't just money!" I yelled back while he kept my face in his death grip and still had me pinned to the bookshelf. I braced my hands, which were both around Cyril's right wrist.

"*Just* money can get people killed! He died!"

I pried away Cyril's hand and threw it off, panting raggedly.

In response, Cyril quietly stared at me as he continued to fume.

It didn't seem like this was about money anymore. I felt bad about it—enough to choke up—all because I'd gotten worked up from Cyril's anger.

My own obstinacy and helplessness had upset even Cyril, kind as he was.

Eventually...Cyril said, still eyeing me like a man-eating tiger, "Why are you so selfless, Feil?"

I didn't get what he said right away.

The moment I thought over what he was saying, Cyril's arm was already reaching for me. He grabbed the collar of my shirt and brought his face right up to mine so I couldn't look away.

"*You're* the one who's alive. *You're* the one who's suffering right now, Feil. Your parents aren't here anymore. They're dead, and you won't find them in this world. You don't need to worry about how they feel."

He was insistent, relentless.

I tried to figure out how to respond to him as he rebuked me—me, the person he didn't really know.

"I ain't selfless!"

I got carried away, grabbing Cyril's collar back, snarling and showing him my canines, too.

"After my mom died and we didn't have money, my pa wouldn't take on debt or accept charity from the temple. I'm just doin' this out of spite of 'im. I'm gonna work even harder than my old man. I've gotta become a summoner who'll make everyone proud."

I threw the words at him, telling him about the family I hadn't wanted to talk about and the memories I hadn't wanted to dig up. It felt like leaving out the truth here would be cowardice.

"On top of workin' fields for others, he had a small plot of his own for medicinal herbs. This stuff was nasty, and it'd give ya a rash just touchin' it. He had a handshake agreement with the guild that he'd sell 'em to them, but he actually looked for another place, too, and got a doctor to buy 'em for a high price."

Normally, knowing another person's business like this was just imposing on others, but this was the only way to get Cyril to know how I felt.

"We needed three million by the time I was sixteen. A farmer wasn't gonna be able to get that kind of money together."

I could only pray that he'd get even a fraction of the stuff I'd seen and felt.

"But another person workin' with the guild got jealous an' stabbed him."

"He didn't do anything wrong, though. There's nothing for you to be ashamed about—"

"But he died. An' that's the *worst thing* he coulda done!" I yelled, my voice cracking. Cyril's grip slackened.

"He was an upright fella! An' all he thought about was me! I'm doin' this 'cause even though we were dirt-poor, he didn't leave me with debt—he had the nerve to leave me with money an' also behind on my own! That's why I gotta keep my hands clean when it comes to money, or his whole life'll be a lie!"

Cyril probably wasn't answering because I was in such a sorry state that he couldn't bring himself to. Or maybe he wasn't because I was obstinate about never taking debts, as outlandish as it was.

"I can't really believe heaven exists. That god of death, Croaka, says that he made a land for the dead, but those bastard gods lie as easy as they breathe. When somebody dies, their soul might as well just disappear as far as I know."

"..."

"But there's a chance, however slim. In that little chance that there really is a place the dead go when they die, and if my mom and pa really are there—well, you can bet I'm gonna make 'em regret what they did...! An' I'm gonna tell 'em both off for croakin' and leavin' me behind...!"

"...Feil."

"I went through all this sufferin' to become a summoner and spent all this time thinkin' about the two of 'em—an' look what they did!"

I'd taken advantage of Cyril not being able to stop me and had gone off on a rant, but I'd finally run out of breath right there. I was exhausted, almost as though I'd bled out with the force of every single word. Between my choppy breaths as I sucked in air, I swallowed my spittle and couldn't help but cough.

"...I'm sorry...for suddenly losin' it..." I said. Cyril let go of me and turned his back to me. He put his left hand on his hip and started massaging his temple with his right like when he was trying to keep a headache at bay.

"The *Torrenoxion*, huh... I just want to burn every single copy without a trace."

What he was saying sounded unsettling, but his tone was back to the old Cyril I knew.

"Why does it cost a whole nine hundred thousand? This is just vexing. Who's the author? Do you know who wrote it?"

"......Lakariez Gianpan..."

"You've got to be kidding me. Lakar—Lakariez? …As in the Azure Guide *Lakariez*?"

"What? Well…I got no clue who the Azure Guide is, but the author's name on the spine was Lakariez. So it's gotta be."

"I see… So you're sure it's Lakariez Gianpan…"

"……"

"……"

"……"

"Laka—" Then, in the next moment, I saw the light of the candle cast a shadow on Cyril's face as he suddenly clutched his sides and broke out into a laugh. "Ha-ha-ha! Ha-ha-ha-ha-ha! This is hilarious! What were we even doing—?"

I had no idea what it all meant.

I waited for Cyril's laughing fit to die down until he finally turned to face me as he wiped away his tears with a finger.

"Listen, Feil, my grandfather was a huge fan of Lakariez Gianpan, the summoner. He was a well-known adventurer and even wrote a children's book called *Lakariez's Red Dragon*. That's likely prohibitively and unusually expensive, too. I even wanted to become a summoner in the first place because my grandfather told me all about Lakariez."

"What?!"

"My grandfather has an endless collection of all his works. He even collected hundreds of letters of personal correspondence, so I'm sure he would have a spellbook by the man as well. I'll have someone bring it from home by tomorrow."

"Wait, Cyril, what are you…?"

The sudden and unexpected development had left me glued to the spot, speechless. Cyril abandoned me in my state, threw off his cardigan, tumbled right into bed, and pulled the covers up. Then as though he'd forgotten the fight we'd had just minutes earlier—almost as though it'd never happened in the first place—he turned his back to me and casually said, "I'll let you borrow it, so master it in three days. I don't want to lose at the summons festival, either."

15

The Summoner Is Also Mocked

"I don't remember saying you had to learn everything in *two* days," Cyril said to me as I yawned so wide I thought my jaw was gonna detach.

"I'm super sleep-deprived because of it, though. I almost fell asleep in lecture earlier, an' I clenched my teeth together so hard, my jaw hurts."

"I think you should probably take the day off from work today."

"Like that's an option, Myfila. If I took off every time I'm a li'l sleep-deprived, I'd starve to death in an instant."

After we asked the professor questions following the lecture, the three of us trudged down the hall toward our next class. It could be my fatigue getting the better of me, but the books under my arm felt even heavier than usual.

"Maybe I'll sleep during the day. I wanted to see the ranking matches to do some reconnaissance round then, though…"

"Leave that to me and Myfila. Please just sleep, Feil."

"Can I? Sorry for the trouble."

I had daily classes, work at the pub late into the night, and reading from the magical tome *Torrenoxion* to do that left me running ragged, but I felt surprisingly fulfilled and optimistic. It felt good to know what I needed to do now. It was straightforward, enjoyable even, to realize that as long as I did what needed to be done, I'd get results.

"Still, I gotta get through this next lecture first. The high-order magic prof has a voice that just lures ya to sleep."

"Hee-hee. Want me to douse you with water, then?"

"Long as ya got a towel ready for me after."

The next class we were going to was required for first-years. Because over a hundred students were taking it, it was held in a lecture hall that you'd enter on the second floor of the school building. The hall was circular, like a giant mortar cut in half, and it even looked impressive enough to upstage the giant theater in town.

We'd used up time asking questions earlier, so half the seats would probably already be full. There weren't even ten minutes until the bell that signaled the start of the next lecture.

"If you catch me snoozin' during lecture, wake me up. You can even punch me."

"All right, all right. I'll wake you up like a normal person."

I pushed open the large, grand doors, when—"*Bwuh!*"—for some reason, I found myself soaking wet.

An orb of water about big enough to fit in someone's arms had hit the top of the door frame and burst, mostly landing on me. It'd all happened the moment I'd opened the door, and I hadn't even been able to react.

Still dry behind me, Cyril asked, "Want me to get a towel ready for you?"

I launched into the lecture hall, driven by rage.

"Who in the hell did this?!"

But…when I saw the unexpected sight in front of me, even as I had my fist readied in the air, I stopped, and all I could manage was a "What the…?"

The chairs and desks in the staircase-style lecture hall were overturned all over the place on every single tier of the hall. Even the podium at the base of the hall had been flipped over, and the place sure wasn't ready for a class to start.

"…The hell is goin' on…?"

I counted five summons. One water elemental that took the shape of a heavily armed knight standing at four mejals tall. And four bare women with giant wings on their outstretched arms and bird legs from the knee down—harpies.

When the harpies cried out, they would raise up a whirlwind, bringing up desks and chairs to assault the water elemental in the form of a knight. The elemental had turned its left forearm into a thick water shield that it used to block each item of furniture hurled at it.

"Did I get the wrong classroom?"

"No, Feil Fonaf, but how *terribly* unfortunate for you."

I turned toward the direction the voice had come from and found a cheery brunette staring at me and trying to hold back a laugh. It was Lulua Folicker. She was also with her two teammates.

"Ha-ha-ha! Looks like it's your lucky day, Feil, my mate! If that'd hit you straight on, you would have had an appointment with the infirmary!"

"Gh-Ghol, it's rude to laugh."

I wiped my face with my sopping wet sleeve as I headed over to their side. "I'm not following. Startin' up a summonin' battle isn't supposed to be as everyday as droppin' an eraser in class."

The gigantic knight brandished the blue and transparent sword in its right hand. That sent a bunch of water orbs of different sizes flying through the air, but none of them hit the harpies.

Instead, they smashed into the walls and flew at us.

"Holy Shield."

The defensive light-magic spell Lulua incanted blocked the water orbs. It was surprisingly big and enveloped not only her and her teammates, but also me, Cyril, Myfila, and five or six other students nearby.

"Nice."

"You all almost broke the spell, though," she told me.

Once I was in Lulua's safe area, my earlier rage subsided for the moment. Looking at the entirety of the lecture hall from the top level, I more or less gleaned what had happened.

That nasty aristocrat, Bernhart Hadcheck, was fighting a red-headed girl.

"How'd you like that?! What's wrong, Julietta?! Where's that lesson you were gonna teach me?!"

"Urgh. I can't lose. Help me, Olupeia!"

Now that I was thinking about it, that knight was Bernhart's Counterpart, and Bernhart liked the girl, so he'd sometimes pick fights with her.

The fifty or so students who'd already gathered for class had withdrawn into a corner of the hall and were focused on keeping out of the warpath of the desks and water orbs. The only ones hooting and hollering, playing the audience, were Bernhart's own cronies.

"They're fightin'…but why hasn't anybody tried stoppin' them? Nobody's actually 'fraid of Bernhart."

Lulua gave me a strained smile.

"You do realize he's still a summons-festival participant, right? But right, I suppose no one's intervened since Julietta staked her pride on this duel."

"Her *pride*? Then she'd have to duel 'im every time she sees that mug of his."

"It's Julietta's mother… Apparently, well…she works at a brothel. Used to, rather."

"Doesn't sound that unusual to me."

"I didn't hear it directly, though. And then I have no idea how he heard about it, but apparently, Bernhart was talking about it. And then he told Julietta…that since she has the blood of a prostitute, she might as well date him. And that she should be happy for him to have chosen her as his mistress…"

That was pretty bad. I sucked in a breath through my teeth without even realizing it, and Cyril had punched a wall. I could hear him murmuring, "That sorry excuse for an aristocrat…," under his breath with a voice that sounded like it'd rumbled in from the depths of hell.

"I see. Guess we can't stick our noses into this seein' as that's how it is. Honestly, doesn't look like she's doin' too hot."

"You know how Bernhart's been acting a little odd for the last week or two? It's like he doesn't know when to stop talking, and he's been way more aggressive lately…"

"Ain't he always like that? 'Sides, it's not like I keep track of everything Bernhart does or says. I'm annoyed the sleazebag takes up any of my memory, personally."

"I wonder if being selected to take part in the summons festival is what's gotten him into this mood, then...?"

Myfila had taken my wet books from me, so I crossed my free arms. Then I started grumbling to myself, "Julietta...you can't hit him head-on. Overpower 'im with speed, and you gotta aim for the caster... Wait, no, this isn't the time for that."

Next to me, Lulua giggled.

"It's hard not to want to intervene, isn't it?"

"Bernhart's water elemental's pretty powerful, but he's fulla openings. I've never seen an easier opponent in a duel. I've seen her let too many perfect opportunities slip by, and it's got me worked up."

"Well, aren't you the harsh critic? Don't you think it's unfair of you to expect Julietta's combat skills to match your level when you're the best of the first-years at making use of your summons and extempores?"

"Still, who'd think that bulldozin' their way through relyin' on their summons' natural skills would cut it?"

"You have a point. Until she can get close to the elemental, Julietta won't have a chance of winning."

"She'll get worn down. Bernhart's gonna toy with her right up to the end, and that'll be it."

Since the redhead, Julietta, was fighting to defend her and her mom's honor, it'd be a real faux pas to help out. Even if one of her harpies took a direct hit from one of those orbs and the knight—the elemental, that is—trampled the harpy when she fell to the ground.

"One down!! You see that?!! I'm the greatest!!"

Bernhart's voice grated on the ears when he threw out his hands and shouted at the ceiling, but that still wasn't a good enough reason to join the fight. Only thing I could do was impatiently watch him and his cruel harpy hunt.

"You see that, Julietta?! This is what you get for saying no to me!"

He'd waited until the moment the harpies worked up a gust of wind again to serve up another orb at one of them. After the orbs hit the hard walls of the classroom, the water elemental calmly walked to the harpy and grabbed her torso with his left hand.

"Let go of Olupeia!"

As the harpy let out a heart-wrenching scream, Julietta unleashed a blade of air.

That water spirit didn't so much as flinch as the offensive spell hit him directly. His shoulder was gouged out, but it recovered like a pebble dropped in water.

"Not gonna work!"

Bernhart's electricity spell tore through the ground, leaving a path of destruction in its wake as it grazed by Julietta. She let out a curtailed scream as she was sent flying, but she couldn't catch herself in time and tumbled across the lecture hall's floor.

"I never wanted to hurt you, Julietta. But this is what happens when you don't listen to me."

As Bernhart grinned, the water spirit joined his side, still holding the limp harpy. He looked up at the captured summon, then spat on the classroom floor. "Pretty face, but I could do without the bird legs...

"Hey, Julietta, I heard these harpies are all about lust. And they're your Counterparts, huh? Bet you got a lot in common."

Julietta shook as she somehow managed to get up.

Her hurt pride pained me, but that had been Bernhart's target of joy. He laughed—crudely and for a long while.

"If you become mine, that's your ticket to going up in life! Then you won't be stuck with a small-dicked pauper the rest of your life, like that Feil Fonaf!"

Then I finally had my laugh.

"Now you've said it, Bernhart. Expected as much," I murmured, then leaped out without a second thought.

I extempored a gigantic grasshopper that was three mejals tall, jumped onto its head, and cut into the one-on-one battle. The grasshopper made for a grand entrance as it landed right between Julietta and Bernhart. Its legs cracked apart the floor under it.

I looked down at Bernhart from its head.

"Hey, Bernhart."

Bernhart only looked at me like a pigeon that'd been hit with a peashooter. It was like he couldn't process why I'd come out here or why I was grinning.

"Pretty plucky of you to insult me right after Julietta."

Julietta, who'd staggered to stand up behind me, begged, "S-stop, Feil, I'm fighting him to defend my honor."

"Keep it down, Julietta. He dragged my name into this and said I've got a small dick. I ain't gonna keep quiet and let 'im keep yappin'," I said, ignoring her.

Then I heard someone burst out laughing on the topmost level of the lecture hall, filling the whole place with rambunctious cackling. "Ah-ha-ha-ha-ha-ha!!" Lulua was holding her stomach, pointing and snickering at me.

"Right! If you let him make fun of you, that'd be an attack on your honor as a man!"

From next to her, Cyril was disturbingly egging me on with a "You can kill him, you know! It's supposed to be an honor for aristocrats to die in a duel!"

It wasn't just the two of them, either.

The other students who'd been watching the whole state of affairs started hollering when I got involved.

"It's Feil Fonaf! Feil Fonaf's entered the ring!"

"This is what I've been waiting for!"

"We knew you're the kind of guy who gets the job done!"

"You better not lose! You're not the only commoner with a bone to pick against that fob!"

"Please win! Help Julietta!"

"To hell with the lecture!"

Most of them were guys I'd never exchanged a word with before. And there was a girl I'd sometimes nod at when we passed by each

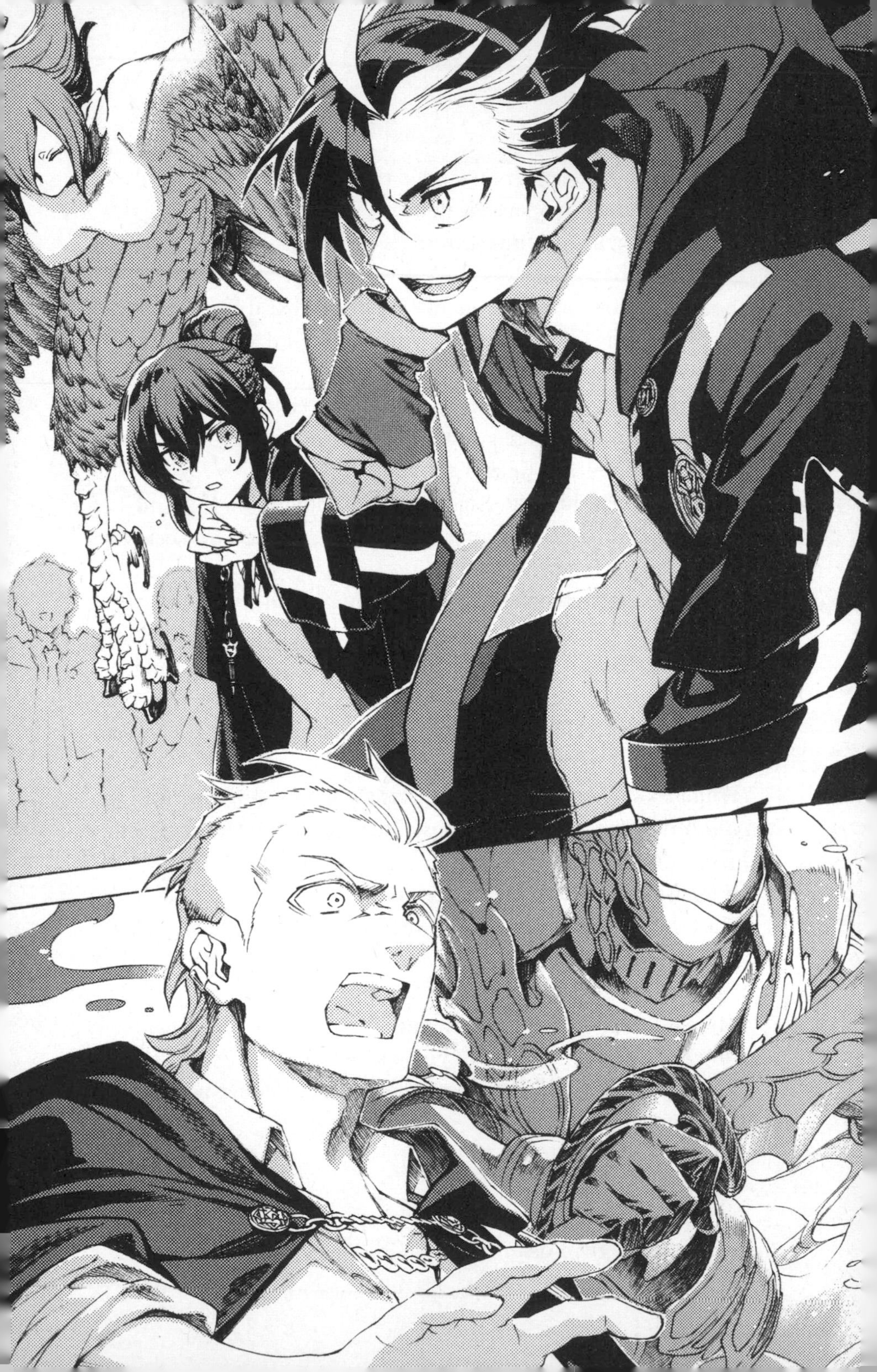

other in the halls. When those guys started cheering for me…well, that made Bernhart fly off the handle.

"You *paupeeers*!!" As he yelled, the water elemental, who'd thrown aside the harpy, rushed at me.

My grasshopper leaped while I was still riding it.

It slammed into the wall, cracking the surface, before using its hind legs to take its second bound no sooner than it'd made contact. It barely dodged the water elemental's orbs.

Then having synced with my grasshopper, I straddled its cold head and kept my balance.

"The water left undiscerned, the hunter creeping soundless. The night may be overturned, but thine shall be boundless. Devoured of its morning dew, anon the wetlands may wither. Now, with thine fangs away from view, the false darkness comes hither."

Even as my breath caught when we sped up, I incanted the summon.

I didn't say it loudly, but the blue light of my summoning circle took shape as I concealed it with the flash of a Thunderbolt spell and yelled, "Haaa-ha-ha! Bernhart! This is how you aim!"

So nobody in the classroom—particularly Bernhart—had any idea I'd cast a summon.

Well, Cyril and Myfila and maybe Lulua probably caught on.

"Don't you dare run, Feil Fonaf! Get off that thing! Get down and fight meee!!"

"Poor little aristocrat boy! Can't even catch one little bug with your big ol' elemental!"

My electricity spell and his water elemental's orbs tempestuously collided.

I had agility overwhelmingly on my side. Because I'd been persistent about hitting Bernhart with high-power electricity spells, he had no choice but to continue casting defensive charms, and the giant water elemental couldn't leave his side. The most he could manage was trying to chase me up with wimpy squirts of water.

Then Bernhart had lost his patience and started to act on it.

"O, beast of the wind-chasers! Clad of dragon scales, one of great incisors! Steal through the woods, indomitable; devour the behemoth of arrogance abominable! Thee, traitorous lion-turned-snake may well slither! For now, the black beast's time to feed comes hither!"

He started to enchant the summon of a scaled weasel, which Cyril and I could've easily extempored.

A gigantic weasel covered in black scales instead of fur appeared.

Anyway, these things were known for being quick, and they were about twice as big as a large dog. As ancient predators, they'd easily be able to hunt down the average bear.

But then a swarm of lice and beetles appeared out of nowhere, surrounding the scaled weasel.

"Why you…, Feil!!"

"That's what happens when you don't think before ya summon!"

There were a lot of summoners who didn't like rote memorization and therefore didn't use extempores, but far as I was concerned, that carelessness could lead to death. Like now, considering how I'd seen through his summon and struck first with an extempore.

Maybe I was the guy synonymous with bug swarms now.

Just by stopping the scaled weasel with a bug extempore, the classroom was already in an uproar. "It's Feil Fonaf's specialty move!" The bell that signaled the start of a lecture had already sounded, but nobody stopped to notice.

When I glanced at the entrance to the hall, some dozen odd stragglers were standing around with the flabbergasted high-order magic professor.

Then I saw that all too eye-catching platinum hair. Sasha Shidoh Zultania was also there, looking grave.

Sasha's way scarier than the professor.

Regardless, I couldn't stop the battle at this point.

He'd worked so hard to call forth his summons, only for me to render them powerless, and to add insult to injury, when the grasshopper landed again, it sent a pebble flying right at the guy's head and made him yelp. With that, Bernhart's rage had reached its peak.

"Garcfoire, go full throttle on the water!! Wash everything away!!"

In response to Bernhart's shout, the water elemental crouched. It grasped its water sword's hilt in both hands and swung the blade to the side with a more dramatic swoop than it had so far.

The sword transformed into an overpowering torrent.

"Ha-ha-ha-ha-ha!! Hya-ha-ha-ha-ha-haa!!"

The water surged through the entire lecture hall, with the water elemental at the center. It swept away the desks and chairs, broke apart the levels of the classroom, and even engulfed the students who had been protecting themselves with defensive spells.

Naturally, this wasn't a development my grasshopper could escape with just its agility.

I used it as a shield instead as I focused everything I had on protecting myself from the approaching deluge. The moment I hid in the grasshopper's shadow, I heard its exoskeleton creak and make a foreboding cracking sound. I could tell from the sharp pain that went through my heart that my summon had died.

"*Tsk*. Sorry," I said.

Eventually, the water subsided...but the entire classroom was flooded. The bottom level was submerged to the knees with water, while most of the class was sopping wet up to their bangs.

"That was close. Thought I was a goner..."

As I grumbled to myself, I crawled out from under my dead grasshopper. My eyes worked their way up the legs of the water elemental in front of me, lingering on each part of it as my eyes traveled up.

Bernhart was standing on top of the transparent knight's shoulders.

"Kneel, pauper. If you do and beg for forgiveness, I'll at least spare your life."

This time, he was looking down on me.

I snorted. "No thanks. Don't think you've won just 'cause you defeated a measly grasshopper," I said as I squeezed the water out of the hem of my conjurer's robes. The water dribbled down, splashing.

"Huh? What else can you do when all you can manage are insect summons, pauper? What? Are you gonna try pulling another underhanded extempore? Whatever you summon, Garcfoire'll blow it away anyway."

"You'll blow it away? You sure you didn't mean you're gonna *be* blown away?"

"What the hell are you—?"

"Ahh, I dunno how to break this to you...but you're so frickin' oblivious, Bernhart. I wanted to make it a surprise attack, but now you've got me wantin' to show you the trick up my sleeve."

The moment after I said that, a faint shadow spread over Bernhart and his summon...the two who had been so sure of their victory shuddered, likely at the giant prismatic, amorphous life-form that had made its way to the ceiling of the lecture hall.

"Th-the hell is that thing...?"

"Thanks. I really owe you one for helping my chameleon slime grow so big."

Like a snake rearing, my slime threw itself onto the water elemental from the side.

The little four-mejals-tall giant knight was nothing compared with my slime, which'd taken over a good 60 percent of the lecture hall's space at some point. It was massive and overwhelming.

The water elemental wasn't even able to retain its shape as a knight as it was blown to pieces all over the walls of the classroom.

Naturally, Bernhart flew into the air, but bits of his knight cushioned him, and he somehow made it out in one piece. I'd actually been making sure the slime held back. I couldn't have him dying on me that easily, or I'd be in trouble.

The students in the class were in an uproar about the summon that had "spontaneously" appeared.

"I-it's humongous! The hell is that thing?!"

"Why, it's a chameleon slime. It must have fed off all that water the elemental created to have grown this large..."

"Wait, when did he even summon that thing?!"

The chameleon slime, a creature that eerily undulated in an oil slick of colors, was normally tiny and barely the size of a full person.

The remarkable thing that was often pointed out about it was that it could shift its body color to blend with its surroundings, but more importantly, it had an abnormal capacity for absorbing water. If you hit the books, you could find countless reports of wild chameleon slimes feeding on an entire wetland and then attacking villages in the mountains.

In other words, it was a water elemental's natural predator.

And this was just what'd happen with them unwittingly watering the slime lingering next to me the entire time. That last blast of water had been what'd sealed the deal.

"So what was it you said again?" I said to Bernhart. "If you kneel and beg—right?"

I scoffed at the image of Bernhart crawling away on all fours and patted the slime as if it were a loyal hound when it slipped over to me.

"You've gotta cut back on the scummy lines. It makes you look like a sleazeball."

I waited until my slime had finished lapping up the stagnant water at my feet before I started walking over.

"It's sleazy, and now, what, are you going to get your henchmen to save you? Or will you acknowledge defeat and apologize for all that crummy stuff you said? Which'll it be? Haven't got all day here."

Bernhart remained on all fours.

Instead, the scaled weasel attacked me, still covered in my bugs.

It was fast—what could I say?

But there were giant clumps of beetles at each of its joints and lice blotting out its eyes.

I drew back, evading the desperate last charge and casting a Linebolt spell—the new spell that I'd memorized—right as it passed by.

A thin thread of electricity formed from the fingers on my right hand, which then clamped down on the scaled weasel's head.

I'd only touched it for a brief moment, but the spell, which only I knew I'd cast, passed through its skull and messed with its brain. I'd barely expended any magic, but the weasel dramatically flopped over, then the chameleon slime squashed the poor thing.

"When you can't extempore, you sure look pitiful during times like these. I ain't going to let you escape, either."

"You…you think I'd run…?!"

Bernhart stood up.

His customary duck hairdo had been ruined, and he'd even lost his weasel, but his face still burned with fury as he looked at me.

"Garcfoire hasn't been defeated YET!!"

He practically yelled himself hoarse.

In response, water spurted up in one corner of the classroom. Apparently, that'd breathed life back into the elemental after it'd gone silent from being blown away by brute force.

The chameleon slime lost no time going on the move. It covered the waterspout, gorging itself on the endless water buffet.

"How long are you gonna rely on that slime?!!"

That slime—he was right. My chameleon slime could only absorb so much water.

That was why I stepped forward.

I ran toward Bernhart, who was still thoughtlessly standing right in the open, and gave him a punch straight to the mug.

Crack.

The light sound echoed throughout the classroom as Bernhart was sent flying back onto his behind. I grabbed him by the collar and glanced at the water elemental.

"Not enough, huh."

I dragged Bernhart up to his feet while he was still too dazed to realize what'd happened, then this time, I head-butted him straight in the bridge of his nose. I didn't want him falling over quite yet, so I kept a hold of his collar. Next, I kneed him in his defenseless crotch.

That moment, Bernhart's face froze, and when I checked for the water elemental, it'd disappeared. "All right, it's gone."

Maintaining a summon took a certain amount of concentration. If you could distract a summoner with pain or render them unconscious, you could force a recall on any monster of a summon. It was an established trick for fighting a summoner, even among kids when playing make-believe hero.

I released my hands and the collar of his clothes with them.

"Y-yo... Ah..."

Unable to support himself, Bernhart crouched down right on the spot.

And in that moment...

"Whoaaaaaa! Feil Fonaf!!"

"You WON!!"

...the other students exploded into a cheer.

In that same moment, five guys ran over toward us. "Bernhart—" They were the nasty noble's henchmen. I could tell right away because of their incredibly tacky appearances—it was those telltale gold bracelets and extravagant rings they wore.

The five of them surrounded me.

"You coward! You resorted to underhanded tricks, Feil Fonaf! You punched Bernhart at the end!"

They started howling at me. "Shut up," I said as my chameleon slime bowled one of them over, and they all turned away from me to retrieve their friend who'd been blown away. They'd ditched Bernhart.

"Who's the coward now?"

When I walked toward them, the fear showed up on their five faces.

That was only natural. They weren't just facing my overgrown slime anymore. Cyril had even summoned up Zylgar, who had appeared from behind me to menace the five lads.

"You gonna wail at me for bein' underhanded while a furious tiger's in front of ya, huh?"

They didn't answer.

One of the five started to say something, but when Zylgar roared at him, he fell right over onto his rump.

"You go around talkin' about people, and now you wanna uphold ranking-match regulations? Seems awfully convenient for you guys. Huh? You agree with me?"

I cocked my head to the side as I threatened them.

They swooped right onto their knees—a little too easily—and rubbed their foreheads right into the ground.

"P-please give us a chance to apologize, Feil Fonaf! We, um…we only did it because we thought it'd make Bernhart happy. We thought he'd pay us for it."

"We won't hang out with him anymore."

"So please just spare our lives. We won't call you poor anymore."

"Please, Feil Fonaf. You can see how it is. It's all the truth."

"I'm begging you!"

I was flabbergasted by how little self-respect these guys seemed to have for themselves, but I just thrust my chin over and ordered them, "Go say that to Julietta."

I watched them scramble off, fighting one another to get there first, then headed back over to Bernhart.

Zylgar was batting Bernhart's head as he was still crouched on the ground. Those giant paws treating him like a toy didn't seem like a good situation, so I had Zylgar move off to the side.

I heard a quivering voice coming from below.

"F-Feil—Feil Fonaf… Feil Fonaf, you…you know what'll happen now that you've upset me…?"

He was trying to lift his bloodied face.

"Are you an imbecile? What're you goin' on about when I've got your life in my hands?" I said. Then Bernhart, his nose smashed, which'd transformed the terrain of his face, started laughing unpleasantly. "Heh-heh-heh-heh.

"I'm the one who's got the key to doom. I'm an apostle of the end."

"Of the end, huh…?"

"You'll be the first one I'll crush at the summons festival. No matter how much anyone struggles, the silver will be unstoppable."

I hadn't gone silent because I'd been caught in Bernhart's weirdo ambience—I'd remembered that strange guy from a few days ago at work.

…That weird customer talked about doom and ends and whatever, too…

I kinda got a bad feeling about this. But Julietta appearing behind me disturbed me from those thoughts. "Feil, thanks for your help."

I didn't say a word as I surrendered my spot right in front of Bernhart's eyes.

I couldn't care less what Julietta and Bernhart were going to talk about, so I recalled my chameleon slime and swarm of insects.

"Cyril, you worrywart. I wasn't gonna lose against a measly five guys in a fight."

I gave Zylgar's giant face a stroke. I was down to my elbow in his plush coat.

"—My mother isn't dirty!!"

I turned around when I heard the sudden outburst to find Julietta had kicked up toward Bernhart's face. His jaw was sent up, and that made Bernhart completely quiet.

His shoulders were still moving, so the guy wasn't dead, but…I didn't think he was getting up for a while.

Then Julietta turned to me.

"I'm so sorry for the trouble I caused. But I'm very grateful. If you hadn't come by, I would have—" She stopped there and bowed her head low.

I smiled awkwardly at her and answered, "Don't think twice about it. I was just irritated he got me soppin' wet is all. Laying him out made me feel a little better."

Then I suddenly looked over and saw both Sasha Shidoh Zultania and the high-order magic professor coming my way.

Julietta stepped in front of me.

"Please wait. Please wait, sir. It was all my—"

She was trying to take all the blame for the mercilessly destroyed lecture hall and wasted lecture time.

Princess Sasha, also a trustee of the Academy, was the one to absolve Julietta of the crime.

"Lulua has explained everything to me. I think it's only proper for Bernhart Hadcheck to take the burden for the full cost of repairs to the lecture hall."

Julietta and I both sighed with relief at that.

Then Sasha took a look at me and smiled.

"It seems you're capable of absolutely everything," she said.

I raised my open hands lightly and shrugged.

"Just learned by example."

I didn't actually know much about fighting with my hands, so I'd learned from watching drunken brawls between the customers at the pub.

"Ah, yes, but there was also that peculiar magic you used. It looked a bit like threads."

"That was just a test…"

"I won't inquire further, then. I'm simply happy to see you've progressed in your preparations for the summons festival."

After that, she started talking with the high-order magic professor about what to do next. I heard things like "supplemental lecture" and "other classroom" and realized then how much trouble I'd caused for both of them.

I waited for them to finish, then tried to apologize, but…Sasha came to me herself eventually and gave me a small smile before saying, "I think this is quite nice in some ways. It feels like we're really in our adolescence."

My eyebrows knit together. The heck was she saying?

Anyway, if high-order magic was canceled, I just wanted to get back to the dorms so I could change out of my wet robes. I felt like if I didn't fight against it happening at every moment, I'd end up with a cold like any other person.

16

The Summoner Talks Fables with the Princess

"Well, like I was sayin', Pandora can't be the *only* monster."

"No, it could only be Pandora. This is the end of the world we're talking about, you realize? Not just the end of humanity—the entire world. No matter how strong the monsters were during the age of gods, it's not like they would be able to end the *world* itself."

"I had the impression that the gods were up to more absurd stuff than the monsters...," I tried.

"Yes, they generally were. But even Flagah, the god of destruction, was put to shame when he failed to cut down the World Tree in his hubris."

"Only the strongest god and Pandora had the power to destroy the world," Myfila said. "That's why they resorted to fighting each other directly."

"See, Feil. I vote for what Myfila just said."

"Agh," I said. "Do we have an expert anywhere in this place—*anyone* who knows mythology in this Academy?"

"Mythology is the temple's specialty. Shall we go ask them?"

"So, a priest? Most of 'em never know when to quit talkin'. Feel like we'll end up gettin' a sermon for bein' rude if things go sideways."

The dining hall at lunch was a hullabaloo of over two hundred students that day.

There were some stuffing themselves in preparation for an afternoon ranking match, others chatting up a storm with their friends, and some grumbling about the heaps of assignments they'd gotten during morning lectures…and also even a handful eating quietly alone.

Among them all, the three of us were waxing poetic about our own theories on mythology.

Our subject: whether there was any being who could usher in the destruction of the world, other than Zen—the Supreme God—and Pandora.

"There sure are fewer to choose from than I'd expect," I said. "I always got the sense the end of the world was a regular thing during the age of gods, though."

"Well, the mythos was created from each locale handing down stories and cobbling that together with the greater elementals' descriptions of the past. So it makes sense that a ton of side stories are parading around as the main story line."

"Still, I can't believe that the fire giants only burned down Mount Galba. They always say they 'burned every mountain,' so here I was convinced that—"

"That was just a slightly worse mountain fire than usual. The Hearth Goddess's Great Blunder was much bigger."

"Sure must've put egg on those giants' faces bein' beat out by a goddess's cookin' disaster."

Encouraged by the teeming conversations around us, Cyril and I started to naturally talk even more loudly. Myfila was the only one who kept her usual tone without being influenced by anyone.

I took a bite of my staple sautéed vegetables as I said, "Well, when it comes down to it, the world's still standin'. Pandora might be the only one, then." I chewed as I looked up at the tall ceiling of the hall. Then I sunk down in my seat, my back dragging along the chair.

"Oh?"

Right as I was on the verge of falling off my seat, a platinum-blond girl walked down the cramped aisle between the long tables.

Like the other students, Sasha Shidoh Zultania was carrying her tray of food as she walked. She stopped—deliberately—and chose that moment to give me advice on my posture.

"I do believe you know that's not the proper way to enjoy a meal."

I sat up in my chair. "Of course. *Right*, Sasha." A thought had occurred to me. "Say, Sasha, we've got an open seat right here. Why don't ya join us for once?"

"For once? Don't you mean for the *first* time?" Sasha just smiled wanly at my sudden proposal.

The two girls behind her, on the other hand, were staring like hell had frozen over. One of her overly serious teammates scowled and hesitatingly asked, "Feil Fonaf, are you…inviting Lady Sasha to eat with you as though you two…are friends?"

I wrestled with some tough rye bread that was giving my jaw a workout.

"Princess or not, in the Academy, we're just classmates. Haven't got to be so formal."

"I am suggesting that you *do* have to be!"

She was suddenly screeching at me—I'd been expecting the strait-laced one to act like that. The students around us were all so surprised that they turned to look at us at the same time.

"Oh—I didn't…"

That made her go silent.

There was an awkward pause before Sasha saved the situation. She set her tray down gently next to me. "Yes, I should spend some lunches deepening my bonds with schoolmates." Then she pulled out a chair. That was enough to dispel the tension.

"Come, Mireille. Dorothea, you as well. Why don't you have a seat?"

The students around stirred a little from Princess Sasha sitting down with us, but that was it. They all went right back to their own meals.

I took a peek at Sasha's lunch—it was the daily special. Unexpectedly ordinary.

"Don't often see you in the dining hall," I commented.

"I carved some time out of my day so I could. I can't eat a sandwich with one hand while continuing to work every day. I daresay it's not a healthy habit."

"Well, don't push yourself too hard, bein' a princess *and* an Academy trustee an' all, or you'll end up sick someday."

"I ought to say that to you. You forced your way into Julietta's battle earlier, after all. Do you make a habit of saving people?"

"'Course not. Just lost my patience."

When they saw Sasha and me talking, it wasn't just Sasha's teammates who gave each other dubious looks, but Cyril and Myfila, too.

Suddenly, Sasha said, nearly laughing, to Cyril, who was sitting across from me, "We haven't spoken over a meal like this since we were children, have we, Cyril?"

The most handsome guy in the Academy gave her a fond smile before he replied, "It's not the same, Sasha. Back then, I wasn't even allowed to address you by name, and there wasn't anyone as rambunctious as Feil around."

They sounded a whole lot like childhood friends when they talked.

As I stuffed my face with the mountain of veggies on my plate, one of Sasha's teammates chose to quietly blurt out, "I didn't even know vegetable stir-fry was on the menu as a set meal."

"So, Feil Fonaf, I know you well enough. What did you need from me?" asked Sasha.

"Good instincts," I said.

"Of course I'd be able to tell."

Then she finally started eating her own meal. She trimmed her fish with unbelievably graceful skill using her knife and fork, then brought a morsel to her mouth. She didn't speak with her mouth full, either.

I decided to keep the conversation going while she was eating.

I started off with a "Sorry, but it's just normal chitchat—"

I didn't look at her as I stabbed at my vegetables with a fork and asked her, "Who do you think was the strongest being in mythology?

It can be a god, a monster, whatever, anything goes. We were talkin'
about who was the strongest, but Cyril and Myfila insist it's the
Supreme God and Pandora, and they just won't listen to reason."

Sasha was shocked enough to blurt out, "What? How nonsensical."

"Don't even start. Look, I know, I know. Talking about who's the
strongest seems so immature, but there's somethin' I wanna figure out."

"Please don't tell me you're writing a novel about an invincible
summoner."

"'Course I'm not. I just keep hearin' people bring up disturbing
crap about doom an' the end an' whatnot lately. Had a drunk grum-
blin' to himself about it at work, too."

"So you're wondering what could bring about the end?"

"I figure a princess of one of the eight grand kingdoms has got to
know about the mythos. You'd at least know more than me, considering I only go to temple once in a blue moon."

"You overestimate my knowledge."

"Then which caused more damage: the fire giants or the hearth
goddess's mistake?"

"Why, the hearth goddess, of course."

"See, you've already got me beat. I know 'bout the Supreme God
and Pandora, obviously. But what I wanna know is whether there were
any others linked directly with the end of the world."

Then Cyril chimed in, "Myfila and I told him there weren't any."
He brought a cut of steak to his mouth. Then he quietly told Sasha
our theories until now.

"The prime suspects I would say are the origin elementals, the
World Serpent, and also Leviathan—though I suppose someone who
couldn't so much as pierce Pandora's armor should be struck from the
list. Leviathan likely wouldn't be able to destroy anything like the sun
or the planet."

"What about Pearla, the goddess of love and trickery?" she asked.

"I suppose she could be called the biggest 'nuisance' in the mythos,
but we figured battle prowess was ultimately most important. The
power to directly bring about the end of the world... No matter how

smart or sagacious Pearla is, she wouldn't have any future after being tossed into a wasteland on her own. Pandora, on the other hand, would destroy the wasteland and the rest of the world with it."

"Do you mean that Pearla commanded Pandora to cause those calamities...?"

"So talking about who could directly cause the world's destruction on their own or in a small group, there aren't actually a lot of candidates."

"You're right. It really does narrow it down with those conditions."

The drunk I'd come across at work and Bernhart Hadcheck had both talked about similar ends.

I'd told Cyril and Myfila about the strangeness I'd felt about what he'd said so we could talk about the world ending. Cyril laughed it off, saying it was silly, but since I wouldn't back down, he ended up humoring me and talked it through.

It wasn't like I was actually worried the world was gonna end or anything.

It had to be a coincidence anyway. Some sort of fool's practical joke.

Sasha took a bite of her simmered fish as she thought. Eventually, she swallowed, then finally answered, "I'm in agreement with Cyril and Myfila."

I didn't try to argue with that.

"Ah, well. If you say so, Sasha, then it must be true," I grumbled softly as I forced myself to accept the conclusion.

"However, that's only true if we limit the discussion to gods and monsters."

"Yeah?"

"Did you two forget?" she said to Myfila and Cyril. "Do you remember the Supreme God, Zen—who fought Pandora—as being a good god? There was one particular story of his brutal deeds that might come to mind."

Despite Sasha's clue, nothing came to mind for me since I barely knew anything about mythology. Besides, weren't most of the stories dealing with the Supreme God pretty violent?

"Right...the Six Executioners of Metal..."

I'd never heard of whatever Cyril had said just then, so I just pretended to by saying, "Right, the Executioners," and nodded.

Myfila started to count off on her fingers. "Um…the Grace-Crusher of Iron, the Dawn-Guide of Gold, the Angel-Eater of Silver, the Night-Delusion of Copper, and—"

"The Incantation-Inciter of Lead, and the Dream-Lurker of Salt."

Wait, I hadn't heard of any of these before. What was up with that? What the hell were these guys?

They'd probably noticed the confusion on my face. Sasha continued gently and politely as she explained as though giving a sermon at the temple.

"The Executioners were dealt with cleanly even in the mythology, and there are many who dislike the story, so it seems the temple sometimes glosses over them. This is what has been said about them: The Supreme God, Zen, formed the Six Executioners of Metal from the corpse of a perished god to cloak the sky, the land, and the oceans. These were the Grace-Crusher of Iron, the Dawn-Guide of Gold, the Angel-Eater of Silver, the Night-Delusion of Copper, the Incantation-Inciter of Lead, and the Dream-Lurker of Salt. By the evening of the morrow, the Executioners one and all fell to the Legendary Beast of the Last Realm—and they say the perished god was the goddess Yana, who was Zen's mistress and sacrifice."

"But wait, didn't she already go through a ton of terrible stuff?"

"Exactly. That's exactly why women in particular dislike the story of the Executioners. She gave everything to the man she loved, and in the end, even her own corpse was used by him."

"So that's why I had no clue. The temple must've been tryin' to be considerate of the little ol' ladies around."

"The Supreme God's popularity among women is catastrophic enough as it is, after all."

"But, Sasha, could these Executioners *actually* destroy the world? 'Specially if they got clobbered by Pandora?"

"They did fight Pandora through an entire night. The other gods who'd banded together were killed with one strike, so I daresay the Executioners put up some fight."

"Right, right."

"And the Supreme God also used his lover's corpse to create them. He wouldn't have done that believing they had no chance... Though, I may personally just want to believe that."

"Hmm. So I'm not sure it's them, but seems like a good lead."

I kept working on my stir-fry and felt relieved. It wasn't like Zen's relics would suddenly make an appearance in this age. Worst case, even if they did by some blunder, it wasn't like any human could use a god's weapon or anything.

"Guess I'm just worryin' too much...," I said to myself, and that was where our debate about the strongest being in mythology ended. Our mealtime conversation drifted to discussing the summons festival, which was starting ten days from now.

"Even if it'll give us a chance of winnin', we'll only resort to it when we're in dire straits. If we managed to beat you, Sasha, I've got no clue how upset you'd be with us."

"We still decided that there was value in trying it," Cyril added.

"We'll just use all options available to us, same as always."

"Hold on. What in the world are you three up to this time—?" Sasha looked at us dubiously as we started making insinuations on what was coming.

We all smirked like kids hiding a mischievous secret. And as though we'd timed it perfectly, we all said, "Don't worry. We aren't breaking any of the festival's rules."

17

The Summoner Sees an Angel in the Dark of Night

The evening winds of December dried the sweat on my face.

I sat cross-legged on top of a towering mountain of rock and was half in a daze. The powerful winds that brought along the snow-laden clouds from the northwest made my cloak whip around me, but I didn't bother closing the front buttons.

I was all alone looking up at the night sky, the moon hidden.

"Haah…"

My breath was warm. Until just then, I'd been using magic continuously, and honestly, I was pretty much running on empty. I was assaulted by such strong fatigue, even moving a single finger seemed like a monumental task I couldn't bother with.

But despite how lousy I felt, my mood was great.

If I could move, I would've raised my fists in the air and hollered out of joy. I felt a sense of accomplishment…or maybe it was relief. Even as I was surrounded by the cold, dry, lonely night, my heart was filled with something warm. Right then, I didn't feel any sense of impatience, irritation, or envy toward anyone at all.

The only thing occupying my mind—wholly, deeply—was that I'd made it.

That was right. I'd made it for the summons festival within a day. I'd managed. Finally…I'd been able to move Pandora's giant corpse how I wanted to, to a certain extent.

I suddenly laughed into the night air at myself. "Ya nitwit...it's still not gonna be that easy..."

It wasn't like understanding the Linebolt spell from *Torrenoxion* was enough. I had to keep him balanced after I got him to stand up. And when he walked, I needed to understand where to flex and the order of operations to make it work.

Then I needed cooperation from Cyril's flying summons to act as Pandora's eyes.

There were tons of things to do, and whenever we took a step forward, new issues would arise. Since we'd once fully convinced ourselves that me being able to use Linebolt would be enough to be prepped, we'd genuinely started to panic.

I barely remembered the past week.

I'd been busy with one thing after another trying to prepare for mobilizing Pandora's corpse.

Though we'd been careful to hide Pandora's existence at first, we ended up needing even the time we lost on our commute to the deserted wildlands, so instead, we started to go to some mountains near Raddermark at night for our practices.

And I've been asking the boss to let me take a break from work...

Because of that, my already light coin purse had grown even lighter and was so empty, I didn't know how I'd feed myself the next day. I don't know what I would've done if we hadn't made it.

The wind continued to gust.

I stayed where I was, sitting at the top of that mountain.

I'd told Cyril and Myfila to head back to the dorms already, and now I had no idea what time it was because the moon was hidden, but I was sure it had to be late into the night.

I didn't need them to keep me company while I was staring into nothing and letting the night winds buffet me. I'd wait until I'd recovered enough magic to summon my giant grasshopper to go home.

"Uh..."

In the darkness, I searched for the small leather-bound book in my inner pocket—my *Summoner Incantations*—and pulled it out.

I could hardly see anything, but when I opened it, I just traced the parchment with my index finger.

I started to recite the Legendary Beast of the Last Realm Pandora's summon incantation without imbuing the words with magic.

"Arise, O beast that thwarts despair… Over darkened sea, your wings claim the air. An ending world entrusts a prayer to the beast from its fate to spare as the ice of morn echoes the grief to bear."

I didn't fully get what it meant, but the more I heard it, the sweeter it sounded.

"Cry not for the morrows through loss ye acquire. Rejoice for the flower that blooms from the fire."

The verses, which didn't seem fitting for a beast that had killed the gods, fascinated me.

"The lonesome beast offers a hymn come night…to the plunging stars upon their plight…… Anon, a far journey awaits thee, one of deep mercy, to alight with the prayer-granting beast when thee unite…"

I looked down and went into thought.

Had my Pandora…the one I'd summoned with such a selfless incantation…really caused a war that ended the age of gods? Was it really true?

"What a lovely verse."

Right then, I heard a beautiful voice from overhead.

I didn't turn to look. I was surprised by the familiar voice, but not flustered.

Eventually, I looked up.

"Is that the verse to call your Counterpart?"

In the sky, I saw that platinum hair dancing along, and Sasha. Her archangel glowed faintly as she stood on the angel's palm looking down at me.

She only wore a nightgown and a fur coat over top. It seemed like she'd rushed out of the dorms. I caught glimpses of her beautiful legs as the strong wind gusted at her.

"Hey, Sasha."

She replied to me, "Good evening, Feil Fonaf."

"Nice night out," I said.

"Is it? The moon isn't out, and it seems likely to snow to me."

"I just got to see a beautiful princess and an archangel up close. That's a lot better than any ol' moon to me."

"Um…were you just coming on to me?"

"What are you talkin' about?"

"Well, that aside—are you all right? You look quite haggard."

"That was 'cause I was training like a dyin' man until now."

"Here in the mountains and all alone?"

"Wasn't alone. Tomorrow's the summons festival, so I had Cyril and Myfila go home ahead of me. I'm just here staring into nothin' because I wanna. Once I've recovered enough magic, I'll get right home."

I glanced over to find the archangel's giant face, big as ten adult men, the silver mask hiding her eyes, and her scant armor. I tilted my head to the side, trying to catch a glimpse beneath the mask, but in that moment, the archangel gently pulled her chin away. Didn't seem like she was going to let me get a peek that easily. In the thick of darkness, the angel's white skin emitted a soft light. Like the light of a hazy moon.

"How 'bout you, Sasha? Can't imagine you came out for a nighttime stroll in that outfit just to see what your rival's doin', did ya?"

The archangel's light had probably illuminated the "mountain" I was sitting on. Then again, it was currently covered in dirt, hiding the smooth surface and strange bluish-blackishness of it.

"Some townspeople convened in the Academy…," she finally answered.

"What?"

We were in the dark night, where even the moon and stars were hidden from view. Unless someone was already suspicious, no one would have noticed that I wasn't actually sitting on a hill of dirt. Even Sasha hadn't noticed yet—that I was sitting on top of Pandora's head.

"They were panicking about strange sounds coming from the mountains. They said they'd heard the sounds for the last few days, but today was the worst thus far. They were so frightened, they could hardly sleep, and they asked the Academy to look into it."

"Oh, geez… Sorry about that…" Now that Sasha had told me, I could only apologize to her frankly.

"You mean to say that the sounds of your practicing reached Raddermark?"

"Seems like it. Thought this was enough distance, but looks like we underestimated."

"What in the world were you even doing in the middle of these mountains?"

"I was just doin'…somethin'…with my partner."

"Something? It took Cecelia five minutes to travel here by flight from the Academy, you do realize?"

"Five minutes, huh? It'd take my grasshopper over thirty."

"Please don't make light of this. Even a dragon's call would reach Raddermark from here…but the townspeople informed me that they thought they heard the footsteps of a heavy giant—they even claimed they heard a volcano's eruption tonight. We have no such thing anywhere near Raddermark. What in the world did they hear, then?"

"I'm sorry. I'm real sorry. That was all my fault."

"Then give me a proper answer, Feil Fonaf."

"Well, I— Right."

Sasha's tone was composed, as though she was shutting out her anger and distrust with reasoning.

But right then, I was trying to work out whether I could come up with some excuse. If Sasha hadn't noticed Pandora, I was wholeheartedly devoted to keeping his existence a secret from her. I could have told her I'd suddenly used my Counterpart's abilities to strengthen my electromagic, which must have been when the town had heard a clap of thunder—that was the excuse I'd been able to come up with, but for some reason, I couldn't get the lie out into words.

In the end, still conflicted, I murmured, "Dammit. I don't know what to do."

Apparently, I just didn't want to lie to the girl in front of me. The eighteen years of morals that had shaped who I was just refused to let me lie to Sasha to get out of this situation.

Why did it have to be the third princess of the land of Shidoh here instead of one of the Academy professors? And why did she have to come all the way to the mountains in nothing but a jacket-covered nightgown?

Actually, that must have been what she was wearing when she'd talked to the townspeople like that and told them not to worry because she would investigate it with her angel personally.

She knew what her responsibilities were, and she was the type of princess to fulfill her duties without complaint.

"If only I'd gone back with the others," I mused.

I cursed my idiocy and the situation as I clambered to my feet. I lightly kicked the ground, knocking off some of the mountain I'd blown apart to hide Pandora's head and exposing what was underneath.

I hadn't actually wanted to bother anyone. I didn't want to reveal Pandora for tactical reasons, but I also didn't want to trick Sasha.

But still, the reality was that Pandora did exist here right now. And he was too big to hide, and it was way too late to recall him.

If I *didn't* trick her somehow, didn't figure out a cunning way to deceive her, she'd probably see through it right away. Dozens of confident lies and excuses formed in my head that I could have bet on just barely deceiving her, and I settled on using them.

When I raised my head nonchalantly...

"Oh..."

...the archangel had extended her hand toward me.

Sasha was trying to get down to stand on Pandora's head without realizing what it was. I saw a look cross her face as she realized there was something odd about the mountain I was on, but the light of the angel's skin wasn't enough to reveal the truth.

Once she joined me on the head, she suddenly approached me, closing the distance between us.

"Wh-what...?" I said, drawing a step back, but she'd already grabbed my right hand so I couldn't escape.

I had no idea how quickly she must have rushed here, but her hand was cold as ice.

The moment she stopped me from moving away, she brushed away my sweat-soaked hair with her fingertips. She did it roughly, like she was getting revenge for when I'd done the same to her in the past.

"I was worried. It's much more difficult than you would think to search for a person's presence through Cecelia's senses."

I lightly brushed away her hand and gave her a small, rueful smile as I said, "But you couldn't have known we caused it."

"These were abnormal circumstances, so we had an impromptu roll call, of course."

"I see. And that's how you realized I wasn't in the dorms."

"I've given the residential adviser full discretion to punish you for leaving without permission. You'll have a scolding to look forward to in a few days."

"I'm really sorry..."

"Once I return, I'm sure the town will settle back down, but I need a reason for what happened."

"Right..."

"So, Feil Fonaf—what in the world were the three of you doing out here? Regardless of whether the town is told the truth, I should at least know what really happened as the person who will need to tell them."

Her tone was like a mother trying to reason with a child. It shocked me for a moment, like I was hearing my dead mom's voice in the back of my ears, like I could hear her in Sasha's words.

"Uh, ahh..."

I let out a long sigh as I looked up at the layer of clouds above threatening snow.

Even with Sasha plucking at my heartstrings, I couldn't betray Cyril and Myfila, who'd come all this way with me. I'd prepared myself to tell the lie of a century just as I saw the moon appear.

Its face peeked down at us from between the rifts of the cloud-covered sky. The silent moonlight streamed down, vividly illuminating the December night. The mantle of darkness enveloping the rocky terrain was pulled off one peak at a time.

We were in a ravine deep in the mountain range that had been eroded by a river. Though we were in a spot where we were looking down at the precipitous cliffs, only the one that Sasha and I stood on was a unique shape.

It looked almost as though an unbelievably massive devil had sat itself down right in the ravine. And the contrast with the surroundings revealed just how odd it looked. Naturally, there was something unnatural about it. The giant mountain didn't seem like something that should have existed in the ravine.

"Now even the moon's seen it...," I murmured and scratched at my neck. *Guess this is it*, I thought.

A moment ago, I'd just decided to lie my way through this, but now that the place was illuminated, I wouldn't be able to hide it. Something like this wouldn't get by Sasha.

It was just a coincidence. Or maybe the god of justice and truth or something simply wouldn't allow me to lie. Either way, the only path left for me was now in the opposite direction of where I'd been heading.

"All right, Sasha. I'll let you get a good look, so keep your eyes open."

After Pandora had been exposed by the moonlight and I'd decided to make my confession, I didn't even need to complete my thought. "W-wait, please... What is this?!" she blurted out.

As the moonlight spread and Sasha saw the scene, she looked all around.

I kicked the dirt under my feet again and stomped—slightly dramatically—on the ground.

"This is my Counterpart."

Sasha looked at me in shock. Our eyes met.

"The Legendary Beast of the Last Realm, Pandora. Kind of puts ya off, right?"

I'd never seen Sasha Shidoh Zultania's beautiful face freeze from alarm or terror before...and I couldn't help but grin when I saw the invincible summoner so dismayed. It felt like I'd seen something rare, and that just got me more stirred up—so worked up, I couldn't even stop myself and what I did next:

"Though, right now, he's dead and can't move."

And then, right after I'd said that, almost reflexively, I turned pale and thought—*Oh. Crap.*

18.

The Summoner Appears on the Honorable Stage

The wind gusted by. The bustling roads of Raddermark rushed past below my feet. If I listened carefully, I could probably faintly catch the sounds of the high-spirited hawkers and the rhythmic sound of blacksmithing.

And during all that...

"I'm really sorry. I just happened to let it slip..."

...I was currently clutched by the collar of my cloak and hanging in midair off a giant beak.

"You just so *happened* to? You realize you told her our most important secret?"

"That's a fatal mistake," Myfila added. "It's not like you, Feil."

"Did Sasha seduce you or something? That's how bad this looks."

"I just wasn't thinkin'... I just went with the flow, and it ended up slippin' out..."

"What kind of idiot goes around revealing our weak point to the most likely person who's going to win? It'd at least have been better if she was someone we could win against without Pandora."

"Dammit. Why did I do it...?"

Normally, flying over Raddermark on a summon was prohibited, but today was the summons festival. It was the one time of year when summoners were *supposed* to shine.

Smaller versions of the ranking-match relay equipment usually reserved for the great hall of the Academy had been set up all around

Raddermark, sending the three-hundred-thousand-person town into a frenzy.

I'd heard that it was an exciting sight to see the citizens leave all the buildings to overflow the streets. Apparently, even the most strait-laced government officials would set aside their work and gather to watch the screens with a beer in one hand once the matches started.

People old and young, rich and poor participated.

These screens broadcasted to the affluent neighborhoods of the aristocrats, the jam-packed streets filled with people of all kinds, and even the slums, where the residents scrambled to find the next day's meal. Everyone was going to see the summoners as they bravely rushed in to fight.

And as part of that, the best summoners who would rise to the stage were allowed the one-day privilege to enter town with their summons on the morning of the summons festival. It was even more or less compulsory so we could act as an advertisement.

While we were circling leisurely overhead from the back of Cyril's large bird summon, I looked down to see an herbivore as large as a hill plodding down main street. A trail of kids had formed at its feet to look at the summon, which was several thousand times larger than themselves, and some were even shaking hands with the summoner.

Kids looked up to summoners in any time and age. It was always easily the top career by a large margin whenever there was a *What do you want to be when you grow up?* survey. Having a dragon or large beast, a beautiful elemental, or really any kind of partner that went beyond the human existence probably tickled their fancy.

Light snow flitted down through the wintry sky.

"Huh? Why are you the only one riding in such a unique place, Feil Fonaf?"

A voice *also* came down to me, along with the snow.

I looked up to find Lulua Folicker and her two teammates.

She was snickering at me from on top of her fluffy white dragon as I hung from the large bird's beak. Then the dragon gyrated through the air and appeared directly below the bird.

She matched us in speed.

We started talking—her straddling the neck of her dragon and me hanging off the bird's beak—like we were just jabbering in class.

"...Got in trouble with Cyril and Myfila," I explained.

"On the day of the festival? Wow, you've really done it, then."

"This time, it was a hundred percent my own fault. Was a huge idiot."

"So you're saying they're having you reflect here? Your strongest point is that perverse sense of camaraderie you all have together, so be sure to make up."

Cyril decided to cut in from on top of the bird's back right then. "He told Sasha our secret weapon's weakness."

Lulua clapped her hands together and burst out laughing right away. Her bright giggle filled the air under the heavy span of clouds.

"Well, no wonder you're upset. I would be, too! Ah-ha-ha-ha! I never would have taken you for doing something like that, Feil Fonaf! Did Sasha seduce you or something?"

I let my head droop. "Don't even... Cyril already said that..."

"So? So what is it? What's your secret weapon? And what's that weak point you mentioned? You already told Princess Sasha, so I'm sure you can tell me, too."

"Don't be silly. Cyril'll actually murder me if I do that."

"Not even for a peek at my thigh?"

"You could come at me in the nude for all I care. Ain't talkin'," I spat out, which just made Lulua laugh louder. Her summon even joined in, bleating melodically.

"Oh, the princess is so lucky. She actually knows what you guys will do, and nobody can predict what mischief you'd get up to."

Myfila's grumbling right after that hit me straight in the heart. "Thanks to him, we need to figure out a counterplan for that. It's been a *lot* of work."

Cyril and Myfila knew that Sasha seeing Pandora had been unavoidable. What they were really mad about was that I'd gone ahead and revealed Pandora was dead and couldn't move.

Sure, I'd been so excited to see the top student in the Academy flustered, but I'd been an idiot to run my mouth and tell her such a big secret. Sasha's archangel would be able to just target me the moment I tried to get into Pandora.

"I'm sorry," I said.

Lulua laughed again when she saw my shoulders droop as I still hung in midair. Then she changed the subject. "So actually, have you guys heard about Bernhart?"

I just shook my head without saying anything, but it seemed like Cyril knew more about what was up than me.

"I heard no one's seen him since the incident. He's been missing from lectures and hasn't returned to the dorms, so his teammates went to visit him at his house, didn't they?"

"Yeah, exactly. His flunkies—the guys who were following him around for the allowances he gave them—could all abandon him, but his match teammates aren't so lucky."

"They're still participating in the festival, after all. If they had to bow out because he was missing, they'd become the laughingstock of the whole Academy for being cowards. That'd make them desperate."

"So what do you think happened?"

"He's still missing, as far as I'm aware. Actually, just yesterday, Bernhart's teammates threw themselves at me, begging me to know if there was some sort of underground aristocrat's salon and wanting me to tell them about it. I sent them away and let them know there's no such thing."

"Well, it looks like he actually is doing something now."

"Someone found him?"

"Not *found* so much as *spotted*."

"Oh?"

"Last night was the opening of a Conjurer Society members-only auction, and that's where he was seen—by Erica and Hayana. You remember how those two collect things from famous, deceased conjurers, right? They said it was difficult to tell since he was wearing a hood, but it sure looked like Bernhart."

"At the Conjurer Society? That's almost next door to the Academy."

"So he must have been close by—much closer than any of us thought. And can you guess what he bid on at the auction?"

"I'm not particularly interested to know…but it's the Conjurer Society, isn't it? So maybe a painting that makes anyone who looks at it go insane."

"Obviously not! It was a summoning stone. One that can summon an angel."

"Why would a summoner—even a bad one—need a summoning stone? Normally, those are just used by the rich as protection. The strongest thing those can summon would be about as strong as the average conjurer anyway."

"Apparently, it went for a very high price, all because it was an angel."

"I'm sure it did. But no summoner would use their money on that. Why would they spend an exorbitant amount of money on a one-time summon when they could just take the time to make a contract with an angel?"

"I wonder if that'd even be possible. It *is* Bernhart."

"Well, if all his memories of everything except how to be a summoner were wiped and he went through a full personality change, then maybe."

"Ah-ha-ha! Well, I think that it must be a counterplan to extempores. Especially after he got pummeled by one Mr. Feil Fonaf."

"So he wanted a summoning stone that wouldn't require an incantation? That seems like an extravagant waste of his money."

"Maybe he's thinking of what'll happen if he can't get support from his teammates? The whole thing with Julietta showed that he's powerless if he's put in that kind of situation."

"Well, no one's going to be happy with this."

"All of Raddermark's put off by it. And of course they would be with a summoner who relies on a summoning stone going up on the grand stage. Then again, I can sympathize with his obsession over winning at the festival."

"We'll need to face upperclassmen even in our first matches," Cyril said. "It doesn't matter if they laugh at us as long as we win."

"Right. It might not be a big deal to Princess Sasha, but the rest of us have to face more experienced second- and third-years."

"Your first match is against third-years, right?"

"And you're against second-years. Let's all do our best to get our victories, then. Well, we're off. Sorry for bugging you. And please forgive poor Feil Fonaf."

After having a much longer conversation with us than expected, Lulua's dragon rapidly ascended into the air.

Then her beautiful, downy dragon seemed to dance as it wheeled around the skies of Raddermark. On the ground right about now, the people who were witnessing the dance were likely cheering.

The streets seemed like they could have stretched all the way into the horizon. The vast sky of the giant town of three hundred thousand was filled with flying summons from gigantic dragons and huge birds to large serpents clad in electricity, a herd of pegasi, and even a flying whale.

Even as I absentmindedly watched the town while hanging from the giant bird's beak, I didn't feel like I'd ever get tired of looking at it.

We'd just gotten to the great market on the east of Raddermark, so I tried searching for the Horse's Drool Pavilion from the sky.

"Huh?"

Right then, I saw a girl waving her hand like mad from one of the roads to the great market.

She was a brunette and looked pretty young—I realized it was Ilecia, who was in charge of the dining room at work. Had she seen me from over two hundred mejals away on the streets? If she had, her eyes must have been really good.

I was about to wave back when I heard Cyril suddenly say, "So that's how it is, Feil," so I turned my attention to him instead.

"Sorry. What is?"

"Bernhart. It looks like he's got his own plans."

"Yeah, seems like. He's been up to plenty gettin' an angel summoning stone. I'm sure he could've picked up a different one if he just needed it as a counter to extempores."

"So that part bothered you, too?"

"Personally, I woulda looked for lots of cheaper ones an' fought with numbers. Then again, cheap in this case means enough to build an entire house for just one stone."

"Bernhart or not, I'm sure the angel's stone couldn't have been a casual purchase."

"So he must've been desperate for it to be an angel, huh…"

"But here's the rub. How powerful is an angel from a summoning stone, really? It'd probably be an even match for your bugs, wouldn't it?"

"Maybe. But anythin' summoned by a stone isn't synced with the owner. That's an obvious weakness."

"So what do you think is happening, Feil?"

"Right… I think we've gotta wait an' see first. Either way, both our teams have gotta win to make it on."

"You have a point there. We might not even make it to the final round with Sasha, whom you so kindly informed of our secret."

"If there's any way I could apologize to make it better, I would…"

Right then, the bells of Sedra Cathedral, which was visible from anywhere we flew in the sky over Raddermark, went off.

Its ten gathered steeples were round, giving the cathedral an organic look. Each steeple contained a hanging bell, and when every one of them went off together, their rings built up to be heard all across Raddermark.

The tolls told us it was ten in the morning.

It also let us know that the summons festival had begun.

"It's time," Cyril said as the giant bird flapped its wings. It circled around wide over the great market and headed to the north, cutting through the wind.

The little bits of snow hanging out in the air started running into me, so I covered my face with both my arms out of irritation and kept an eye in front of me through the gap.

Raddermark itself had no town walls, but to the north, where the Academy and its field lay, there was a thick wall of eighty mejals that bordered the width of the urban area. That was there to protect the ordinary lives of the townspeople as the summons clashed in the Academy ranking matches. The two gigantic and mismatching fortresslike buildings that made up the Academy served as the one and only gate leading beyond the wall.

Going past those buildings led to a field conspicuously full of boulders—that entire area from one end to the other was owned by the Academy and served as the grounds for the Academy ranking matches.

During this season, it just looked like a sprawling field of withered grass, but in actuality, the entirety of it was supposed to be over ten times bigger than all of Raddermark, and it even boasted three impressive lakes.

Cyril muttered, "Now that I can see the meeting point, I'm actually starting to feel a little nervous…"

Myfila chimed in, very concisely, "Don't worry. We'll manage."

I could see all the summons gathering one after another behind the Academy buildings at the entrance to the sprawling field. I even saw Lulua's dragon touching down on the withered grass.

Right in that moment, I said, "Looks like all the hotshots are gettin' together for a huddle, huh," trying to sound braver than I felt.

Even though it was called a summons festival, we didn't have a special meeting ground where it was being held or anything like that. There weren't many differences between this and our usual ranking matches. The biggest changes were that only fifteen teams were selected from among all the year levels to have a tournament-style match, the whole thing would be broadcast across Raddermark, and powerful artifacts were allowed. Otherwise, it was no different from any other match.

But my heart still raced, my fingertips went numb, and my lips started to twitch.

I gave myself a light slap on the cheek with one of my hands and took a step on the field right as the giant bird gently landed. As soon

as my feet hit the ground, I made sure not to twist anything and immediately looked for Sasha.

I met eyes with the platinum-haired beauty who'd made it ahead
of us...

"Hey."

That was all I said before giving her a bold smile.

A casual declaration of war to the top-choice contender. An
announcement that we'd win this time around.

"Hey, look, Feil."

But then Myfila yanked on the sleeve of my robe, so I turned
around. "What's up?"

"What's wrong, Bernhart?" someone was saying.

Bernhart Hadcheck had just come out of one of the Academy's
buildings and was spotted walking toward us.

"But—but what's the plan? You *just* came back, and now you're saying it's time to get started...but we have no idea what you want us to do."

Today, Bernhart didn't have his signature hairdo. His face looked
haggard, and dark circles had even formed under his eyes. He almost
looked like a half-dead fiend, based off the vibe he was giving off.

"Bernhart, are you listening to us?!"

"Please stop muttering all those weird things under your breath.
Let's get a plan set up!"

It seemed like they were arguing as they walked—or more like
Bernhart's teammates were attempting a heartfelt negotiation with
him as he completely ignored them. Even when they both tried to grab
his shoulders and tugged on his clothes instead, he brushed them off
and kept walking over our way.

When the participants of the festival turned to look at Bernhart,
every single one of them seemed calm and composed. Not one person seemed intimidated by Bernhart's behavior.

In fact...

"Well then, we'll now go over the summons festival's rules."

...when the Academy professor arrived and announced that, the
air seemed to stir much more.

The Summoner Shudders at the Commencement of the Silver

A one-day tournament of fifteen teams meant fourteen matches in a day. For that purpose, the Academy's expansive yard had been sectioned off so we could hold three matches at once.

A library on the third floor of one building had also been set up as a waiting room for the participants. The bookshelves, which didn't have the *Torrenoxion* but did contain spellbooks from every age and nation, had been covered by relay screens of the matches so we could watch all three.

"Sasha sure looks calm. She's readin' a book at a time like this."

"That's just how royalty should be. We should take a page from her."

Most teams were gathered in front of each screen, but when I happened to turn around, I found Sasha there sitting down to elegantly read a book.

It seemed like she must've brought it in herself. She could hold it in one hand, and it looked like it could've come from any old bookshelf, unlike the spellbooks around here. A black leather cover hid the front of the book.

"But the size of that... You don't suppose it could be a manga?"

"No way. Has to be some super-formal specialized tome or somethin'."

But Sasha liked manga. I was sure she was reading a shoujo one to kill time.

I brushed Cyril off just when he'd been about to realize it, but before I turned back around, my eyes suddenly met Sasha's. She gave me a small smile and brought a finger up to her lips, giving me a "Shh." She looked ridiculously beautiful while doing it.

I knew she was telling me to keep quiet about her manga hobby, but there was something a little suggestive about it, too.

The first matches had just started on the relay screens.

"So, Feil, which match do you think we should focus on?" Cyril asked beside me. He was wearing a military uniform with a stand-up collar under his robes. He had a sheathed longsword by his hip that made him look less like a smart summoner and more like a charming commanding officer. Tall and handsome, he was going to show up on screen all over Raddermark. Whether he wanted it or not, he was definitely going to get a ton more fangirls.

"Every match besides Bernhart's—is what I'd like to say, but…," I said, which drew a brief sigh from Cyril.

"Right. I thought so…"

"Guy's face didn't have an honest look to it. I reckon he's got somethin' planned."

Myfila, who'd been caught by Cyril and was getting her hair combed out, looked up at me with a cryptic look. "The unskilled rich boy might do something?"

"He might have somethin' up his sleeve like we do. Well, even if he hasn't got talent, he can do most things by puttin' his money where his mouth is."

"You mean an artifact? An old powerful one?"

"Probably," I said.

"The Six Executioners of Metal we talked about with the princess are also technically artifacts," Myfila said.

"Ya nitwit. Why would a divine weapon show up in a tournament like this?" I said.

I scoffed and then turned my eyes to the screen where Bernhart's team was displayed.

The match had just begun, but it was clearly progressing in one direction.

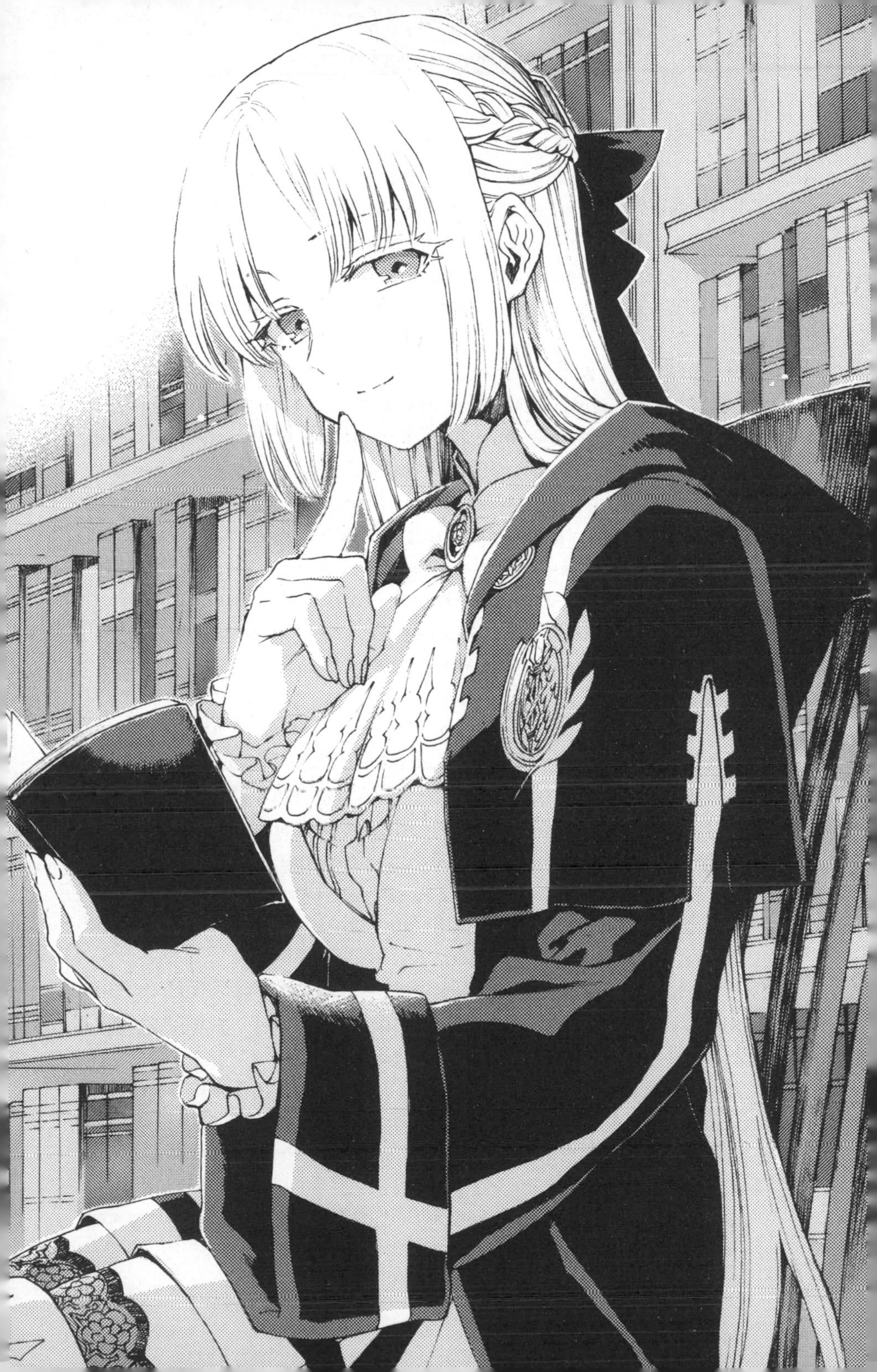

All three members of Bernhart's team had been forced to go on the defensive as they were cornered by a trio of blazing fire elementals summoned by the second-years they were up against. Wait…no… more accurately, this wasn't really even a match.

It was just a pair-up of the hunters and the prey. Like rabbits against tigers.

I hadn't expected that things would end with Bernhart's knight-shaped water elemental powerless when he had such an advantage.

Immediately after the match had started, the second-year team had come out with the three fire elementals and blasted the ground and rocks below their feet with as much firepower as possible, then started throwing all the hot rocks at the water elemental.

Even cold water ends up turning to steam when it's exposed to hot rocks, and not every water elemental could deal with hot water or ice, either. Though they were amorphous and had an infinite water supply, they were susceptible to large changes in temperature— particularly the younger ones with less power.

Once Bernhart's water elemental had tons of hot stones inside it, it wasn't able to maintain its form. Actually, it didn't *just* lose its form— it turned straight to steam and was absorbed right into the dry ground.

"…Bernhart's team just doesn't compare with second-years. Guess there was nothing he could do with 'em throwing out that firepower right from the start," I grumbled as I crossed my arms.

Cyril asked me, "What would you have done in his position, Feil?"

I snorted before I replied, "Fled, obviously. Would've run for my life and used the time to make the water elemental bigger. That way, no little hot stones could've made it boil away."

"So you think they got it all wrong from the start. They must have thought they had an advantage and wanted to see what'd happen."

"Ha-ha-ha—watchin' 'em ain't a good strategy against upper-classmen."

Even though the end-of-match bell hadn't gone off, the winners and losers were basically settled.

The second-years had trapped Bernhart's team in a fire funnel and were launching a barrage of flame spells at them from outside. Their attacks were ferocious—merciless without any hope of finding an opening.

Once the defensive spells Bernhart's teammates had cast were broken, that'd be it.

"Has Bernhart really got nothin' up his sleeve...? We should've watched Lulua's match if this was how it was gonna turn out."

The screen just continued to show the nasty aristocrat being tormented.

"Why'd he even buy that angel summonin' stone...?"

The other participants around me started leaving the screen once they were sure of Bernhart's loss...but I stayed to watch. Cyril and Myfila also didn't budge.

"Huh?"

I unintentionally grunted when I saw Bernhart pulling artifacts from his robes as he was surrounded in his hopeless situation.

The relay zoomed in on him right then.

Though the waiting room had no speakers so we could concentrate on our upcoming matches, Raddermark would have likely been ringing with Bernhart's laughter right around then.

"What the heck is that thing...? Is it really worth guffawin' over like that...?"

Bernhart had raised both his hands. In his left was a fist-sized blue gem—likely the angel summoning stone—but his right hand held a silver chalice I didn't recognize.

The summoning stone broke apart in Bernhart's hand, and a two-winged angel appeared above him.

She wore a snow-white robe and held a slender sword in her hand. She was just human-sized.

How'll she be able to help fight in the situation they're in?

My brows furrowed as I thought that.

"Whaaat the...?! Wait! Wait!"

I left the screen and ran at full speed to the one of the library windows.

I practically threw myself at the north-facing window as I yanked it open and hung outside, looking at the summons-festival battlefield and glaring in the direction where Bernhart's team should have been.

Since I'd panicked out of nowhere, the participants who hadn't been watching Bernhart, including Sasha, seemed genuinely perturbed as they looked between me and the relay screen.

But they wouldn't have been able to tell from that. The screen that should have been showing Bernhart was currently blank.

"Huh? What happened? Wasn't the match basically over?"

"No idea. But one of the first-years suddenly started making a scene and—"

The waiting room began to stir. People started to gather at the window where I was. "Huh? Seriously?" "Did something bad happen?" They were all making random comments as they tried to follow my gaze.

"Silver...," someone murmured in amazement.

That's right, silver.

Far into the distance of the wide, vast field—in a corner—was a giant surge of liquid silver.

At first glance, it looked like some sort of endless geyser of water... but it was firmly blocking and reflecting the weak rays of sun that came down with the snow as it glittered. It had to be easily spouting a hundred mejals tall. The spout of water was also pretty thick in circumference, and once it reached the atmosphere, it fell headlong back to the ground—not like rain, but more like a gigantic waterfall.

It didn't fit in at all with the flitting snow scene around it; something was extremely ominous about it.

"What the heck is that thing? What happened?" someone watching the scene out the window said. But it wasn't me or Cyril or Myfila who answered—apparently, others had also been watching Bernhart's match out of curiosity—and a third-year girl replied, "It was some sort of artifact I've never seen before. There was an angel summoning stone—that one, I recognized—but there was something else that suddenly swallowed up the angel that came from the stone. What was that? Some sort of magical slime creature? What was inside that cup?"

It seemed like even she was confused after witnessing everything, though. When she realized everyone there was staring at her, she cleared her throat lightly and explained, "Um, so the son of the Hadcheck nobles used two artifacts. One was an angel summoning stone, but the other seemed to be a cuplike artifact that housed some sort of magical creature…"

She stopped there and turned to look at the window, where the unusual events were progressing.

"And that silver geyser is what came out of the cup artifact. As soon as the creature—which was waterier than a slime—swallowed up the angel, it started to expand. It swallowed up the Hadchecks' son and also even the flying relay camera."

One of the second-year boys spoke up. "What happened to Gerald's team? They were up against him."

The third-year replied, "They weren't on-screen, but they were really close, so…" She didn't clarify any further.

"But it increased in volume so quickly. What's it using to expand like that? The magic floating around in the air wouldn't account for that much growth."

"The thing's probably usin' the magic from the angel it swallowed first."

"But it's just a summoning-stone angel. I don't think it would have the power to make something like this possible."

"Right. You've got a point."

"Perhaps the artifact itself was storing magic?"

"Well, that seems like it'd be reasonable, but is there any material that *could* store that much magic?"

They all sure seemed worthy of being participants in the festival just from their conversation. Everyone had naturally started analyzing and trying to identify the phenomenon in front of them. It didn't matter what year they were in or their position.

"This is... Feil...?"

Cyril had said my name after making his way next to me. He sounded bewildered, as if he was seeking answers.

But...

"Sorry. Could ya wait a sec?"

...I didn't have the wherewithal to give him what he wanted. No matter how much I wanted to deny it, my mind automatically filled with images that made me shudder.

That silver spectacle in front of me—I didn't know why, but I couldn't help but think it was the beginning of the end of this world.

That was what the drunk from my workplace had been going on about.

And for some reason, Bernhart had been fully confident he could bring about the destruction of the world.

Then there were those beings from mythology that no one fully knew the particulars of, which Sasha had told me about in the Academy dining hall.

All those things that couldn't be easily connected were instinctually and insistently coming together in my head—giving me a nasty and foreboding premonition.

Finally, I grabbed hard onto the sides of the open window as I murmured, "The Executioners..."

When I practically growled my words, they seemed to have reached the discussion happening behind me.

"The Executioners?" someone said. "As in the Six Metal ones?"

"What were they again? The Grace-Crusher of Iron, the Dawn-Guide of Gold, the Angel-Eater of Silver—?" And that was where the conversation stopped.

"No—*nononono*!! There's no possible way!! That's utterly inconceivable!!"

"Is that seriously the Angel-Eater of Silver for real?!"

They were all knowledgeable summoners. But even as they denied it, they all rushed at the windows with enough force to almost throw me out.

They threw open all four large windows, and the temperature in the library dropped precipitously.

"B-b-but…that…might just be true?"

"A relic of the gods—of the Supreme God? No way."

"No, I refuse to accept it. If that's supposed to be a divine creature, then anything could happen."

"You mean like it could swallow anything whole to create an infinite magical supply through transmutation? Or it could transform the matter into any form it wants?"

"That's right. That's not anything like what we've learned."

"Then try explaining how a single artifact and an angel could be causing this to happen."

The spring of silvery water hadn't stopped and was spreading across the ground. Instead of being absorbed into the earth, it seemed to stretch endlessly, engulfing most of the field that we could see before we knew it.

It looked almost like a sea of silver rising as though it was a tide.

"What do we do…?"

"How far is it going to spread…?"

Even as the bell for the end of the match rang out wildly, the silver water showed no signs of stopping. It was already attempting to creep up to the base of the Academy buildings below.

It seemed like fear had finally trumped intellectual curiosity for the brilliant summoners. At some point, they'd stopped talking, and the waiting room fell into a deathly silence even quieter than when it was used as a library. The end-of-match bell that continued to clamor was ear-piercing.

"Feil Fonaf," someone said abruptly, bringing me to turn around.

I found Princess Sasha and her two teammates there. Even though they were first-years, they were the strongest team around, and all the other school years had opened up a path for them.

"How do you know that's the Angel-Eater of Silver from the Six Executioners of Metal?"

"Just a gut feelin'. Haven't got any solid evidence for it."

Then only Sasha approached my side. Myfila, Cyril, me, and Sasha in that order from right to left were all taking up one of the windows.

"My head hurts," she said. "I've seen legends two days in a row."

"How's this happenin'? A drunk's nonsense 'bout doom and destruction comin' to life…"

"Do you think Bernhart is able to control it?"

"Pretty sure he can't."

"Did you see him get absorbed?"

"Yeah, right before the feed cut off. Looked pretty frightful as he got swallowed up. His teammates, too. I reckon they wouldn't run from the silver water if they coulda controlled it."

"…The feeds for Lulua and the other matches also just cut off a moment ago. From what I saw, it seems the silver substance attempts to assimilate anything that moves."

"Why's a myth actin' same as a slime…?"

"This is no longer a matter of the summons festival. The Academy must devote all its resources toward stopping it."

"Just don't summon your archangel no matter what. Even if we only know about it from its name, it's still called an Angel-Eater. An' the thing ended up like this after it ate an angel."

"I know."

"You're goin' to the professors now, right?"

"Yes… Though, I'm not sure any of them would know of a way to stop it."

"So it's a matter of whether the summoner corps under the royalty's direct command make it in time."

"I'll use my royal rights or even insist as the king's daughter to have them dispatched as soon as possible. So, Feil Fonaf, will you please help me as well?"

When Sasha asked me that, I just managed a sound from my throat. "Huh?"

I reflexively turned to look at her and found her amethyst eyes staring back at me. Those royal eyes were filled with a noble sense of responsibility and heartfelt kindness.

I almost started to joke, "You want me to have Pandora splash around in a puddle for ya?" but considering the dire situation didn't call for it, I stopped myself. Instead, I just gave her a plain and direct assent.

"All right. I'll do whatever I can."

I couldn't let the world go ending just because of Bernhart.

Also, losing the actual Academy would've killed me, and I wanted to also protect my boss and my coworker Ilecia after all they'd done for me.

Sasha smiled faintly at my response.

Then Cyril and Myfila were right there beside me.

"If Feil says so, then I won't object, either. I swear upon the name of the Ojlocks that I'll do all in my power to help."

"We practiced getting him to move lots and needed a way to debut him."

I couldn't actually mobilize Pandora on my own. I needed help from Cyril—who acted as Pandora's eyes—and Myfila, too.

Whether Sasha realized that or not, the princess looked at us and smiled again. This time, it was a full smile. One that was filled with trust in all three of us.

"Good. You make an excellent team."

It was a tad embarrassing, but I was also kinda proud in a way. The edge of my mouth naturally twitched up.

Then...

So now what? What should we do? I'm willing to buy time or act as a decoy.

...the moment I tried to tell Sasha that...

"Get away from the window!!" someone yelled as a new development had broken out.

The sea of silver, which had only continued to grow, sweeping along the ground without showing any other movement, now had clearly displayed a sign of sentience as it attacked the Academy building.

And since the third-floor library was facing the field, we were directly affected.

The silver ocean rose like a giant tidal wave and smashed into the building again and again. The glass of the window next to us cracked, and I heard a giant crash like brick had started crumbling.

The sound of a girl's scream intermingled with the sound.

"Sashaaa!!"

I immediately stretched a hand out to Sasha in front of me. Myfila was safe. I saw Cyril immediately pull her into his arms.

At the same time, as I held Sasha tight in my arms, I used an extempore. A swarm of tens of thousands of insects instantly appeared and shielded us against the silver wave. The swarm reached Cyril as well.

It was like a punch from a giant.

"Gah!"

As the wave pushed in from the open window, Sasha and I were both blown away, tumbling along the floor like dead leaves in a strong gust of wind.

If I hadn't summoned the swarm, we likely would have been swallowed by the silver ocean, too. Even Cyril and Myfila. After taking most of the insects I'd summoned, the silver wave retreated.

"Dammit. That had some force to it."

As I cursed and got up, I saw just how bad the situation was on the northern side of the library where the tidal wave had hit. Parts of the wall had crumbled away, and none of the windows had retained their original shape.

"Everyone okay? You're all alive?" someone called.

"I'm fine." "Okay here, too." Seemed like no one had been swept off.

As I grabbed Sasha's hand and stood her up, I murmured, "Blasted Angel-Eater...tryin' to swallow up the Academy and get over the town wall..."

She was looking at me with worry.

"Are you all right? You didn't get hurt?"

"I'm fine, just sore all over. More importantly, we've done what we could just then."

Then once Sasha stood up, she looked around.

....

All nine teams and twenty-six people—the best of the summoners who'd been waiting for their own matches save for Sasha herself—
were staring right at her.

"Whew..."

We had no time to hesitate. She only took two seconds to suck in
a breath.

The next moment, she began a dignified speech as the strongest
summoner in the Academy—the one fated to become a hero—and as
the third princess of the land of Shidoh, whose duty was to love her
people.

"A danger the likes of which Raddermark has never seen is now
imminent. Though we have yet to identify what it is, the enemy we
are facing is likely one of the Six Executioners of Metal—the Angel-
Eater of Silver."

The moment the sea of silver—or rather the Angel-Eater—had
actually started to mobilize, we'd lost all ability to postpone action.

Beyond the wall that separated the summons festival battle-
grounds and the town were three hundred thousand spectators likely
waiting even now for the resumption of the festival. If the Angel-Eater
surged into the crowd, it would be a disaster for the history books.

We had to evacuate everyone without a minute—or a moment—
to lose.

"No matter what fear we may feel, we are summoners. We are the
ones who have protected humanity since the gods all left the world.
We who are present now are the successors of knowledge and crafts
passed down from summoners who faced great dangers since ancient
times."

The third princess Sasha Shidoh Zultania's resolute voice bolstered
the courage of those of us who had recoiled at the appearance of the
legendary Angel-Eater—and she had also shared with us the responsibility of protecting the people.

"A line of heroes cannot tuck tail and run now simply because of
one measly Executioner. We must protect the meek this day once more.

Those of you able to take to the skies must halt the progress of the Executioner. Those on the ground should take the people to safety—we are all equipped with the power to do that."

Once Sasha finished, all the summoners present looked firm about what their roles were. They would dash out of this room as quickly as they could with their proud summons and head to Raddermark.

Cyril, Myfila, and I would be doing the same.

If the Angel-Eater of Silver had its targets set on Raddermark, then we needed to prioritize evacuating the citizens.

It wasn't time for Pandora to mobilize yet.

Since all Pandora could do was brawl, he wouldn't be any use against the slime Angel-Eater. And even if we did fight with him, the battle would likely immediately get pushed into Raddermark. Before deploying a beast over three-hundred-fifty mejals tall, it would make more sense to first create a field where no one would die.

"Now!" Sasha stretched her right hand in front of her, giving the signal, and several had already started their summoning verses. "Let's go, summoners!"

20.
The Summoner Rages at the Unreasonable Legend

"So you were alive, Lulua!"

A familiar white dragon passed by me overhead, and I couldn't help but shout.

In the next moment, the dragon's long, lithe body twisted through the air and abruptly came to a halt.

I doubted she'd heard me in the pandemonium of hundreds of people running. It was more likely she'd spotted me in the middle of the great market, straddling a giant grasshopper as I helped guide people in east Raddermark.

"Is everyone on?! Rest assured this centipede won't harm you! So please don't worry!"

In front of my eyes was the giant centipede of over ten mejals that I'd summoned.

At that moment, about twenty people were on my summon's wide back—they were the sick and elderly who couldn't evacuate on their own, but they were staring at me as I rode on my giant grasshopper seeming anxious and like they were close to bursting into tears at any second.

Then I gave them a wide, toothy smile.

"We're taking the shortest route to Sedra Cathedral! The cathedral is being protected by several summoners from the Academy, so it'll definitely be safe! Have a pleasant trip!"

The giant centipede took off running like it was gliding across the ground.

I gave them a big wave as they headed off...

...then I immediately switched gears and started urging everyone in the market along.

"Ruuuun!! If you don't wanna die, dash for the cathedraaal!!"

Not a single person had a word of complaint about my threatening shouts—and naturally so. Even now, anyone could see the giant silver slime that was trying to climb up the wall just to the north.

One of its enormous feelers glooped over the wall, and in that moment, a dragon flying by that area let out a blast of fire.

Though that wasn't enough to burn away the feeler, the thing didn't seem to like the more than three thousand degrees of heat and had already pulled its appendage back.

It'd been more than half an hour since that idiot Bernhart had set off the artifact.

The Angel-Eater of Silver had first started out as an ocean of silver that grabbed whatever it could, but it'd progressed, turning into a gigantic and mobile slime.

Though it was attempting to get into Raddermark using the shortest route possible by crossing over the wall that spanned the length of the city, the high-level spells and barrage of summons attacking it were keeping it at bay.

It faced dragons and air elementals clad in electricity, gigantic birds of fire, and even grand devils carrying large swords. Over a hundred airborne summons were halting the Angel-Eater's invasion at the wall.

"Feil Fonaf! Is that really the Angel-Eater of Silver?!"

As the white dragon came down right above me, Lulua Folicker's head peeked over from its long neck. She was also with her two teammates.

"No clue! Whether it's the Angel-Eater or a new species of slime, that still doesn't change what we gotta do! If you can fly, then get over to that wall and start defendin' it!"

"That silver ocean flowed in right when we were in the middle of a match, and we almost died!"

"Well, sorry ya had to deal with that! Go tell it to that nitwit, Bernhart!"

It wasn't just the summoners from the festival in this. Over three hundred students from the Academy and all the professors had come to the town and were working to save the three hundred thousand people.

All of Raddermark was filled with summons right now.

Gigantic beasts and frightening dragons were being used in place of wagons to get people to each of the designated evacuation centers of the districts. Apparently, the headmaster and Sasha had decided a full evacuation of all three hundred thousand citizens out of the city would be infeasible, and the head of Raddermark had agreed.

"Esteemed summoners! Please allow us to handle this area!"

As Lulua and I were shouting at each other, some town guards with swords at their sides ran over.

"Thank you!" I said. "Please run if you think it's too risky!" Then I had my giant grasshopper hop off. I had it leap onto the rooftop of a butcher, then made it jump even higher. We were heading over to the great market by rooftop.

Lulua and the rest of her team followed me.

"We just need to protect the town until the summoner corps of Shidoh come, then we'll win, right?!"

"They're the strongest group around! If they can't fight against it, then this world is done for anyway!"

"Where are Cyril and Myfila?!"

"I'm joinin' them at the market entrance! Actually, stop worryin' about us and hurry and get to work! If you got time to shoot the breeze, least you could do is cast a spell!"

After I yelled at them, Lulua pouted. "Well, sorry for feeling scared!"

"We'll go! We're going to go!" she said. "We are summoners, after all!"

She stuck out her tongue and gave me the best confident face she could muster, then sent her giant dragon flying up. After her dragon let out a roar overhead, it headed off, lightning fast, toward the northern wall.

For a few seconds, I watched Lulua walk away, then I immediately used transmission magic for a Voice Link spell, which was a type of magic that allowed you to talk to someone from a long distance as long as it was set up beforehand. It was priceless during emergencies like these and such a basic spell that people basically claimed you couldn't be a conjurer or summoner without being able to cast it.

When I invoked the spell, the small summoning circles had probably appeared on my tongue and at the back of my ears.

"Cyril, good news. Lulua was actually alive and kickin'."

I didn't wait for Cyril's voice to come through as I cast my eyes down.

When I looked at the people running through the wide roads, I checked for whether there were any who needed help. Then I murmured, "I can just leave the guards to handle that."

But right then, I met eyes with a guy who was staring straight into the sky.

—?!

That moment, my whole mind was going at full blast.

I wasn't going to let him go that easy—not the guy in the dark-green robes full of pockets who looked like a traveler. I stopped my grasshopper quick as I passed him overhead, then when I was right in front of his eyes, I got off.

The man started to scram at full speed when he saw a summon suddenly appear in front of him.

I jumped off the grasshopper and went after him, grabbing the shoulder of his cloak.

He tried his best to beat me off, but I was desperate. If I let him escape now, I'd lose my one clue and my one chance of saving Raddermark.

"Where do you think you're goin'?!"

"S-stop, please!"

I tugged the cloak and dragged him to the nearby wall of a shop. Then I pushed him into the hard brick wall. I held his neck with my right arm to keep him from struggling.

"You're that drunk from before! Would ya care to have a chat with me?"

I had no clue what my face must have looked like after blowing my lid. The thirty-something man was practically in tears when faced with me, an eighteen-year-old.

"I-it wasn't my fault!" he said, looking genuinely terrified. "It was all the voice! The voice!" He kept going on about some mumbo jumbo, but when I pressed my right arm against his throat, he stopped.

"I haven't got time for your babble! Just answer the questions I ask ya!"

I was being openly hostile, but I didn't have time to be nice to him right now. I kept pressing into his neck until he finally couldn't stand having his air cut off and he nodded.

I pointed at the northern wall with my left hand.

"What the heck is that?! Is that the silver-whatever thing you were talkin' about before?!"

The silvery feelers were flashing in and out of view above the wall the same as before. After looking at it just once, he looked frightful as he said, "It's the beginning of the end. The thing that will open the door to our demise. It hasn't forgotten the mission engraved into its very being itself or the wrath of the god."

Partway through, I pressed on the guy's throat again.

"Just the practical parts! None of this metaphorical nonsense!"

"I-it's an Executioner. One of the Six Executioners of Metal. The Angel-Eater of Silver."

It seemed like we were right on the money. Something I never wanted confirmed. Just then, my anger and impatience reached their peak, and I punched the wall next to the guy's face with my left hand.

"Why?! Why'd you bring that thing into Raddermark?!"

The man couldn't put up resistance against me anymore at that point. Tears were forming in his eyes as he gave up all attempts at evasion or lying. "It needs the Shidoh princess—Sasha Shidoh Zultania. That's what the Angel-Eater of Silver was ordered to do," he confessed.

I hadn't expected Sasha's name here.

Even less understanding of the situation, I ended up baring my teeth at the guy as I screwed up my face into an even worse scowl.

"It was ordered, huh…?!"

"I-I'm just a temple researcher. I travel to the ruins of legends and look for miracles left behind by the gods."

"Seems like dire times if an academic from the temple's hailin' in world destruction. Is the nitwit pope tryin' to destroy the world?!"

"No! J-just listen to me! I'll tell you everything!"

I bit my lip until I tasted blood to keep my impatience at bay. I stared into the guy's face practically with the eyes of a devil as I tried to judge whether the guy was sober and had all his marbles together.

"I-it was exactly half a year ago. The research team I was with excavated it on Cape Millegranna in the land of Kudoh… When we took it out of the ground, it was just a lump of silver, but it turned into a chalice overnight. At that point, when we realized it was some sort of artifact, we began our research."

Even though he seemed terrified by my threatening attitude, he still looked like he had his wits about him based on the look on his face.

He wasn't spouting nonsense anymore, that was for sure.

"We had our suspicions from the start that it was some remnant of the Angel-Eater of Silver. *Millegranna* is a local old word that means 'silver headdress.' Among mythological researchers, it's believed to be the spot where Pandora fought the Angel-Eater of Silver."

"Oh…? So you're sayin' you were chosen from among 'em, huh?!"

"Th-that's right. I was. Sometimes—just sometimes, I'd hear the voice."

"You're tryin' to tell me you were just controlled by the Angel-Eater's voice?! Ya really want me to believe that?!"

"Please believe me! Please, really. There wasn't anything special about me. To the Angel-Eater of Silver, humans are just tools. We were there to help it move, that's it!"

"What did the Angel-Eater say?! Why's it tryin' to move?!"

"It's trying to fully revive itself so it can restart its destruction. In order to resurrect itself after being defeated by Pandora, it needed something to serve in place of its core—an archangel. The voice in my head told me to bring it a powerful angel and to kill the beast and the world."

"And that's Sasha?!"

"She's just the only person I know who can summon an archangel."

"And why's the thing gotta also destroy the world?! Pandora's long gone! The Supreme God killed him eons ago! Doesn't that mean the Executioner's done its duty?!"

"It's the goddess Yana."

"Yana?"

"That's right. The goddess's corpse was supposedly used to create the Executioners. Her dying wish—her hatred—has turned into a curse that's made the Executioners into the world's destroyers. Though their original target was Pandora, it's since also become the world itself."

"*Tsk.*" I couldn't help but sharply cluck my tongue.

I could get Yana's mortification at being used as a sacrifice by her own lover, but blaming that on the whole world was completely off the mark. She should have limited her grudge to just that bastard of a Supreme God. She'd involved everyone who was only trying to survive in the world in her revenge.

I wanted to come right out and say that, but there wouldn't be any god anywhere to hear it anyway.

"How'd it get from you to Bernhart Hadcheck, then?"

"B-Bernhart? I'm not sure—I have no idea. I don't even know who Bernhart is. I'm telling the truth."

Then, next, he showed me his right hand and that its four fingers had cruelly been lopped off right at their bases, leaving only his thumb.

"I stole a valuable object of research from the temple. There were many chasing me, and it's possible one of the people the temple sought help from might have gone by that name."

Seeing that gave me a start, but it wasn't enough to cool me down now that I was seething.

Actually, I almost wanted to laugh it off by telling him the pursuer must've been kind only taking four fingers. What probably happened was that he'd refused to let go of the silver chalice and had lost it along with his digits.

"So somebody must've sold it to Bernhart on the black market...! I wanna find 'em and give 'em an ass-kickin', but now's not the time..."

After coming to that conclusion, I decided not to ask more about Bernhart.

He'd been looking for an artifact to use for the summons festival and must have bought information on the Angel-Eater of Silver. Even if he might've gotten his hands on it that way, it was all already too late to change at this point.

Anyway, right now, I needed to know how to stop the Angel-Eater, so I asked the man firmly, "What happens if it eats a weak angel instead of an archangel? Will it stop eventually?"

But after refusing to meet my eyes for a while, the man finally shook his head weakly.

"No. It'll probably stay in that incomplete state and keep looking for the archangel."

"An' what makes you say that?"

"The Angel-Eater of Silver's power source isn't angels. It's the linchpin that stabilizes its liquid form. The reason why it's so persistent about taking the archangel is because its foremost priority is to construct a form that can kill Pandora. When I traveled with the Angel-Eater, there was a vision I always saw... It was likely one of its own memories... When the seven Angel-Eaters faced Pandora, only two were able to harm the beast."

This was new—that the Angel-Eater had multiple bodies.

I didn't pursue that line of thought and instead ground my teeth out of anger at my classmate again.

"He got manipulated tryin' to win... Figures for Bernhart. Thought he could just use some random angel to do it...!"

Then, while I still kept him pinned, the man stared at one of the giant silver feelers quivering at the wall and murmured, "I didn't see the Angel-Eater look so formless in my visions. I don't think that's what the Angel-Eater wanted to turn out like, either."

Even in my flustered state, his voice seemed ridiculously soft to me. I finally let go of his neck and faced him directly as I talked.

"Please tell me what the summoners need to do in order to beat that thing."

The man looked directly at me as he shook his head.

"I'm not sure."

"Ya didn't see anythin' in your visions? You said the Angel-Eater had seven bodies in the past. How'd Pandora defeat 'em back then?"

"Through plain brute force. He used his fists to break the angels that made up their cores. That thing over there... It doesn't look or act like the Angel-Eaters Pandora defeated. I don't think you'd be able to defeat it in the same way."

After that, the man suddenly looked behind me and turned his eyes down right away. "...Princess Sasha..."

"Sasha?"

I'd been so focused on the man in front of me that I hadn't been paying attention to the changes around me. When I turned around, I saw Zylgar and Cyril, Myfila, and also Sasha riding on top of him.

They must have seen my giant grasshopper in the road and come down here.

"When did ya start listenin' in?" I asked, instead of explaining. Cyril was the one to answer.

"We just got here, but we know everything."

"What?"

"Feil, you yell way too loud. I thought my ears were going to burst." Cyril stuck out his tongue at me as he dismounted Zylgar. The Voice Link circle was on his tongue...then I realized right then I'd had transmission magic invoked that entire time.

"Sorry. Forgot to turn it off."

Cyril didn't really complain, though. "It's fine. Saves us the hassle of having you explain again." He helped Myfila and Sasha off the giant tiger.

I had no clue why Sasha was also riding with them. Thinking she might've come up with a way to stop the Angel-Eater, I started walking over to her.

Then I… No, not just me—everyone in the place realized that "night" had suddenly come overhead.

"Y-you gotta be kiddin' me!!"

When I looked up at the sky, I didn't find it overhead.

Instead of the overcast clouds and light flecks of snow, I saw a smooth surface that fully cut off the sunlight in an unnatural way, even for the winter. Not only that, but the various flying summons that had been protecting the northern wall until that very minute were all being driven away by the flat surface that had appeared.

It was the Angel-Eater of Silver.

The Angel-Eater, which had been retreating whenever the flying beasts and summoners intercepted it, had finally made a full appearance despite its behavior until now.

Its massive body had worked itself over the wall.

The dragons blasted it with their full power, scorching the air.

I saw the blinding flashes of the summoners' desperate attempts at last-ditch feats of magic. But they could no longer make the Angel-Eater budge now that it'd overtaken the entire sky. It easily accepted every blow humanity could give it but didn't stop in the slightest in its pursuit.

It was trying to engulf the entirety of Raddermark now.

"…Wait…please, not yet…," I could only murmur to myself… After that, I couldn't breathe as I watched the sky of despair start to come down on us like an avalanche. I felt helpless in a way I'd never felt before as I almost fell over.

There wasn't anything we could do anymore.

No hero or heroine could come to save us.

And I realized that a lot of people were probably going to die. People of all ages huddled in the shelters, the good people carrying their elderly parents on their backs as they ran, even the thieves who were probably taking advantage of the situation, and the good guards who had kept their posts until the very end—my boss and Ilecia, who had always been there for me, and we, the summoners, who were supposed to have powers beyond human understanding... We were all going to be swallowed by the Angel-Eater of Silver and die.

The sky slowly fell on us.

I wouldn't have felt satisfied unless I saw the scene through to the end, so I willed myself to keep my eyes open.

That was how I saw the warm light near me.

"Sasha?"

At the same time I saw Sasha engulfed in a glow in front of me, a beautiful six-winged archangel like a goddess stood up in the spacious road. She was easily tall enough to stand higher than the buildings around her. Her long platinum hair fluttered in the strong wind that had been stirred by the Angel-Eater's giant movements.

I looked up at the archangel's face from her feet.

"...Wait, Sasha...you're not gonna—"

I watched her gracefully remove her mask with a hand several times larger than a person.

It was Sasha Shidoh Zultania's beautiful face that appeared beneath. It wouldn't have been an exaggeration to say it was the most beautiful face in not just the Academy but all of Shidoh.

A Volte-face—when a summoner becomes one with their summon.

Right now, I was sure Sasha could have brought down an evil god on her own. She was the strongest summoner in the Academy and Raddermark's last hope.

"Feil Fonaf." Her amethyst eyes looked down at me; her lips said my name. "I'm truly glad you were the one to summon Pandora."

Even though we were probably just ten seconds from total destruction in this god-awful situation, her gentle eyes and out-of-place dreadfully calm voice ousted the fear from my heart.

"Wait, Sasha. Not yet. We're not done yet. There has to be somethin' we can do, so don't go—"

But in its place, anger took root in me.

Finally, Sasha flapped her glowing six wings and floated into the air. Even then, the beautiful girl was looking at tiny me.

"I'm leaving the rest to you," she said. Finally—at the very end—she said with a small smile, "Please protect the town and our world."

In the next moment, she flew straight into the sky like a meteor and opened a hole in the Angel-Eater of Silver's massive form.

"You damn nitwit!!"

She'd gone so fast that I knew my yelling would never reach her.

I could see the actual sky through the giant hole in the Angel-Eater.

At its center, Sasha had spread her six wings and was brandishing a flaming sword as she fought off the many silver feelers coming at her from around the outside of the hole.

Whenever Sasha waved her sword, two or three of the feelers would be obliterated, but the Angel-Eater was able to cover practically the entire sky of Raddermark. Whenever her sword burned away one feeler, a new one would form on the body and doggedly pursue her.

She struck down five, and ten wriggled back out.

When she struck down ten, fifty leaped at her.

When she struck down a hundred of them, three hundred didn't stop pursuing her.

The archangel it'd been waiting for all this time was right there for the taking. The Angel-Eater of Silver was probably feeling frenzied.

And soon, it was clear there was too much of a difference in how much of the Angel-Eater there was.

"STOP IT!!" I yelled again in vain as Sasha was taken by surprise and a feeler caught her.

All four of her limbs were restrained, and even more of the feelers relentlessly swarmed her. Like a powerless butterfly caught in a giant spider's web, she couldn't even put up a struggle as it swallowed her.

And in that moment…

"Please protect the town and our world."

…Sasha's voice rang again in my ears. "Fine! That's exactly what I'll do!!" I pulled my *Summoner Incantations* out of my robes. I sped through the pages, then as Cyril placed a hand on my shoulder and Myfila latched onto my side, I firmly started to chant the Legendary Beast of the Last Realm Pandora's summoning verses.

"Arise, O beast that thwarts despair! Over darkened sea, your wings claim the air!"

All three of us glared at the sky with everything we could muster.

"An ending world entrusts a prayer to the beast from its fate to spare! As the ice of morn echoes the grief to bear!"

At that point, the "night" brought on by the Angel-Eater of Silver broke, and the wide swath of silver began to collect into one spot. It moved faster than the wind. It immediately started to form into a humanoid shape where it had swallowed Sasha—right at the center of where the six-winged archangel had been.

"Cry not for the morrows through loss ye acquire! Rejoice for the flower that blooms from the fire!"

There, it formed into a nude angel that must have been three hundred mejals tall—that was probably the best way to describe the Angel-Eater as she changed form and descended from the overcast sky.

"The lonesome beast offers a hymn come night! To the plunging stars upon their plight!"

But to me, as I summoned the god-killing beast, she was just the divine form of a being I wanted to beat to death.

"Anon! A far journey awaits thee! One of deep mercy, to alight! With the prayer-granting beast when thee unite!!"

The Summoner, Together with Hope

Back when Raddermark had first been founded, the people who'd gathered had probably been fully dedicated to the future expansion of the town. They must have wholeheartedly wished for their descendants' peace and welfare.

They probably never expected it to be the stage of some revenge match dredged up from the days of myths and legends.

"Pandora's eyes are fully set up."

I heard Cyril in my ear. We were using Voice Link to let us talk from afar. At that moment, Cyril was outside Pandora, directing his large avian summons through the sky.

"Don't worry about what's under your feet. You can rampage as much as you want, Feil."

There were a bunch of images projected onto the wall of Pandora's skull. I had a view from Pandora's perspective, one from the side, and even a long-range view. I also had one pointing down at him from directly above, a view from directly behind him like it was in third person, and exhaustive views of him from the sides and from behind.

I was focused on the first-person perspective, staring straight at the bare-naked angel.

"Thanks, Angel-Eater. You gave me enough time to stand up."

I laughed ominously like a beast myself.

Then suddenly…

"Cyril!! Wh-what is this?!" I heard Lulua Folicker on the communications line.

...it seemed like all the summoners who'd been sent into confusion over Pandora suddenly showing up had started gathering around Cyril, who was still outside.

"Did Feil Fonaf summon him?! That—that can't be true...?! This wasn't the trick up your sleeve, was it?! This is more like a secret weapon—you summoned the strongest and oldest god-killer!!"

It sounded like there was a commotion going on outside, but I didn't have the time to listen to all that right now.

"Feil, let me know if you don't have enough magic. I'll inject the tonic right away."

"Yeah, try your best not to kill me."

Even while Pandora was just standing, I was on all fours and continuously feeding electricity through the arm I had in Pandora's brain as my Linebolt consumed my magical reserves.

Next to me, Myfila was on her knees and eyeing the Angel-Eater. She murmured, "She's pretty...but there's something about her that gets on my nerves..."

I just let out a curt laugh in agreement.

"Also seems in real poor taste for her to look so much like Sasha."

After absorbing the six-winged archangel, the Angel-Eater of Silver had been made whole again.

Though she was smaller than Pandora, she was still a weapon that had been made by the Supreme God, and she had a dignity and grandeur to her that fit her name as an Executioner. Even though she wasn't clothed, she wasn't just beautiful—her silver skin was unblemished, but there were odd plantlike symbols carved all over her skin that gave the Angel-Eater's beauty a strangely conspicuous sense that something was off.

And I could also see the two silver wings behind her that looked like a whole bunch of outstretched swords of different sizes.

But the wings weren't connected to her back. Instead, they seemed to float nearby through some supernatural power, like they could be used as weapons at any time.

And her face was like a peaceful Sleeping Beauty's.

Only her long, undulating hair still retained hints of her earlier indeterminate form.

She was clearly divine... She wasn't the kind of opponent humanity or summoners could have won against. Even the Shidoh royal family's summoner corps likely would have been powerless against her fully recovered form.

"But the princess asked us to fight," Myfila was suddenly saying.

"That's right," I replied, not fearful of the enemy in front of me in the slightest.

"Sasha Shidoh Zultania herself risked her life to make sure we'd be in a position to do this. That's enough for me to put my own life on the line."

"Do you think fate linked you two?"

"...Maybe. Dunno."

So sometimes, even a genius like Myfila would talk about things like fate. At the same time, a ton of miracles had to have occurred for this fight against the Angel-Eater and Pandora to have been made so conveniently possible, so I could fully understand why she wanted to call it that.

I didn't think we'd taken the best road here, but the truth was still this. In this situation now, where the Angel-Eater of Silver of the Six Executioners of Metal had been revived, humanity and this world, where so many lived, had been given a path to survival.

Sasha Shidoh Zultania had sacrificed her own archangel in order to allow the Angel-Eater to fully revive so that the Angel Eater's one weakness—her linchpin, which also served as her core—could be revived as well to allow Pandora to stop her.

If Sasha hadn't seen Pandora under the moonlight the previous day; if today, Sasha hadn't trusted us; if my partner, dead or not, weren't the Legendary Beast of the Last Realm, Pandora...

"We never would've been able to punch the daylights outta the Angel-Eater."

I grinned as I licked my lips like a starving beast.

"All right—let's do this, Cyril, Myfila. It's our time to shine," I said and looked off into the distance.

Under the overcast sky was Raddermark, large and sprawling.

And two legends stood facing each other right at its center. To the north, the Angel-Eater of Silver. To the south, the Legendary Beast of the Last Realm, Pandora.

Compared with the Angel-Eater of Silver, who stood with perfect posture, the blue-black beast, Pandora, slouched a lot. He had two tails and ten whole wings on his back, at any rate. I didn't know what he'd been like while alive, but my Pandora stood hunchbacked like this. Then finally, I fed a new electrical impulse through Pandora's cranial nerves from my fingertips.

"Wh-what? Cyril! Pandora—Pandora's moving!!"

"You should get far away from here, Lulua. From here on out, this place is for the legends."

After waiting for this very moment, we were finally mobilizing.

From the long-range view, Pandora's first step looked slow as he touched down on the terrain and brought up a cloud of whatever was on the ground, but then right after that, he rapidly accelerated.

As he kicked aside the houses and large shops under his feet like pebbles, he made a beeline for the Angel-Eater.

The Angel-Eater didn't fail to also get a move on.

Her right arm liquefied, turning into a gigantic spear, as she drew a leg back into a fighting pose immediately and met Pandora's charge with a strike from her weapon.

She had a much longer reach.

The silver spearhead reached Pandora's left breast first, but the unidentified material of his exoskeleton was impenetrable. The point of the spear was crushed as easily as syrup and continued to crumple as Pandora approached. It couldn't even hold him at bay.

While the Angel-Eater seemed dismayed by the loss of her weapon, Pandora grabbed her face with his right hand.

"Aaaaaaah!!" I yelled with gusto and increased the output in my Linebolt.

Even the giant Angel-Eater—her face still in a vice grip—was being pushed by Pandora's charge.

She tried to brace herself to hold out, but Pandora's seemingly limitless power rendered all her efforts moot. After all, Pandora was much larger and heavier than her.

I could hear a rumble, even from within Pandora's skull.

Under the feet of my gigantic summon, everything was flying into the air —the houses, the carriages, even the streets themselves. All of it.

"Feil, don't pay attention to it! Keep going!"

"I know, dammiiiit!"

I was just glad that I didn't see any people in the mess. I held on to the one hope that the evacuation had finished fast enough and that no one was under Pandora's feet right now.

"Don't die!! Please, I'm begging for no one—not even one person to die!!"

As he pushed the Angel-Eater, relying on pure strength, Pandora charged through the great market. In just barely five or six seconds, we were past that, too, and stepping into the sprawling residential streets.

Even the biggest streets couldn't accommodate Pandora at three hundred fifty mejals.

The only thing I could do was avoid the designated evacuation points, where the citizens were gathered. I destroyed the houses they'd never be able to go home to, crushed the roads where they'd made memories—but even then, I didn't let up on the Angel-Eater. I prayed hard and fast that the evacuation was already over in the area and that no one would die.

"No backing out NOW!!"

I increased the output on my Linebolt even more, driving Pandora's huge build further.

We were reaching the northern wall.

"Get outta the waaaay!!"

We crashed straight through the thick wall, which barely reached Pandora's or the Angel-Eater's knees, scattering gigantic pieces of

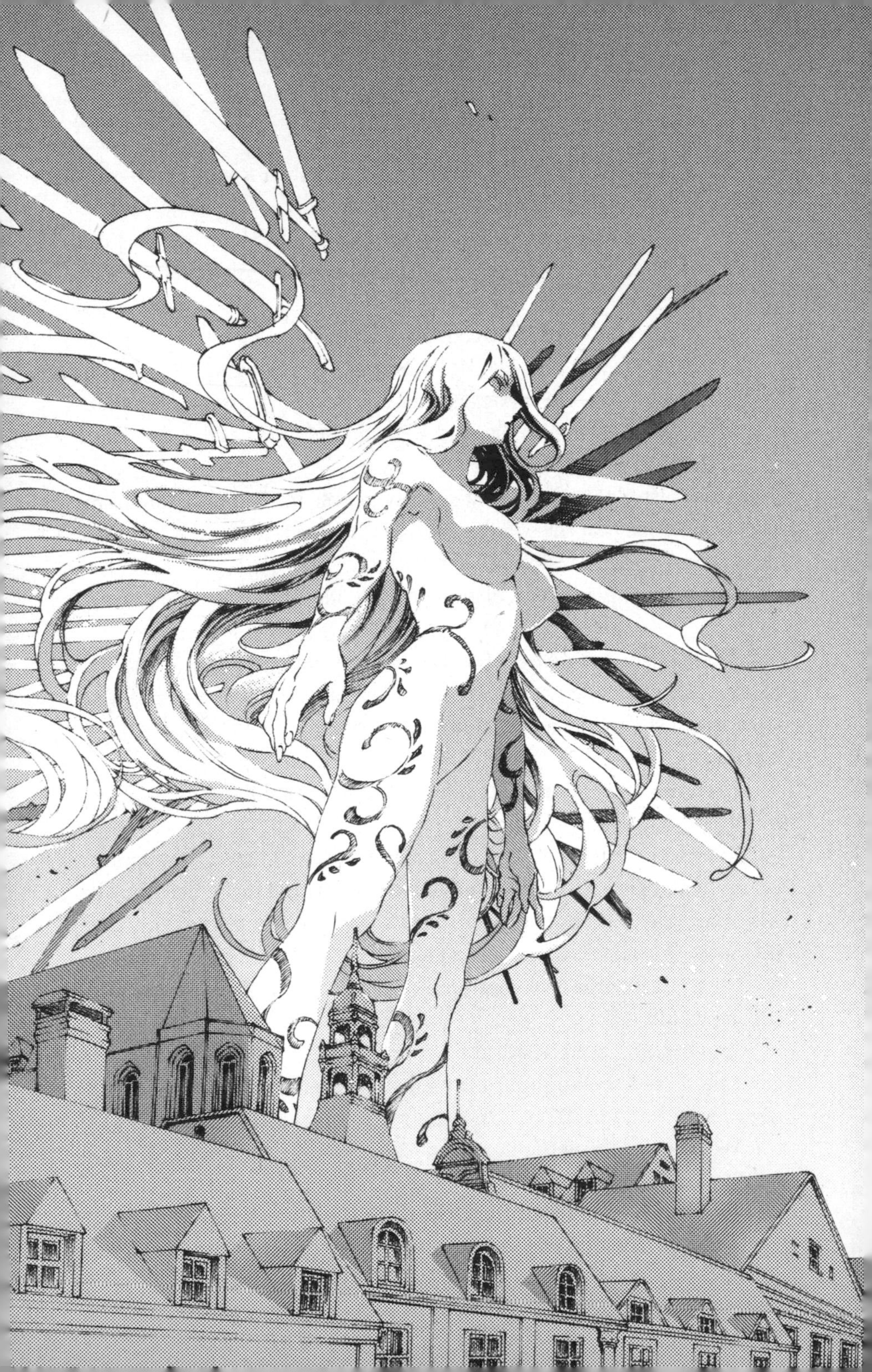

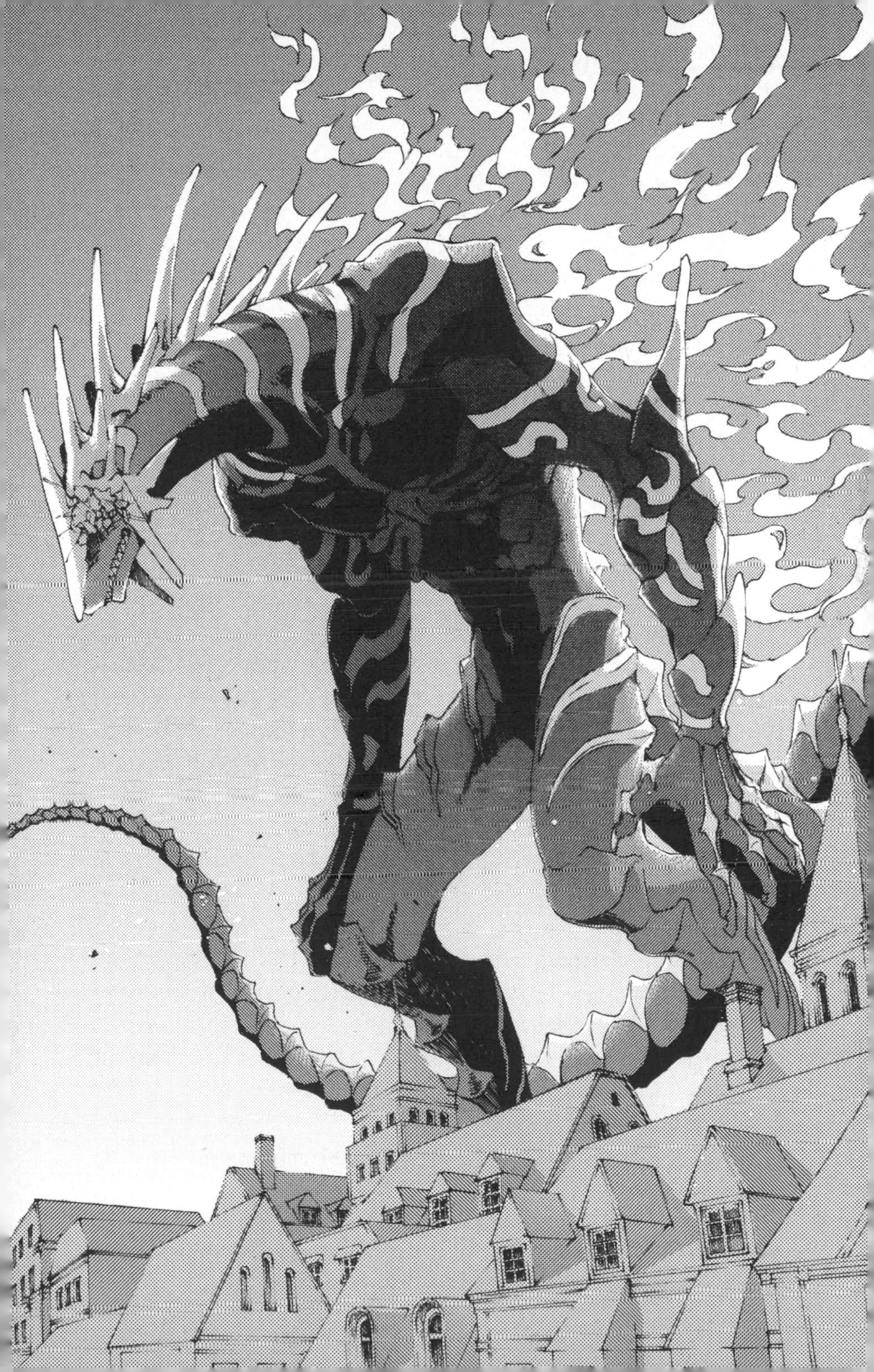

rubble near to the field that served as the Academy matches' stage. I sped up, not caring what was below us.

I charged farther back into the field, nearing the center of it and getting the Angel-Eater even slightly farther away from Raddermark!

Instead of bringing up the stone paving of Raddermark, Pandora's charge created a gigantic cloud of dirt, and finally, the view behind Pandora showed no sign of Raddermark at all.

"Gah-haah!"

Right then, right as I sputtered while my magic was nearly running dry, I gathered up the remaining strength I had to wallop the Angel-Eater right in the face with Pandora's left hand.

There was force behind it, but I'd aimed too close, and it hadn't done any damage. It just made her stagger only slightly.

So...

"M-Myfilaaa."

...when I asked her for help at the last moment before my Linebolt was about to cut out, I had Pandora turn around. His two long, reaching tails boomed—the tips had probably easily broken the sound barrier.

They kept going, whipping around to strike the Angel-Eater right in the side to send her flying away.

I wasn't even able to check the direction she'd gone in. That moment, my vision started fading to black, and I was right on the verge of losing consciousness.

"Bwuh—Ah!"

Myfila's special tonic had just barely worked in time. I was woken by my own hacking as I sputtered out the lump of air that seemed to have settled deep in the back of my lungs.

"It's not over yet." With the needles and test tube still sticking out of my neck, I reinvoked the Linebolt. First, I stood Pandora up after he'd almost fallen to his knees.

I was perspiring from every pore of my body—both sweat and snot dripped off me.

The tonic was actual dragon's blood—basically a lethal poison. Even with Myfila's efforts, it still had an effect on my body. Though I'd replenished my magic, I felt like throwing up on the spot.

"Haah, haah, haah—" I panted raggedly as I eyed the image on the skull wall and couldn't find the Angel-Eater in the first-person view.

Where was she?

The moment I thought that, I heard Cyril in my ear. "Feil, look up!"

When I raised Pandora's head on reflex, I saw her feet fill the first-person.

She drop-kicked us, practically trampling us in the process.

It didn't matter then how much heavier Pandora was or how firm Pandora's neck and muscles were.

"Ahh?!"

"Give me a sec!"

The inside of Pandora's skull was chaos.

As I was on all fours, an arm in Pandora's brain, and Myfila was trying to pull the test tube out of my neck, we were suddenly sent flying.

Had Myfila not instantly summoned a gigantic rotting corpse to act as a cushion for us, we probably would have bounced off Pandora's hard skull and been goners.

It was some sort of midsize whale carcass. I couldn't even guess why Myfila had this thing as a summon in the first place. Then again, we'd been saved when we fell into the organs that spilled out of its belly. I didn't have even a moment to breathe out in relief, though.

"Tsk!"

As I got up in the fibrous goop and unidentifiable flesh that fell down on me, I scrambled on my arms and legs back to my original position, where I could control Pandora. I thrust an arm deep into his brain.

"You're not goin' anywheeeere!!"

That moment, Pandora's right hand broke the speed of sound as it shot into the sky.

He leaped up slightly, grabbing the right ankle of the Angel-Eater right after she'd kicked Pandora in the face. His overpowering grip crushed her ankle as he landed back down.

Then keeping the momentum going, he threw the Angel-Eater on her back atop the giant field.

The ground crumbled.

The shock wave and heat it brought up was like a meteor striking the ground as the sudden large-scale explosion created a crater in the middle of the field. The terrain had peeled up in layers dozens of mejals thick. Under that, the tough bedrock had cracked deeply, spreading extensively.

Right as Pandora was sinking down after tripping on the broken terrain, everything except the first-person perspective and the ones from afar cut off.

"Are you okay, Cyril?!"

"Don't worry about me!! Keep fighting, Feil!!"

The shock wave must have devastated Pandora's surroundings. The sound of wind buffeting him covered up Cyril's voice in the Voice Link and made him hard to make out.

"Feil!" Myfila was yelling at me.

The Angel-Eater, who had been buried under the bedrock and was pinned down by Pandora, had raised her open right hand at him. Before I could react, five pure-white beams of destruction were let loose from her fingertips.

The beams shot directly at Pandora's chest.

…But that hadn't affected Pandora's exoskeleton in the slightest. The beams, which were probably thousands of times more magically potent than the bombardment we'd suffered at the floating cemetery, had no effect on Pandora.

I had Pandora ram his gigantic left fist into the Angel-Eater's face from above, and the already broken bedrock gave way to let the Angel-Eater sink even deeper into the ground. The blow was accompanied by a small earthquake.

"Dammit! The ground's too weak!"

It was a clean hit, but it hadn't done the damage I'd intended. The cracked bedrock had ended up cushioning the Angel-Eater.

I had Pandora grab hold of the Angel-Eater's neck, then force it to stay in place as I made his other hand pummel her in the mug.

That single blow was enough to crush her face in devastatingly.

It was like I'd smashed a fist into a delicate clay masterpiece—but even then, the Angel-Eater kept functioning as though nothing had happened. She transformed her arms into swords and aimed for Pandora's joints.

Her left sword headed for the base of Pandora's right arm, but the point couldn't drive its way in, and the whole blade crumpled.

Her right sword tried to lop off a piece of Pandora's inner elbow but anticlimactically bounced off. She brandished the sword again, striking the blade at him another time, but it couldn't cut through. Instead, the other blade also broke.

"You think that blunt sword's gonna cut it?!!"

Even if the Angel-Eater could shape-shift into whatever she wanted, there was no point if she couldn't get through his armor.

So I showed an opening without having to worry about any counterattacks. I brought Pandora's fist as far back as I could.

When I drew back the fist like I was drawing the string of a bow and brought it down, the moment it touched the Angel-Eater's face, her solidified silver form turned back to its original liquid state.

Her entire head splattered to the ground behind her. Not even a fragment remained.

She was now a *headless* buck naked angel.

I didn't assume that I'd won, but I wanted to believe we were out ahead.

I drew Pandora's fist back for a follow-up.

Then right at that moment, I shouted, "You little?! You're still—!!"

The Angel-Eater had suddenly brought her knees up and kicked Pandora in the stomach. I clung to his brains. Suddenly, I was floating. The Angel-Eater's kick had sent Pandora's giant body into the air.

"Myfila! Hold on ta somethin'!" I yelled as I focused all my attention on feeling the same sensations as my summon. I was basically working on instinct as I made Pandora regain his posture, getting his left and right legs to land, then his right hand, his left, and the two tails on the ground in order.

Pandora had been kicked clear out of the crater and back onto the field, but the shock of his landing combined with his massive weight was too much for the ground to hold. As soon as we touched it, it started to crumble... Eventually, even while standing, Pandora had been buried to his knees into the earth.

"Haah. Haah. Haah. Haah. Hah—" I panted as my magic ran out again. Myfila, who'd gathered what was happening, told me anxiously, "This next one might be your limit..." Then she administered the second vial of the tonic.

The effects were immediate.

"Hurk—"

While still on all fours, I hacked up all the contents of my stomach on the spot.

"Gah! Guh! Hurk..."

Finally, I was throwing up stomach acid directly onto Pandora's brain. I wiped my mouth off with my robes.

"Just got dizzy from controllin' Pandora. Don't worry about me."

When I glanced over, Myfila's whole face was ash white as she stared at me.

"Feil, do you see this?" Suddenly, Cyril was talking to us again. "The Angel-Eater's getting up. She's transforming again."

"'Course she would. A lackluster kick like that wouldn't get through Pandora's armor. She's gonna come at us with whatever she's got to attack with now."

The broken-off views all came back online.

The different views Cyril was delivering through his flying summons showed something strange. The inside of the crater had filled with a surge of pure-white flames.

From inside the tall and large inferno, I could see the wavering shape of a curvy woman.

After almost all her attacks had been blocked by Pandora's exoskeleton and her head had been crushed, she was rebuilding her form. She was likely transforming her shape to dedicate everything into her offensive capabilities.

"Seriously...I'm already goin' all out as it is..."

The same moment I got Pandora out of the crumbling ground, a woman's willowy fingertips emerged from the wall of flames.

Then...

...with the same grace as someone opening up the curtain of a dressing room, *it* appeared...

"......Sasha..."

I hadn't been the one to murmur that—that had been Cyril, who'd been watching the scene with his own eyes outside Pandora.

I could only *tsk* lightly.

A silver Sasha Shidoh Zultania had appeared. The Angel-Eater's new wingless form was a nightmare that could only be put into those words. Her incomparable beauty, that long platinum hair, amethyst eyes, and her captivating nude form that could have been mistaken for a goddess's had all been reproduced and looked exactly like the Sasha I knew.

The only perceivable differences were probably the halo floating above her head, the silver skin, and the giant rose in bloom at her chest—and also the three-hundred-mejal height she towered at.

....

On the giant field that had been trampled to smithereens by the two legends, the legendary beast Pandora and the silver beauty faced each other.

At first, neither held a weapon, but the Angel-Eater wordlessly raised her arms, and the flames behind her went on the move. They engulfed her hands, absorbing into her and forming a pair of slender swords.

To be frank, it didn't matter how much magic they were imbued with or how sharp they seemed, because these weapons went beyond that.

Myfila, who'd been keeping me from total exhaustion, seemed to have noticed, too.

"Careful, Feil. I think those swords must—"

"Yeah, yeah. She's reproduced the ability of the god who could cut through anything... I know that they'll probably be able to cut through Pandora."

But that didn't change anything.

Even if the Angel-Eater of Silver could use a god's abilities, that didn't change the fact that Pandora was the legendary god-killer.

"In that case, right here and right now, we're gonna have to kill another god," I bluffed and had Pandora advance.

He leaned forward precariously as he approached the Angel-Eater—first, I had him bring down his right fist.

In that moment, the Angel-Eater disappeared from the first-person view.

"Guh?!"

A sharp, searing hot pain raced through my right side. It was the first time I'd felt such distinct pain since summoning Pandora.

Even though Pandora was dead, his pain receptors clearly weren't. Since I'd synced as much as I could with Pandora to control his corpse, it felt like my own body.

The Angel-Eater had cut through Pandora's side once she was close enough.

"Gah! Ow!"

This time, I felt my back and the back of my thigh burning.

She'd moved around to Pandora's back with unbelievable speed, cutting lengthwise all the way to the base of Pandora's ten wings; with a flowing movement, she had sliced up to his femur.

I wouldn't be able to see her just from the first-person perspective. So I relied on the distant views to use Pandora's thick, long tails to restrain her.

She just barely escaped them and tried to cut through a blue-black tail with her sword, but she didn't manage. The endoskeleton also hiding within Pandora had firmly stopped the Angel-Eater's sword, making her open Sasha's amethyst eyes wide.

"Dammit! Nobody told me it'd even hurt *my* rear!"

It felt like she'd actually cut through my flesh and been stopped at the bone.

I contracted the muscles of the tail until the Angel-Eater's left sword was stuck in place, then brought down a karate chop as soon as we were facing her.

Right then, Pandora's right hand broke the sound barrier and cut through the Angel-Eater's left shoulder.

This was what had happened as a result of the Angel-Eater's own choices. Her body, which had been specialized entirely for combat, broke to pieces as easily as glasswork. Her left arm, which was no longer connected to her main body, cracked and shattered. It didn't regenerate after that, either.

She tried to back away immediately.

But I didn't move Pandora. I already knew I wouldn't win against her in a battle of speed anyway. Even as I panted from my magic deficit, I chuckled to myself. "Of course the legendary beast Pandora could stand up to a god's power."

I had no idea how long the wounded Pandora and the wounded Angel-Eater—Sasha and I—faced each other without a word.

When I stared at Sasha's beautiful face and she stared back at me, I suddenly murmured, "Real nuisance of a job ya left me with…"

Then my eyes traveled to the silver rose blooming at the Angel-Eater's chest as I said, "I know there's still a chance of saving you… This is way better than with my pa, at least…"

The silver rose—Sasha had to be in there. And she had to be alive.

Call it conviction, but I had a strangely certain feeling it was true.

That was right. Sasha Shidoh Zultania wouldn't have died just because she'd been turned into the Angel-Eater of Silver's linchpin. The strongest person in the school—someone who'd assimilated with an archangel—wasn't going down that easy.

No matter how bad things got, she'd always ride through it with that same unruffled look on her face. That was why she was the most powerful one out of all of us.

She had to be holding out even now within the Angel-Eater.

I'll save you, so just hold out a little longer, I willed her.

To be frank, I didn't care whether she wanted to be saved or not. I had a word or two for her after the nitwit had run off to sacrifice herself for the world. I hadn't even gotten to challenge her again since the ranking match, and I wasn't gonna let her just quit while she was ahead.

The only reason I needed to risk my life saving Sasha were those emotions that overflowed from my chest—that was probably enough.

"...Sorry, Sasha, today's the day *I'm* gonna be tellin' *you* off."

Those were the last easygoing words I was able to manage.

Suddenly, the Angel-Eater rammed into Pandora with one arm and one sword.

I tried to meet her with a fist, but she went even faster, and there was no way I'd be hitting that. She was quicker than I could perceive, practically moving like a sword dancer as she tore through Pandora's outstretched right arm.

"Tsk!!"

I realized I'd never be able to land a fist on her like this. I tried to whip Pandora's left arm at her, but even that didn't hit her. The only thing Pandora could manage to make contact with was the lingering end of a lock of her silvery hair as she somersaulted through the air. In that moment, I realized I needed to prepare for the long haul.

"Myfila! Don't think! Inject it!" I yelled, and she administered a third round of the tonic.

When I breathed in through the nose, it was followed by a bunch of blood. "Gah!! Gah-hah! Gah!!" I threw up more bile, along with a wad of blood, but kept my eyes trained in front of me.

The first-person perspective wasn't useful anymore. Even the long-range view just made me painfully aware of how much faster she was.

Still, I kept my eyes ahead of me.

Even as she kept cutting into Pandora, I brought up his fist.

From the long-range view, all I saw under the thick overhang of clouds was the Legendary Beast of the Last Realm's entire body spurting blood as he rampaged. The Angel-Eater of Silver just barely managed to avoid his fists, slicing through the beast as she pleased.

We had no other secret plans.

We had no secret weapons beyond Pandora.

I'd keep moving no matter how many times she sliced through him. I'd continue to flail until my last moment, just as if I were a beast. That was the one and only hope that remained for Pandora and me.

"Myfila! One more!" I'd used my magic up before I knew it and was calling out to Myfila.

"Y-you can't! Any more and you'll die, Feil!"

After seeing my bloody nose and the blood in my vomit, Myfila gripped the tonic in her hand tightly. She shook her head furiously despite my demands.

I didn't hesitate...

"This isn't the time to be scared—!"

It was the first time I'd done anything like this to Myfila. I'd reached out to her where she'd approached me, wrestling the test tube away from her by force.

"Feil, stop! Please!"

I ignored her tears and her cries to stop as I injected the needles into my neck.

"I'm a summoner...!! Even if my heart stops, even if my skull ruptures, I ain't backin' down here!!"

The left side of my vision was turning red. Tears of blood spilled from my left eye. I tried to fix my vision by rubbing the left side of my face hard with my robes, but all I managed was to smear the blood all over. My left side stayed red, and my vision didn't come back.

So what? How did that change anything?

The Angel-Eater was way faster than I could see anyway. Pandora and I pushed through the pain of our entire body and entrails being hacked up as we could only wave around our fists at random.

Just one!! Just one blow would be enough!! I kept saying to myself.

"Even if I'm up against Sasha an' an Executioner, I've got the god-killin' beast on my side! At this point, it's just a battle of wills!!" I spat up blood as I shouted to amp myself up.

Pandora's revolving backhand struck both of the Angel-Eater's legs as she leaped through the air. Didn't seem too bad for a lucky blow after being sliced to pieces.

Once she lost both of her legs, the Angel-Eater couldn't even stand, so she simply tumbled along the ground, still holding her sword.

My Pandora, the bluish-black grotesque beast, remained upright. He was so beat up, I had no idea if there was any part of his body that hadn't been sliced open, but regardless of that, both his feet were flat on the ground as he looked down on the Angel-Eater.

Finally, in the end, it looked like the shoe was on the other foot.

Then the moment I had Pandora take a step forward to finish her off...

"Huh?"

...I'd lost all ability to even hold myself up and fell face-first into Pandora's brain. As part of the natural progression of things, I couldn't keep up Linebolt, either, and Pandora slowly fell to his knee.

I could feel the tremors of his landing even from within his skull.

"Hey, Feil! What happened, Feil?! Are you okay—?" Cyril's voice, which should have been coming in directly through my ear, sounded far-off.

I'd run out of magic again. I forced myself to look at Myfila, even as my body refused to budge.

"No. You can't anymore!!"

In an attempt to save my life, Myfila smashed the last vial of tonic.

...The broken pieces of glass and dragon's blood were scattered over the ground.

....

But I wasn't done yet. I still had something left to squeeze out of me.

I pressed out what little remaining strength I had to plunge my hand into the neck of my robes, pulling out my cherished pouch, and throwing all the contents out.

The paper notes and grimy coins spilled out, including the gold and silver coins my old man had given to me when he died.

"Power—"

I haphazardly grabbed my father's coins and stuck them in my mouth.

"I need power—"

As I thought long and hard about my dead father, I gnashed down on the coins with my back teeth, practically trying to break through the silvers, then I raised my hand up high and yelled to the heavens like my life depended on it, "Lend me your poweeeer!!"

What I relied on as a last resort was my own soul, the pent-up emotions still burning strong in the back of my heart.

In that moment, Pandora, who should have still been dead, finally responded to my feelings for the first time.

"ROOOOAAARRR!!"

He bellowed heroically even without me feeding magic through his brain.

Still on one knee, he turned up to the heavens, just like me, and let out a cry I was sure the entire world had heard.

The Angel-Eater was coming to attack us from straight overhead after having forced herself to leap even without her legs.

She brought down the sword she had brandished high in the air.

"Pandoraaaa!!" I shouted.

But now, in just this moment, Pandora and I were freer than the Angel-Eater.

Pandora's ten wings suddenly began to open.

His right hand, which should have been slack, flew even faster into the air than the Angel-Eater.

—!!

His outstretched right hand had opened all its fingers, as though seeking something—until it reached the blooming flower on the Angel-Eater of Silver's chest and tore through it.

The same moment Pandora's right hand went through her chest, the bright-blue sky reappeared.

The impact of Pandora's fist hadn't stopped at piercing the Angel-Eater—it sent a shock wave overhead through the giant field, through

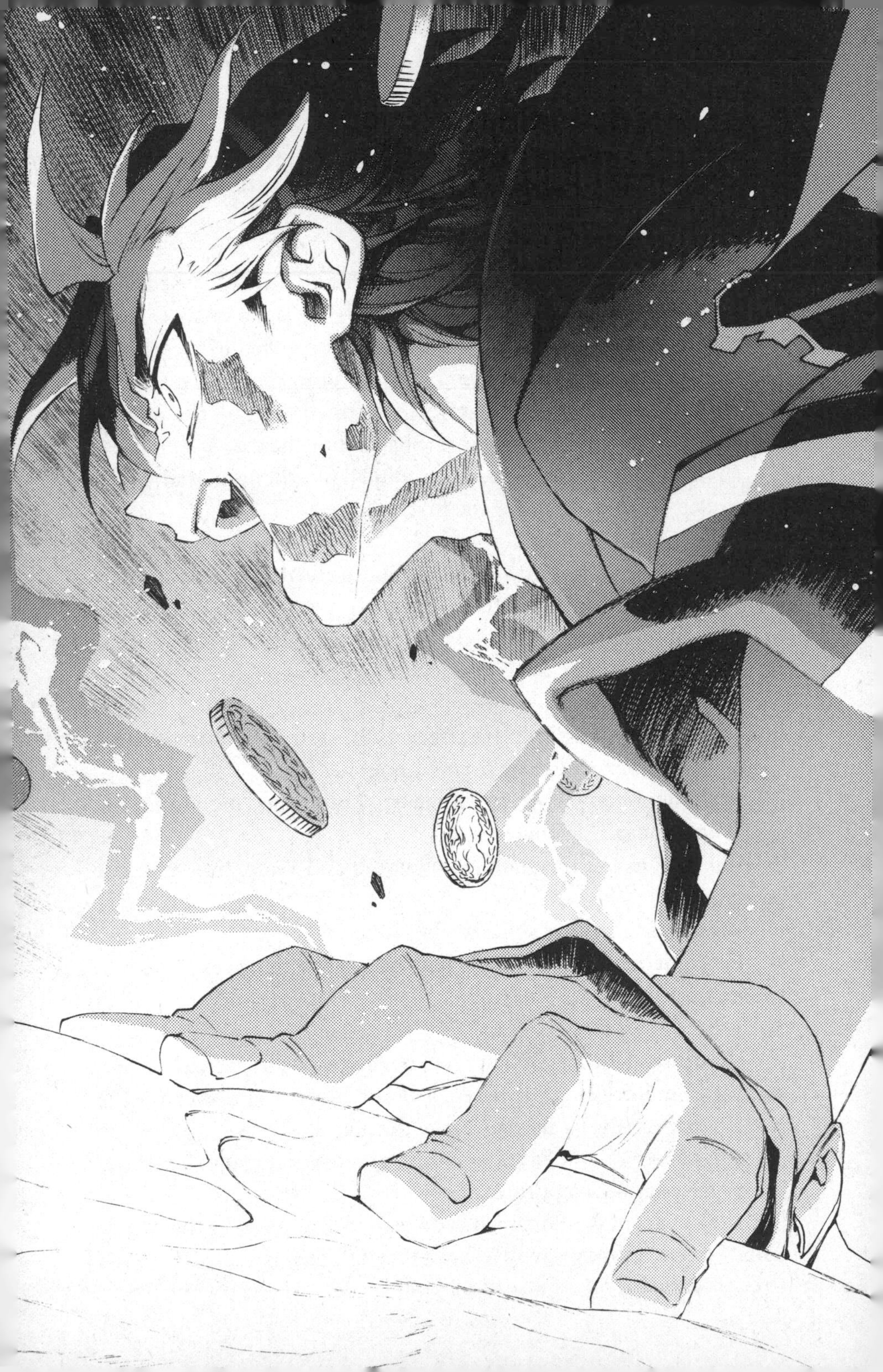

Raddermark's sky, and even beyond into the mountain ranges, clearing all the heavy snow-laden clouds from the atmosphere.

....

....

....

The world, now overflowing with light as the Angel-Eater turned to dust and flowed away into the wind, was blindingly bright.

Then in the next moment, Pandora's large form went limp and fell to his knees in the great plains.

He went back to being a gigantic corpse, quiet almost as though the earlier shout heard round the world had never happened.

And then right after that...

"Feil! Feil!! You—you did it! You defeated the Angel-Eater!"

...an excited Cyril, along with the giant bird he'd been riding, leaped into Pandora's skull.

Myfila was just crying. "Feil. Feil, don't die."

......*I'm still alive. Don't kill me off already.*

All I could do was think the words as I heard Myfila's adorable voice while I lay facedown, devoid of any mental or physical strength.

Eventually, I coughed out the slobbery gold and silver coins.

"Didja see, Pa...Mom...?"

I lifted only my face—just slightly—as I looked at the first-person view.

There, I saw Pandora's open right hand after he'd landed back in the field. On top of his palm rested the core he had stolen from the Angel-Eater's breast—the six-winged archangel Sasha had assimilated with slowly rose up.

She looked around in mute amazement at the bright world around her as sunlight streamed over her.

Eventually, as she looked surprised she was even alive, she turned up to look at Pandora's face.

"...I...survived... I saved her..."

22.

The Summoner and Something More Important than Millions and Millions of Accolades

"P-please wait, Cyril! My butt and my thighs. My rear end is cramping!" I shouted that without thinking when I felt pain suddenly shoot through those body parts.

Then Cyril, who'd been supporting me at the waist, said, "Maybe we should call it quits? You're not even supposed to get out of bed, you know?" He sighed.

I still didn't give up.

I clung to Cyril's military uniform as I slowly lowered myself to the soft carpet.

"I can still move my arms. If I hold on to you like this, I can get on one knee at least—Myfilaaa! Get off my back! I'm soft as a cicada straight from the cocoon!"

"Feil, your muscles feel soft as a slime," she said.

"'Course they do, my muscle fibers are all messed up! You haven't got to call it out!"

Right then, my left knee had touched down on the carpet, but this time, I couldn't let go of Cyril's pants. I couldn't even hold myself up with my own strength on my knee. I couldn't flex my muscles at all.

I gingerly let go of Cyril's pants and almost fell over, then reclaimed my hold on him.

"It's a pretty light price to pay for overdosing on dragon's blood, though. You should be thanking Myfila."

"I'm— That was close. I'm very aware of that. Still, a complete recovery's gonna take a whole month. I'm all broken up about this stuff. Can't even take a bath on my own for a while."

"Like I said, I'll take care of you."

"I don't even get to keep my dignity."

"Cyril, I could help Feil with his baths, too," Myfila offered.

"Sorry, but the law says opposite genders aren't allowed to help with bathing until you're at least twenty."

"Plus, I feel like you won't do a good job anyway."

"Grr..."

It'd already been five days since the Angel-Eater of Silver had appeared in the summons festival at Raddermark.

I was wearing the required conjurer's robes of the Academy, but I was actually fully bandaged up underneath.

That'd been a side effect of overdosing on Myfila's magic tonic.

Even after using up your magic, you could use dragon's blood to force yourself to replenish, but because I'd done so too many times in such a short period, my muscles, which were the storehouse of the magic, had surpassed their limits. I'd basically strained and caused small hemorrhages all over my body. If I didn't have the bandages holding everything together, I might not have even looked a humanoid shape.

The only parts of me that were up and ready to go were above the neck.

"Even His Majesty is going to smile out of pity, Feil."

"Are you saying I look like I'm worse for wear? Because I am. If you had any idea how hard I'm working just to stay on one knee right now..."

A large gauze eyepatch also covered my eye, and I still hadn't regained sight in it.

I was injured and wounded.

No matter how anyone looked at me, I shouldn't have been out of bed.

At that moment, I was in a guest room within the land of Shidoh's palace and was trying to practice greeting King Jikfrit Shidoh Zultania for when I'd have an audience with him.

"I think that's enough, Feil. Sure, it's a rule to go down on one knee in front of His Majesty, but it's not an absolute. If you request it ahead of time, you'll be allowed to forgo it."

"I guess it's time… If I'm strugglin' this much, it'll only be rude," I grumbled at myself after working so hard at staying on one knee. Cyril swooped in right then. He wrapped a hand around my back and under my knees, easily picking me up—basically like how a groom picks up a bride. Then he carried me to a leather couch.

"He'd probably worry about you. His Majesty knew your condition when he called for you. The content of a conversation is much more important than any pomp and circumstance."

I sank into the thick cushion of the couch, and the backing solidly took on my body weight so I could finally catch my breath.

"Haah…" I sighed as I turned my head to look over the large guest room.

The sunlight pierced through the magnificent window, where there wasn't a cloud in the sky, and hit the white walls of the room. The ceiling was tall. It was extravagant, but not gaudy. Flower motifs had been engraved into the walls and pillars, but oddly, nothing looked particularly flashy. It was pleasing to the eye and put me at ease.

Even the furnishings in the room—including the round table, chairs, and grand piano—all looked harmonious together. The winter blossoms in the vase by the window were probably the showiest part of the room.

"I don't know what I'll do if he wants to talk about Pandora, though…"

When I murmured that, Cyril started talking me through it from where he'd sat and crossed his legs on a chair. The old seat creaked under his tall physique.

"His Majesty is a summoner with ties to dragons. He won't say anything cruel about it."

"But he's not going to be like 'Great job stoppin' the Angel-Eater's path of destruction, thanks, you're all good to go,' right?"

"That would be— Well, you have a point."

"He'll say somethin' or ask me somethin'. Either way, gives me a stomachache just thinkin' 'bout it."

Right then, Myfila plunked herself down next to me. She stared into my face and eventually said something that hit me right where it hurt.

"You can talk to the princess just fine, but her father makes you nervous?"

I smiled awkwardly.

"When he summoned me, he signed off as the monarch. I'm not here to see him as Sasha's dad. Right now, this is a commoner meeting a king. 'Course I'm anxious."

"You're worrying too much."

"Everyone thinks you're always breaking the mold, but you really do make a distinction when there's a time and a place for things."

"Hmph. Whatever you say."

I looked over at the big window, trying to lighten my mood even slightly. Beyond it was the balcony and a beautiful blue sky.

The clouds were moving quickly across it. A strong wind must've been blowing.

Right around now...Raddermark was probably fast at work trying to fix up the great market and houses my Pandora had trampled over. At my workplace, the Horse's Drool Pavilion, my boss was probably flying off the handle from being down a worker and being so busy, and Ilecia was likely consoling him.

The whole clash between my Pandora and the Angel-Eater...

Apparently, from what I'd heard, despite two legendary beings duking it out, there'd been extremely few casualties, so they'd been calling it the miracle of Raddermark.

The only people who'd died were the summoners who the Angel-Eater had absorbed to begin with...and there were even some rumors that none of the civilians had been killed. As of right now, Cyril and I had assumed that there was no way something like that could've happened and that the town and Academy must've been telling us that so we wouldn't feel bad...but if it *was* true, my prayers in Pandora on that day for no one to die might've all been worthwhile.

Come to think of it, the one who'd started it all—Bernhart Hadcheck—had disappeared into the Angel-Eater, so his family, the Hadchecks, were shouldering his blame.

Then again, the adults had said they'd handle that stuff so us students hadn't even been informed about what was happening for the most part. They'd likely have to forfeit their fiefs and fortune to act as the funds for the Raddermark reconstruction.

Anyway...

...our world had been saved by the legendary beast Pandora, and though it was slow, we were settling back down into our normal lives. The only people who still had anything to worry about were us—after we'd gotten a summons from the king.

"What are you going to say if His Majesty asks about that final blow?"

"The final one... Why?"

"It was right after Pandora roared and punched through the Angel-Eater. You said you hadn't been using Linebolt right then," Cyril explained.

"Well, yeah."

"Even watching from outside, it looked different. Apparently, the summoner corps prepared a long-sight spell for His Majesty, so he saw the Angel-Eater fight, too. He's probably heard about it. So does that mean Pandora was alive then?"

"Probably... I'm pretty sure he's dead."

"Then how—? You're not planning on claiming it was an act of god, are you?"

"Right, that. That'd be too convenient. I'd be doing a dishonor to my fellow students claimin' that."

"Oh? Looks like you know what it was, then?"

"Since Myfila and I came to the same conclusion separately, I think it's pretty good reasonin'."

"It was probably a Volte-face."

"Really? You think so, Myfila—?"

"But it ain't anythin' as perfect as Sasha's and her archangel's. And I was on the verge of death, so I dunno if I just so happened to sync with Pandora's corpse or if I had a foot in the grave and Pandora just so happened to help me out from the world beyond this one. The only thing I know is that if it hadn't happened, we would've been in trouble."

We still had tons of time before we had to have our audience.

The palace servants who'd been there to bring tea and snacks for Cyril and Myfila until now had made themselves scarce, so the only things occupying the beautiful, giant guest room were us and our voices.

Then suddenly—*Knock, knock, knock, knock.*

An elegant sound rang out from the door, which was framed by flowers, and we all suddenly looked over.

"Excuse me."

"Our master has arrived to greet you."

Right after the knock, the newcomers waited for an appropriate amount of time, then young palace servants reverentially entered the room. The two girls in matching black-and-white maid uniforms were Sasha Shidoh Zultania's two teammates back at the academy— which meant there could've only been one VIP possibly standing behind them.

I immediately whispered to Cyril, "Why would Sasha be here to greet us?"

"Not sure. Probably to see how you're doing, Feil?"

Then in the next moment, the third princess of Shidoh appeared in front of me for the first time in five days, in the flesh.

I caught sight of her flowing platinum hair and amethyst eyes.

The long skirt of her blue off-shoulder dress, which featured gold embroidery, fell loosely from her waist, but the bodice was made to fit her body perfectly. Apparently, she wasn't trying to cover up her curves.

...She's as gorgeous as always...

I could only smile wanly at her and the full royal aura she gave off. "Sorry, Cyril." "Really? You're so fastidious about the oddest things."

Cyril loaned me his shoulder so I could stand up.

"Owww—"

"Your whole body's floppy, so you may as well stay sitting down."

In the end, even Myfila helped, and I somehow greeted the third princess Sasha Shidoh Zultania and her retinue of two while standing.

....

The six of us summoners silently faced each other.

Or really, the silence lasted barely a second. Sasha immediately gave us a greeting fit for royalty.

"Welcome to my father's castle. I welcome you, students of Raddermark."

She lifted her voluminous skirt with both her hands and drew her left leg sideways and behind her, lowering her head slightly without bending her knee.

Then as though they were kneeling in place of the princess, who wouldn't kowtow in front of the common people, the two girls to her sides both bent deeply, following the same etiquette as Sasha.

It was way too showy for just a curtsy.

In response, I only nodded at them, saying, "Excuse me for intrudin' in your home." It was pathetic, but even that rude greeting was all I could manage in my current state.

"You don't get to see that every day, Feil. That was the highest form of greeting a subject can get," Cyril told me.

"Was it? Looks like this son of a farmer's goin' up in the world."

I didn't get to openly celebrate, though.

Sasha had begun to scowl as she watched Cyril and Myfila return me to the couch. *What's up with her...?* I thought until she finally admonished me.

"Please don't bring a canteen into the royal castle, Feil Fonaf."

Apparently, she wasn't looking at us but at my leather canteen on the couch. So she'd figured out that I'd refused the hospitality from the castle and been drinking water this entire time.

"You really are just so..."

She let out a long sigh as though she'd given up.

Internally, I was a little worried I'd be in trouble for a while…

"I suppose you never change, Feil Fonaf."

Whether she knew what I'd been thinking or not, she sighed and suddenly smiled, which made my eyes go wide for a second.

"I'm simply glad you're in good health," she said.

"Same to you. 'Specially since you've been out five days after goin' to explain things to your old man."

"I was being held captive by the royal physicians, more like. I insisted I was fine, but they were scrupulous about their examinations. I head home to Raddermark tomorrow."

"That's good. Then I gotta work hard to get back, too."

"…"

Then she addressed the two girls who were accompanying her. "Mireille, Dorothea, I'd like to be alone." They didn't say anything in particular as they bowed deeply before leaving the room.

"Cyril, I want to go to the bathroom. Come with me?" Myfila said.

"The castle *is* very easy to get lost in," Cyril commented.

Then right after the two servants had left, the two of them had that conversation and headed out themselves.

"But the restroom's right outside the room," I said.

"You haven't heard? The Azure Chamber in this castle is supposed to be the most beautiful toilet in the world."

Sasha thanked their retreating backs as Cyril lightly lifted a hand in response.

The door slammed shut.

Before I knew it, Sasha and I were alone together in the gigantic guest room.

"…"

I couldn't really understand the situation I was in. Still buried in the leather couch, I silently looked up at Sasha.

…………

Then after ten seconds of silence where we could hear even each other's breathing, I finally heard the rustle of clothes.

And just as I was about to yelp in surprise, Sasha was kneeling in front of me.

"Oh, brave hero, I thank you from the bottom of my heart."

That's right. Sasha Shidoh Zultania, third princess of the land of Shidoh who wasn't supposed to kneel to anybody, was on her knees over the carpet now. Not only that, but she held her hands over her chest...almost as though she were praying to a god.

"And I don't thank you simply as Princess Sasha Shidoh Zultania, but as a fellow summoner. I'm proud of you."

"What?"

"Thank you, Summoner Feil Fonaf. Conqueror of legends."

Sasha's jewellike amethyst eyes were trained on me and only me.

"I grant Shidoh's blessings upon your future. Because you were the one to summon Pandora, because you never gave up...the world, Raddermark, and I were all saved."

I was speechless.

I felt pride and gratefulness, embarrassment and guilt, and sentimental like I'd seen the most beautiful thing in the world—but also anger that I had no way of telling my parents about this honor that I was receiving.

My voice escaped me for a while as I felt all those emotions welling up inside me...

"I'm grateful," I finally murmured, then right after that, I blustered out a cut-off silly laugh for a moment. "But who's supposed to be the hero here? We both were reckless."

I met Sasha's eyes.

"You created a situation where we could kill the Angel-Eater, Sasha. Only reason Pandora could punch the Angel-Eater was 'cause you merged with her to give her back her original form."

I probably was giving Sasha the same exact look she was giving me.

It was the peaceful smile of people who'd put every effort they could into a situation. The smile of relief for people who had overcome a day of catastrophe to get to today. We were smiling tenderly at each other, both praising each other.

"We all did everythin' we were capable of doin'," I said.

"Still, I'd like to reward you for your accomplishment."

Suddenly, Sasha stood up and sat next to me. We were close enough that our shoulders would touch if we shifted slightly. Sasha's long, lustrous hair, her pearl-like skin, and her sweet roselike scent wafted toward me.

"What prize shall I foist on you, then?"

"How 'bout a manga?"

"Huh?"

She likely hadn't been expecting an immediate reply. She looked at me with slight surprise.

I looked back at her from the corner of my eye.

"That romance manga about the apothecarist. You said you'd lend it to me before. Your recommended it, didn't ya?"

"...And here I thought you didn't read manga?"

"I've been lyin' around every day, so might as well read it now."

"..."

"The main character's name was Akasha? Rifris's drawings were pretty spiffy, too."

"...All right. I'm sure you won't be able to read it in that state, so I'll sit next to you for all fifteen volumes and turn the pages for you."

Now Sasha was blurting out nonsense suddenly. My voice cracked as I stopped her.

"Th-that's all right. Just the manga'll do."

But the next moment, Sasha was reaching out and doing whatever she wanted with me while I couldn't move.

"Hey— Ouch. Don't touch there, ya nitwit. You're acting just like Myfila."

She was poking me everywhere like she was trying to see how badly my wounds hurt.

"So...I see... If we use a healing spell, you'd need to sacrifice quite a bit of your immune system. And you've already lost enough of that from fatigue."

"That's right! If I up my regenerative abilities, then that'd eat away at my immune system, and I'd croak from a cold! So my only option's to sleep it off!"

Even when I yelled at her to stop, her fair fingers kept poking. At the end of her immature teasing, we both ended up falling onto the soft cushion of the couch with a muffled *thud*.

She hadn't pushed me over so much as suddenly lost her balance, and I hadn't been able to stop her from falling.

....

Before I knew it, she was on top of my torso and staring into my face. Her beautiful face and her curtain of platinum hair took up my entire vision.

Her pointer finger was caressing the gauze on my left eye, which still couldn't see anything.

"...?"

I was fully convinced she'd start poking around my eyeball next, but it didn't seem like that'd been her plan.

....

Eventually, she both seemed to smile and look worried as she murmured, looking indescribably tender, "Back then...I ended up making you shoulder the world's fate all on your own."

Then I sighed and turned my eyes down...but I looked back at Sasha right away and clearly told her, "Cyril and Myfila, too."

"Huh?" Sasha's eyes immediately went wide, but I kept going.

"You've got the wrong idea, Sasha. Cyril was the one outside and bein' my eyes watchin' Pandora pummelin' the Angel-Eater."

"Feil—"

"And without Myfila's tonic and help, I never woulda been able to finish the fight."

As Sasha brightened the more she understood how I felt, the smile on my face also grew. In the end, I was giving her a toothy grin that went all the way to my canines.

"Like I coulda saved the world on my own—I'm just a student."

The same was true for Sasha.

"...You really do make an excellent team."

That moment, Sasha gave me her best smile yet—a smile without any gloom or regret—one that was kind and heartfelt.

"We ain't done yet. We'll keep improvin' even more from here on out...!" I said, and she seemed to gather that I'd tried to stand up right then. She got off me and didn't say a word as she offered a hand and a shoulder.

Then she pulled me up with more strength than I thought was in her.

"You'll hurt yourself at this rate."

"Nonsense. I'm country-raised."

As we stuck right by each other, we bobbed along to the large window.

Sasha opened it, leading us to the balcony and allowing a cold breeze to come in.

"It's amazin'. Ya got a whole view of the capital."

"You should be proud, Feil Fonaf. This is just one of the views you and your friends protected."

When we set foot on the large, semicircular balcony, the land of Shidoh's capital—also renowned as the "white-walled town"—was right below our eyes.

The imposing castle had been built by cutting through a knoll in the middle of the plain. And this guest room was on the castle's topmost floor. Beyond the railing spread the townscape of one million surrounded by alabaster walls.

The hem of her dress caught in the breeze, as did my conjurer's robes.

The azure sky of lingering clouds connected to the ground at the horizon, and as I looked out at the blue of the sky and the white of the ground alongside Sasha, I genuinely marveled at its beauty. I'd just come out to the balcony hoping to get a breath of fresh air, but I'd been so overpowered by the view that I forgot to breathe.

"Do you think you'll be able to speak all right in front of my father?" she suddenly asked me, which brought me back to reality and forced a strained smile onto my face.

"I'm used to figurin' things out as I go, and it'll be nothin' compared with you, Sasha."

"What's that supposed to mean?"

"I'm sayin' I was a lot more nervous at the prospect of goin' head-to-head against you in the ranking matches. So don't worry 'bout me."

That seemed to remind Sasha of five days ago. As though she'd remembered the several summoners who'd been sacrificed and the promise that we hadn't been able to fulfill with each other, she suddenly, earnestly said, "...It's a shame the summons festival had to be canceled..."

I didn't share her sentiments—instead, I put on my usual grin.

"Just ya wait at the top. I'll catch up soon."

Sasha looked at me, and I looked at Sasha.

"So it seems you're up to one of your schemes again?"

A smile graced her beautiful face, almost as though she was part of my mischief.

"I got a mountain of stuff to do after I heal up." I turned to face ahead of me.

I slowly lifted my right arm, which could move a lot more than it had five days ago, and reached toward the distant, distant horizon.

"Can't rest on my laurels after defeating one measly ol' Angel-Eater."

The blue sky and white capital were so beautiful on this brisk winter day. Once I got this audience with the king over with, I wanted to see the town and what lay beyond the horizon, though Sasha'd probably have a few choice words for me if I told her. Or she might have just smiled in exasperation.

"No wonder you're Pandora's summoner. That's grit only fitting for a god-killing beast."

"I gotta live for my partner, too, since he's already dead."

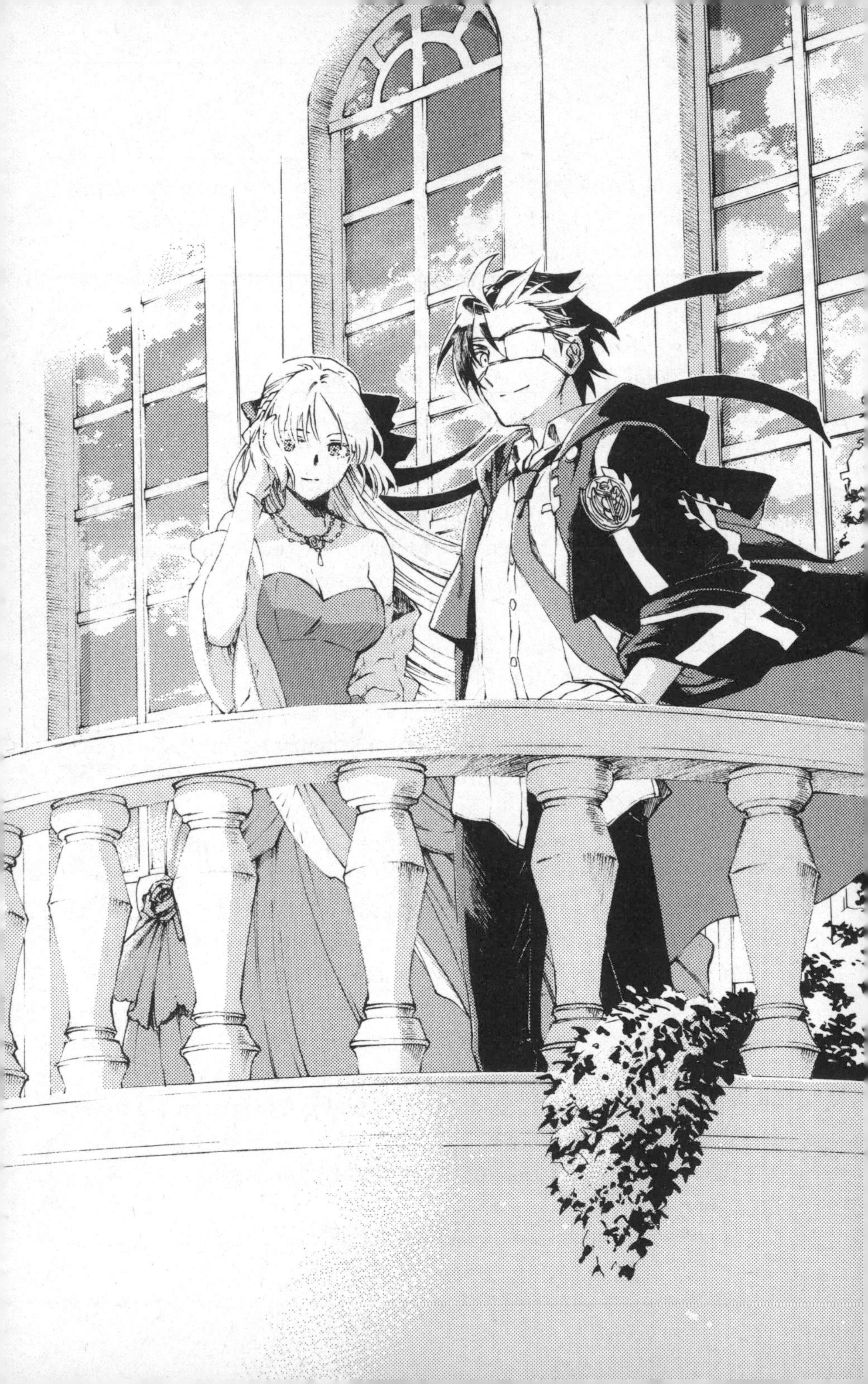

"…I feel like I understand slightly…why your Pandora is a corpse."

"Why is he?"

"Maybe his regrets upon dying—or no, rather, Pandora's final *wish* might have formed a bond between you. So the moment you had the same wish, Pandora came to you."

She had no evidence or logic to support what she was saying, but I felt like her conjecture might have been unexpectedly accurate.

"Ha-ha-ha! Great!"

I didn't even stop to think before I was laughing toward the sky.

Then I said, in a voice so composed even I marveled at it:

"People gather burdens just livin'. I've got my mom's, my pa's, and now it looks like Pandora's wishes, too. But that's not gonna change how I'll live."

"My…that really is such a Feil Fonaf thing to say."

"I'm always like this. I'm always cryin' out about what was 'entrusted' to me, but in the end, the only talent I've got is to survive another day."

Right in that moment, a strong wind gusted by.

But I didn't squint at either that or the sunlight as I exhaled a puff of white breath and my robes whipped around me. I resolved myself to get my next new start today, right now.

"My summon is dead, so I gotta live for all my life's worth."

My mom passed early, I lost my old man, and even my own summon was dead, but I was still standing in this world. I exhaled and inhaled, thinking about what could come next and what I'd do in the future.

My life was just getting started.

I had tons of things I still needed to do, tons I still wanted to do, and an endless world stretching all around me to do it in.

Seemed like I had a long way to go before I could come back to my village as a respectable summoner.

AFTERWORD

Nice to meet you. I'm Rakuzan.

This book, *My Summon Is Dead*, came from an author hounded by work day in, day out who wanted to travel through a gigantic other world and partner up with a humongous monster.

So the main character's partner obviously had to be a dragon, right? No, no, it'd be a giant wolf. Or the open sea would be the stage, and in a novel twist, the summoners would control fish.

Then one day, while I was trying to figure out which monster the lead, Feil Fonaf, would summon, for whatever reason, the partner that makes up the basis of the story suddenly ended up being dead.

So the lead's summon is the world's strongest magical beast's corpse.

I suddenly decided on that story with just the idea in my heart—then decided to let the me of tomorrow figure out the rest. After I threw around a lot of ideas, it turned into a comedy with a group of three friends, and I added school battles, and finally, it took shape.

So this is the revised version of the story that won the special prize of the sixth Kakuyomu Web Novel Contest for the Isekai Fantasy Division. Thanks to my editor, I was also given some pages to write a completely new epilogue.

I tried to make it an invigorating scene that would be fitting after the ferocious battle. What did you think of it? And just as I touched upon in the epilogue, the world in front of the main character is so large and so bright, it's dazzlingly brilliant.

Maybe his next adventure will be to search for the saint who disappeared without a trace three thousand years ago?

Or perhaps an attempt to conquer a living labyrinth slumbering under a certain castle?

Or maybe a friendly match against a summoner training school in a foreign country might be unexpectedly exciting?

....

And so on, I kept adding to the list as I came up with things, but like this story, that's something for future me to think about—that's the spirit, right? I say that there's always tomorrow—that's the kind of person I am.

Speaking of tomorrows—or the future, rather—the manga version of *My Summon Is Dead* will be starting around spring in *Dengeki Maoh*. I hope you'll enjoy the story of the young summoners drawn by the manga artist Konsai Neko. I'm looking forward to it as well.

Finally, I'd like to express my gratitude toward everyone who was involved in the publication of this book.

To Miyuu, my illustrator, thank you so very much for drawing beautiful illustrations that show not just the characters, but every little detail. I felt the bottom of my heart quiver the moment I saw the school insignias drawn with angel and devil wings to symbolize the story of summoners who are open to everything, both good and bad.

To my editor, I believe the new scene and epilogue you encouraged me to add made this a story that others would really want to read.

And most importantly, to the readers who picked up this book. *This story,* My Summoned Beast Is Dead, *is supposed to be a superflashy and fun fantasy!!*—that was my motto while writing it. If you enjoyed the world that the main character, Feil Fonaf, lives in even in the slightest, I couldn't be happier.

I hope that we will meet again. In the meantime, I'll write a little each day.